LI

If it's not one thing,

it's a

MURDER

A Skye Donovan Photographic Mystery

PRESS ®

Medallion Press, Inc.
Printed in the USA

DEDICATION:

For Patricia LaCaria, Pamela Cournoyer, and
Penny Schufreider.
Because sisters make the best friends.

Published 2008 by Medallion Press, Inc.

The MEDALLION PRESS LOGO
is a registered tradmark of Medallion Press, Inc.

Printed in the United States of America
Typeset in Adobe Caslon Pro

ISBN# 9781933836393

10 9 8 7 6 5 4 3 2 1
First Edition

ACKNOWLEDGEMENTS:

I want to thank my critique partners, Theresa Stevens, Bobbie Cole, Alexis Fleming, and Sara Hanz. This book would not have been possible without their invaluable input.

Thanks also to my husband, Keith, for his incredible support, and for making my dreams come true.

CHAPTER ONE

I held the lingerie up by its tiny straps. A froth of cheap, bubblegum pink nylon with little round doilies of gold lace over the nipple areas. Matching lace ruffles around the legs. Open crotch.

Not mine.

"I'm going to kill him." The thought formed slowly and the words were whispered behind clenched teeth.

"Then, I'll kill her." I didn't even know who she was, but I was damn well going to find out.

Blood pounded in my head and I felt sick to my stomach. A little dizzy. Then I realized I was hyperventilating. I sat down on the unmade bed and tried to breathe normally.

It was hard because this wasn't normal.

I knew what normal was. It was my life. I took care of my husband, our eighteen year old daughter, Sheridan; and our home. I decorated the house, orchestrated our schedules, volunteered at Sheridan's

1

school, and played hostess to Craig's business associates. I played tennis at the country club, grew flowers in the front yard and tomatoes and strawberries in the back. My hobby was taking photographs that chronicled our lives, a selection was included with the family newsletter every Christmas. My life was the definition of normal. Until now. When the nausea faded, I looked at the dreadful evidence of his unfaithfulness again.

Outside of being wrinkled, it didn't appear to have been used. At least it hadn't been laundered, from the condition of the papery tag sewn into the back seam. I fingered the tag and squinted at the information printed in English, Spanish, and French. Nylon/acrylic. Hand wash, line dry. Size XXL.

XXL? Craig Williams, my husband of nineteen years, was having an affair with a fat woman. I cringed at my attitude. There was nothing wrong with being fat. My friend, Lily, was plump. I was carrying a few extra pounds myself. Nothing wrong with it. Besides, XXL didn't necessarily mean fat. She could be big boned. Or tall. Maybe statuesque.

She was probably a freaking Amazon goddess.

In *my* bed. With *my* husband.

That certainly explained why we rarely had sex anymore. Craig was having Amazon-sex with his voluptuous mistress instead of Pygmy-sex with his five-foot-two-inch wife.

"Skye?" Craig's voice floated up the stairwell to me. "I'm home."

I froze like I'd been caught sweeping dirt under a rug. I glanced around the room, searching for a place to hide the lingerie. What the hell was I thinking? I didn't need to hide the damn thing. I wasn't the one who'd hidden it under his side of the bed.

"Hey." Craig walked into the bedroom, looked at the sleazy pink confection in my hand, and stopped. His mouth opened, then closed into a grim line.

At that point, I really had no choice. I would have preferred to confront him at a different time, in a different place. Perhaps with all my wits about me. Even with some of my wits within arm's reach.

"What is this?" I held out the handful of wrinkled pink and gold teddy.

He looked confused. It was a decent attempt. Genuine, almost. Maybe it was more surprised than confused.

"What do you mean?"

What did I mean? Oh, okay. We were doing the *I-have-no-idea-what-you-are-talking-about* thing.

"I mean, what was this," I shook the thing at him, "doing under the mattress on your side of the bed?"

"Why were you looking under my side of the mattress?" he asked.

Oh, no. I was not going there. I wasn't about to play his game of making me feel guilty for doing something he construed as snooping. I'd played that

3

game before and lost every time. Besides, I had *not* been snooping. I'd been changing the sheets and the mattress pad. As any good housewife would every freaking Wednesday for the past nineteen years. I lifted an eyebrow.

He stared at me.

I glared back.

I watched several emotions flicker in his eyes and wondered why I couldn't put a name to any of them. A smile wavered on his lips.

"I bought it for you, sweetie."

Bullshit!

Any possibility that I might believe him was killed when he said "sweetie." Craig never used endearments with me. A fact that had annoyed me to no end the first few years, but I'd adjusted. He just wasn't an endearment kind of guy.

"Liar!" I threw the lingerie on the still unmade bed and stomped out of the bedroom.

"Why would I lie?" Craig followed me down the hall and stopped at the stairs.

"I have no idea, Craig. But I know that you did not buy that cheesy piece of garbage for me. For one thing, it's not my size. By a long shot. For another, you know I'd never wear anything like *that*."

"Well, maybe you should."

I stopped at the bottom of the stairs and turned to

look up at him. He had a sheepish grin on his face that just pissed me off even more. "Are you saying that I am somehow lacking as a woman because I don't wear trashy lingerie?" I turned on my heel and continued into the kitchen. Craig followed me.

"I'm saying maybe I'd like to see you in something like that."

I stopped in front of the refrigerator and turned to him. Had he lost his mind?

"You would? You want to see me in that pink piece of dreck?"

"Why not?" Craig lifted his shoulders and grinned.

"I don't think so. I think you want to see someone else in that." I held up a finger. "Correction. I think you have *already* seen someone else in it." I jerked open the refrigerator, pulled out the T-bone steaks I'd marinated for dinner, slammed them down on the counter, and turned back to him.

"You think I'm having an affair with another woman?"

I had to hand it to him. He had the whole shocked-and-disappointed look down pat. I almost felt bad about accusing him.

"Skye, I would never want another woman over you."

Damn, if he didn't sound sincere. Craig looked

5

like his feelings were hurt. I had a momentary twinge of regret before righteous indignation boiled up inside me again.

"You really expect me to believe that? You are so full of shit!"

"Skye, I swear. There is no woman in my life but you." He laid a hand on my shoulder and I shrugged it off.

"Just get away from me."

Craig shook his head in a sad way, held his hands up in defeat, and walked out of the kitchen.

Nice try. I looked down at the plastic bag of steaks swimming in red wine, herbs, and olive oil and realized I hadn't made the salad. Or the garlic bread. I hadn't even fired up the grill yet. I glanced at the clock. Five thirty. I hadn't done all those things because it wasn't dinnertime.

Besides, why should I prepare dinner for that jerk? Bad enough he was screwing around. I certainly didn't want to feed him so he would be strong enough to cheat on me. I threw the steaks back into the refrigerator and grabbed a beer. One of Craig's beers. I'm usually a wine drinker, but the idea of drinking his beer appealed to me. Opening the pantry, I took the last bag of his favorite chips and headed to the patio.

I downed half the beer in one swill, which calmed me down some. Also gave me a little buzz. The buzz felt so good that I decided to switch to wine. Craig came into the kitchen while I was filling my glass with Merlot.

"What's for dinner?"

At least he hadn't asked in a demanding tone. Still, he surely didn't think I was in any mood to cook?

To be fair, I had trained him to expect dinner at seven every night. The only exceptions were when we dined out; the night I'd gone into labor with our daughter, Sheridan; and the night I'd spent in the hospital with her when she had her appendix removed. Our lives were structured and predictable, because that's how Craig wanted it. I'd left my spontaneity at the altar, and after so many years I was accustomed to the structure and predictability.

"I'm having wine." I took my wine back to the patio and listened to Craig fumble around in the kitchen for a while. Finally, I heard the ding of the microwave and then silence.

Once the anger died down to a cold knot in my stomach, I wondered who she was. And when they did it. And why. What had happened in our marriage to make him want someone else? And how had I missed the signs? Weren't there always signs that pointed to this sort of thing? Was I just one of those women who ignored flagrant indications that her husband was cheating? Maybe I was.

There was no point in trying to continue the

conversation with Craig. I was half-drunk and I knew he would be in shutdown mode. I rinsed out my wineglass, threw away the empty chip bag, and went upstairs.

The bedroom was dark and empty. Craig was probably in the den working, which was his usual method of not dealing with something. I changed into a set of short cotton pajamas and looked at the unmade bed. No way was I going to sleep in that bed with him. Fortunately I kept the guest bedroom made up, so I went in there and cried myself to sleep.

I woke up disoriented.

Not quite sure where I was, I closed my eyes again. After I realized I was in the guest room, I tried to think of why I would be there.

Oh, yes! Craig was having an affair. And lying about it.

Rotten bastard.

I opened my eyes again and turned my head. The clock read nine fifteen. Normally, I'm up by seven. I make breakfast for Craig and Sheridan, see him off to work and her to school, then get on with my day. Craig would have left for work already and Sheridan was away at a summer music school, so no breakfast duties today. I could get started on my list of things to do. Shopping for groceries, washing the car, taking old clothes to Goodwill, cleaning the bathrooms.

Considering the events of last night, the list was a bit overwhelming, so I settled for brushing my teeth and putting on a pot of water for tea.

"Skye?"

"Craig, what are you doing here?" He should have been in his office an hour ago.

"I wanted to talk to you."

The teakettle whistled and I poured the hot water in my cup, added a tea bag, and sat at the breakfast table. Craig spooned coffee into the coffeemaker, turned it on, and leaned against the counter, studying his feet. I waited. Years of living with him had taught me if I did anything to try to hurry him along, he would just dig in and take even longer to speak. I was halfway through my tea when he finally spoke.

"About that lingerie." He cleared his throat. I straightened in my chair and watched him. Whatever he was about to say seemed to be a struggle.

"Yes?" My stomach flipped and fluttered.

"This is really hard." Craig turned and poured himself a cup of coffee. "It's mine."

"Excuse me?" I heard his words but my mind just couldn't assimilate them.

"I've been curious about stuff, you know?"

Craig passed his coffee cup from one hand to the

9

other. "About what it would feel like to wear something like that. So, I've been chatting online with some other cross-dressers."

Oh, God, was I married to one of those men who wore evening gowns and pancake makeup and sang show tunes? Weren't they all gay? Craig couldn't be gay. We'd been married forever. We had a daughter. We had sex. Not often, and maybe it wasn't really hot, but still.

"I know it's probably weird to you. But, really, it's not that big a deal." He shrugged. "I was just curious."

Not that big a deal? Just curious? I took a deep breath and thought it would have been easier to deal with the Amazon goddess. I stared at his broad back and long torso, then it hit me. "That *thing* is too small for you."

"I thought it would fit. I wear XXL in a sweater."

He was still turned away from me, and I wished I could see his face so I'd have a clue as to whether he was lying to me.

"I just didn't want you thinking that I was having an affair with another woman. I'd never do that to you."

"Okay." I wasn't sure what I really meant by that. Was I okay with him being a cross-dresser? Did I believe he wouldn't have an affair? I had no idea. But it seemed to work for him.

"I have to get to the office. I'm late." Craig set his cup down, turned, and leaned over to give me a quick peck on the lips.

I don't think I moved for half an hour. Cross-dressing? My Craig?

Eventually an image formed in my mind and I almost fell off my chair laughing. Craig is a big, masculine guy. Six feet three inches, hairy, barrel chest, biceps as big as my thighs. The thought of him in a lacy teddy was not a pretty one. But was it worse than the thought of him in bed with another woman?

I finally set my cold tea down and looked at the phone on the kitchen wall. I really needed to talk to someone about this. I had two friends close enough to share this with. Lily would be busy at her New Age shop, which left Bobbi Jo. The phone rang just as I reached for it.

"Hey, Skye, you won't believe what happened." Bobbi Jo's familiar Texan drawl made me feel like life was normal again.

"What?"

"Edward's car was broken into last night."

"Where?"

"In the garage at his office. He had a late meeting and when he got to the car, the lock was popped off. They stole his laptop."

"That's terrible, Bobbi Jo, but at least they didn't

take the car."

"The police said something must have interrupted them, so they just took what they could get their hands on and ran."

"Didn't the alarm go off?" I asked.

"I guess not. Edward said he couldn't remember if he'd turned it on when he parked it. It's a weird feeling to know somebody's been rooting around in our car."

"Speaking of weird, can you come over?"

"Sure, but why is that weird?"

"Sorry, it isn't. It's just that something weird has happened and I need to talk about it."

"You sound serious, darlin'. What's up?"

"It's too much to go into on the phone."

"I'm at the salon getting my nails done. I'll be there in an hour."

I hung up the phone and headed for the bathroom. After a quick shower, I pulled on shorts and a T-shirt, slathered some mousse onto my hair, slapped on some moisturizer, and called it done. I knew Bobbi Jo would be hungry, so I arranged a small platter with mini-muffins, fruit, and cheese. I'd just put on more water for tea when the doorbell chimed.

"It's open," I called from the kitchen.

"Hey, how ya doin'?" Bobbi Jo whirled into the kitchen, folded her arms around me for a fierce hug, then stepped back. "Now, what's so weird that you want to talk about?"

If I didn't love Bobbi Jo so much, I could hate her for being so perfectly groomed all the time. Something I'd never mastered. Sure, I could pull myself together for a special occasion, but I just didn't have the same raw material. I was short with an average build plus a couple of pounds had crept up on me the past few years. My hair was a light brown with blonde streaks, cut to a medium length.

Bobbi Jo, on the other hand, was tall and slender with a short mop of flaming red curls. At thirty-eight, she could easily pass for ten years younger, and everyone assumed she was a trophy wife to Edward Melrose, her husband of twelve years. They were wrong. Bobbi Jo and Edward were a love match in spite of the twenty-four-year difference in their ages.

"You want something to eat?" I asked. "It's probably going to be a long story." The teapot whistled, and I poured the hot water into a ceramic teapot, set it on a tray with cups, sugar, milk, and lemon, and carried it into the living room. I turned to go back for the tray of food, but Bobbi Jo had picked it up and followed me.

Bobbi Jo poured herself a cup of tea and lifted an eyebrow. "So, tell me everything."

I popped a bite of muffin into my mouth to stall for a little time. Bobbi Jo sat back on the sofa and waited. She tapped her perfectly manicured nails on the arm

13

of the sofa and sipped her tea. I finished chewing the mini-muffin and swallowed.

"Craig is a cross-dresser."

Her blue-gray eyes sparkled under raised eyebrows. A smile slowly spread across her lips. Then she laughed. A big, boisterous belly laugh.

"Oh, my gawd! Skye, that's the funniest thing I've ever heard."

"It's not funny!" It was, of course. Hadn't I just been laughing earlier?

"What makes you think he's a cross-dresser?"

"He told me so. This morning."

"Now, wait a minute." Bobbi Jo set down her teacup and held up a hand. "Craig just woke up and said he's a cross-dresser?"

"Not exactly." I told her about the frothy pink nylon with the gold lace doilies and missing crotch.

"So, that's why."

"What do you mean?"

"A man isn't about to tell his wife he's a cross-dresser unless he's caught with the lingerie. I should know."

"You should know?" I asked.

"My first husband was a cross-dresser. He didn't admit it until I walked in on him in his undies and stockings. Well, his undies. They were my stockings."

"You never told me that!"

"Well, what was the point? He was gone and it didn't seem to matter."

I nodded. Bobbi Jo's first husband had been killed in a boating accident just a year into their marriage.

"I don't know what to think. Last night I was sure he was having an affair and now he tells me he's curious about wearing lingerie. What's next? Is he going to tell me he's gay?"

"There are a lot of regular men who just like to put on women's clothes. Who knows why? But they aren't necessarily gay."

"That's a relief. So what should I expect?"

"It depends. Some men just like to cross-dress as a sexual outlet. Others like to dress up and see if they can pass for a woman. A few of them actually want to be a woman, but that's a whole 'nother issue."

"I don't think Craig wants to be a woman. I doubt he even wants to pass as a woman," I said, unable to picture my tall, masculine husband trying to pass for a woman.

"Yeah, there's no way he could pass. I'd bet with Craig, it's a sexual thing. And, darlin', that part of it can definitely be fun."

"Fun? You mean he'll want to wear stuff when we make love?"

"It was the best sex my husband and I ever had. After a while, I started to think a man in see-through panties was the hottest thing on God's green earth. But I think it was mostly that he was so turned on by wearing them."

I dropped my head into my hands, afraid I was going to hyperventilate again. Was I ready for this? Probably not. On the other hand, Craig and I weren't having much of a love life lately. None actually, for several months.

"Is that why we never make love anymore?"

"What? Problems in the bedroom?"

"Not problems, really. Just nothing. I think it's been five or six months since we've made love." Or had it been longer? Possibly. Mostly I tried to not think about it.

"Darlin', that's just not right. Have you talked to him about it?"

"At first I thought it was his back. He had a bad sprain and had to wear a brace for a couple of months. Then he seemed tired all the time, and then he was working really long hours on a new project."

"But did you talk to him about it?" Bobbi Jo asked.

"Well, I asked him if anything was wrong, but he said no. I didn't want to push him because he had so much other stuff going on."

"And before that, was everything all right?"

"I guess so. I mean, we've been married for a while. It's not like we're on our honeymoon."

"Just how often do you two make love?"

"Not as often as we did in our twenties," I admitted. "But that's normal. It just drops off over the years. I think we usually make love once a month, most of the time."

Bobbi Jo's eyebrows crept toward her hairline. "And you're okay with that?"

"I just think he has a low sex drive. Besides, it's not like we aren't affectionate. Sex isn't everything." I wasn't really comfortable discussing my sex life. Much less, picking it apart.

"Well, of course, everyone's sex drive isn't the same. Still, once a month doesn't seem like much of a sex drive at all." Bobbi Jo sounded concerned enough to make me wonder if that was true.

Had I just gotten used to infrequent sex? More importantly, was this the key to revitalizing our sex life? The comment Bobbi Jo had made about having such great sex with her first husband when he wore panties was intriguing.

"So, you had hot sex when your husband wore panties to bed?" The idea titillated me. More than a little. The thought of Craig in lacy little nothings still made me want to giggle, but the thought of hot, sweaty, screaming sex was nothing to laugh about.

"Oh, darlin'! You would not believe how hot it was. Brings a tear to my eye just thinking about it."

"Maybe I should buy Craig some panties, then."

As soon as the words were out of my mouth I realized I wasn't joking.

"Oh, my gawd! Are you ready for that, Skye?"

"Is anyone ever ready for something like this?" I didn't know what I was ready for. But I wasn't going to let it stop me. "Why not?"

"Great. Fix your hair and get your purse. I know just the place to go."

What was wrong with my hair?

Adult videos and toys.
Rentals and sales.
Obviously, I had lost my mind.

I took a deep breath and fought the urge to hyperventilate. Surely they didn't mean to say they rented adult toys. Next to the sign offering to sell or rent videos and toys, glowing neon script proclaimed the name of the establishment.

"Silky Secrets?" I asked as Bobbi Jo pulled her Range Rover into a parking spot in the strip mall. The display windows held a variety of lingerie. Teddies trimmed with feathers. Stockings with seams up the back and elastic lace at the top. Really, really high heels. There were the usual outfits—French maid, stripper, nurse. Outside of the poorly worded sign, the store wasn't sleazy looking. Still, did I really want to do this?

A Lincoln Navigator pulled up next to us, and a young woman with perfectly streaked hair burst from the vehicle. The enormous diamond on her French-manicured hand drew my attention to the fact that all she carried was a platinum credit card and her car keys as she ran into the store.

"You think she's having an erotic emergency?" I asked.

"Haven't we all, at one time or another?" Bobbi Jo waggled her eyebrows at me. "Let's go buy your husband some panties."

The store was much nicer than I'd thought it would be. The woman from the Navigator stood in front of a rack of videos in a room set off to one side of the store. I wasn't quite curious enough to check out the selection of entertainment. The front of the store was dedicated to the milder lingerie, and the farther back we went, the more imaginative it became. Bobbi Jo pulled me over to a section marked Plus Sizes. I guessed that's what Craig would wear. I picked up a pair of large bikini panties in black nylon with a red glittery design. Bobbi Jo shook her head.

"You want something crotchless."

"Crotchless?"

"Well, how else are you going to get to the goods,

darlin'?"

She had a point. This was supposed to be as much for my benefit as his, and having his family jewels encased in nylon probably wouldn't do me much good. Bobbi Jo pawed through the selection and finally held up a pair of fire-engine-red sheer panties with black sequins and lacy black ruffles around the high-cut legs.

"These are perfect." She stuck her hand through the open crotch and waved it around.

"I think these are nice." I held up a pair of not-quite-sheer white panties with sparkly pink ribbons on the sides. Unfortunately, the crotch was intact.

"Too tame."

"Really? I'd wear them."

"Exactly." She waved her hand in dismissal of the too tame undies, then grabbed my arm. "Oh! Good point. What are you going to wear?"

"Me?" I usually wear an oversized T-shirt and cotton boxers to bed. I didn't think that's what Bobbi Jo wanted to hear. "I have a long negligee. It's black and it's very low cut in the front."

"Can you see through it?"

"Not unless there's a light behind me."

"We need to get you something. Does Craig have any fantasies?"

"Sexual fantasies?"

"That you know about?" she added.

Hell, I hadn't even known about the panty thing until this morning. "None that I'm aware of."

"Okay, we'll just wing it. Go with something standard." Bobbi Jo dragged me back to the front of the store.

Half an hour later, we left with the panties for Craig and a French maid outfit for me, which included high heels, mesh stockings, a garter belt, and a boned black satin teddy with holes for my nipples and a bright green satin bow tie that Bobbi Jo said brought out the green in my hazel eyes. I don't know how because the bow was on my butt.

Bobbi Jo pulled into my driveway and shooed me out of the car. "I want to hear every detail tomorrow. Now, go get ready."

I dumped my purchases on the bed in the guest room and considered my options. How, exactly, should I present this little setup to Craig? I had no idea. Planning and shopping with Bobbi Jo had been fun, but the reality of getting my husband into panties and then seducing him was intimidating.

Could I really look at Craig in frilly see-through panties and not laugh? I reminded myself that hot sex would be my reward. We'd never really had *hot* sex. It was okay, but nothing to scream about. Hot sex would be good. If I could just not laugh or throw up.

I ran a bath and soaked for a while. I shaved my

legs and under my arms. I washed my hair and even used conditioner. I rubbed my expensive lotion everywhere, then styled my hair, taking more than the usual three minutes.

That didn't seem to be really enough, so I painted my toenails a bright red and applied makeup with a heavy hand while they dried. The makeup didn't look so bad, but the toenails were a mess. I spent ten minutes with a box of cotton swabs and nail polish remover to neaten them up a bit. I considered polishing my fingernails, but looking at the job I'd done on my toes, decided I was better off with the natural look.

Bobbie Jo had insisted I forget about dinner. We could always eat later, if we still had the energy. That thought left me a little light-headed and it had the added benefit of me not having anything in my stomach to throw up. I left a note on the table in the entryway telling Craig to meet me in the bedroom. Not that I would be waiting for him there. But I had laid the crotchless, sheer panties on his pillow.

My plan was to wait in the guest room until I heard him arrive. Give him a few minutes to find the undies and get into them, then saunter into the bedroom and let the games get underway. I refused to think about exactly what might happen. I'd be open to everything. I'd go with the flow. I'd give Craig a night to remember. Maybe this would rejuvenate our marriage. We'd start another phase of our lives together. At the very least, I'd get laid.

I poured myself a glass of wine and took it to the guest room to get dressed. Craig was due home in fifteen minutes. I wriggled into the outfit, struggling with the zipper in the back. The boned garment pulled in my tummy and pushed up my breasts. I'd never had such a tiny waist or so much cleavage. I tried to ignore the fact that my nipples protruded from the little lace-trimmed cutouts. Standing in front of the full-length mirror, I regretted that I'd been skipping the gym for the past few weeks. Or was it months? I turned to look at my backside. The big green bow did nothing for my butt, and there was a jiggle to my thighs that I hadn't noticed before. No problem. I'd just keep the lights low.

I'd gotten a really big glass of wine, but it wasn't making a dent in my nerves. I sat on the bed, one mesh-clad knee crossed over the other, my high-heeled foot jumping up and down until my shin started to burn.

Finally, I heard the front door open. Oh, shit! What if he came to the guest room? I lurched across the room and locked the door, then sat on the bed and concentrated on being quiet. That was better than thinking about what I would be doing in just a few minutes.

I heard Craig walk up the stairs. I heard the bedroom door open. The clock read 5:47. I waited until it read 6:01, slugged down the last of my wine, and stood on wobbly four-inch heels.

Showtime!

CHAPTER TWO

I stood a few feet from the bedroom door paralyzed with indecision. I didn't want to keep Craig waiting but I didn't want to walk in on him if he was still putting the panties on. That thought brought up an image of Craig wearing the sequined, lacy panties and I choked back a hysterical giggle.

What if I laughed when I saw him? Oh, God, that would be awful. For both of us. I took as deep a breath as I could in the corseted outfit and had a stern talk with myself.

You will not laugh, giggle, or smirk. You will smile enticingly. Besides, who are you to laugh with your nipples sticking out of fur-trimmed holes and a big bow on your butt? And remember to dim the lights.

I took the few steps to the doorway, turned the knob, and pulled the door open before I could chicken out.

Craig sat on the edge of the bed still fully clothed, his face in his hands, elbows propped on his knees.

The panties were still lying on his pillow. Paralysis set in again. I wanted to turn and run, but I couldn't even breathe. Craig looked up at me and I saw tears trickling down his cheeks. Craig wasn't normally a crier. Outside of a few tears of joy when Sheridan was born, I couldn't remember him ever crying. These didn't seem to be tears of joy. For a moment I wasn't even sure I was looking at my husband. My heart contracted painfully.

"Craig. Honey, what's wrong?"

"This is not what I wanted."

"But you said you had thought about it and you bought that lingerie."

"This isn't about us, Skye. It doesn't have anything to do with you so stay the hell out of it!"

The apology that hovered on my lips slipped away in the face of his anger. Craig was usually so even tempered. I had no idea how to deal with his anger. Suddenly I was horribly aware that he was fully dressed and my nipples were visible. My night of hot, screaming sex was turning into a painful embarrassment.

"Just leave me alone!" Craig balled the panties up and threw them at me, then turned his back.

The panties landed on my exposed nipples, and I automatically clutched at the nylon and stared at his back until it became clear he had nothing more to say. I wanted to say something that would make it all go away. Failing that, I turned and tottered back to the guest room.

I cried myself to sleep and the next morning my first thought was that I was a failure. A complete and total failure.

Which was as good a reason as any to still be lying in bed at nine in the morning. I forced my eyes open, then closed them again when I saw the French maid costume lying over the back of the chair across the room. I should have burned it. And the panties I'd gotten for Craig. Then there would be no physical evidence of my failure.

Seeing him in tears had confused me. Hearing him yell had pissed me off. So, I'd retaliated by stomping off to the guest room to sleep in the full-sized bed while he slept on the incredibly expensive king-sized bed with the adjustable air chambers, the temperature-sensitive foam topper, the down pillows, and the seven-hundred-thread-count sheets. Yeah, I certainly showed him! Not that my guest sheets were crap, but still.

What had I done that was so wrong? Couldn't he have faked being aroused? Even a little? God knows I had on more than one occasion.

It was all Bobbi Jo's fault. The phone rang and I glared at it. No doubt that was the bitch calling now, wanting to know how exciting my evening of kinky sex had been. I could hardly wait to share.

"Hello?"

"Skye?" Bobbi Jo's soft drawl was broken, and I sat straight up in the bed, last night's debacle forgotten.

"What is it?"

"Can you come over?"

"Sure. What's wrong?"

"It's probably nothing, but I need some company."

"Bobbi Jo, will you please tell me what's going on?" I got out of bed and carried the phone into my bedroom looking for clothes. Bobbi Jo had me worried and now I was sorry I'd called her a bitch, even if it was just in my thoughts.

"Edward just called from the office. The police say that someone was murdered last night with my gun."

"Your gun?"

"That little thirty-eight with the mother-of-pearl handle that Edward gave me—"

"I know the gun, Bobbi Jo. Who was murdered with it and how? Wait. I'm getting dressed; I'll be right over." I hung up the phone and pulled on jeans and a short-sleeved shirt. I figured this was going to be a long story and I'd rather hear it in person. Plus, I wanted to tell Bobbi Jo just how wrong she'd been about the damn lingerie. I pulled up at her miniman-sion less than half an hour later.

"Oh, gawd! I'm so glad you're here." Bobbi Jo pulled me inside. I followed her through the great room and dining room to the French doors that led to a spacious patio. Her husband, Edward, and a young man were having coffee at the glass table.

"Skye, this is Sean Castleton, Edward's assistant," Bobbi Jo said as we both took chairs.

Sean and I nodded to each other. Edward had stood when we came out and now leaned down to kiss my cheek.

"Skye, you're looking lovely as ever." Edward was gracious to a fault. I'd barely taken time to run a brush through my hair.

"Okay, now what's going on? Who was murdered? And what does your gun have to do with it?" The doorbell chimed and Bobbi Jo jumped up.

"That must be the police." She hurried back inside.

Edward patted my hand. "Bobbi Jo is making too big a deal of this. I'm sure we'll get it all cleared up now that the police are here." Before I could ask another question, Bobbi Jo returned with two men following her.

"Edward, this is Detective Madison and Detective Spiner," Bobbi Jo said.

Edward rose and shook hands with both of them, introduced them to Sean and me, and offered them coffee, which they both refused.

"We have a few questions we'd like to ask," Detective Spiner said. "Your car was broken into the night before last, Mr. Melrose?" Edward nodded and the detective continued. "The police report lists a laptop as the only item missing from the car."

"That would be my fault," Sean said.

"Your fault?" Detective Madison asked.

"Yes, I had just picked up the gun from the repair shop earlier that day. I left the gun in the car and forgot to tell Mr. Melrose that it was there."

"I see." Spiner made a note. "And you have a receipt from the repair shop?"

"Of course."

"Where were you between nine and eleven last night?" Spiner asked. Edward, Bobbi Jo and Sean all started talking at the same time. Spiner held his hand up. "One at a time, please."

"I was at the office," Sean offered.

"My wife and I were at home all evening," Edward said. "I had two phone calls from people who can confirm that."

"Any phone calls that would confirm your presence, Mrs. Melrose?"

"No. Not that I can remember."

"Detective, I just told you that my wife was with me all evening." Edward's voice was soft but his eyes flared with anger.

"Yes, sir," Detective Madison said and frowned at his partner. "Detective Spiner was asking because of the personal connection your wife had to the victim."

"Personal connection?" Bobbi Jo asked. "How?"

"The victim was Natalie Turner." When Bobbi Jo still looked blank, Madison continued. "She was the girlfriend of David Pearson."

"Oh, my gawd, that's terrible!" Bobbi Jo turned to Edward. "David is my personal trainer."

"I remember, dear." Edward took Bobbi Jo's hand and held it. "Detective, I see your concern here since the victim was vaguely connected to my wife and because my wife's gun was the murder weapon, but I can assure you it's nothing more than a sad coincidence."

"David Pearson is a frequent visitor here, isn't he?" Spiner asked.

"Yes, David comes over two or three mornings a week."

"Usually when your husband is at the office?" Spiner smirked and shook his head.

Edward stood up. "Are you implying something, Detective?"

Spiner shrugged. "Just asking questions."

"I think we're done here," Detective Madison said. "I'm sorry we interrupted your day. Thank you for your time."

"I'll show you out." Sean stood and led the detectives back through the house.

"That son of a bitch!" Bobbi Jo stood up and Edward put his arm around her shoulder.

"Pay him no mind, dear."

"He insinuated there was something going on between me and David."

"He was just fishing for something," Edward said.

"I need to call David. I want to know how he's doing." Bobbi Jo walked inside to make her phone call.

"Skye, thank you so much for coming over. I need to get back to the office and I'd appreciate it if you'd stay here with Bobbi Jo for a while."

"Of course, Edward."

When Edward and Sean left, I went into the kitchen and poured myself a glass of iced tea. I'd just sat down on the patio when Bobbi Jo came out.

"He's just torn up about it. Said he wasn't going to be able to work for a while."

"Poor guy. Did you ever meet his girlfriend?"

"No. He talked about her sometimes. Sounded like they were really in love." Bobbi Jo sat down and rested her elbows on the table. "Let's talk about something else."

I just stared at her.

"Oooooh. What happened last night?"

The doorbell chimed again, preventing me from answering. Bobbi Jo jumped up. "If those detectives are back again, I'm going to give them a piece of my mind about their damn questions." She went inside and came back a minute later with our friend Lily in tow.

"I thought you were going to rip my head off when you answered the door," Lily said.

"Oh, I'm sorry. I'm just in a snit about those detectives."

Our friend Lily was the poster child for the earth-mother-goddess thing. Her clothing tastes ran to loose gauze pants and full skirts topped with a brightly patterned dashiki; her dark blonde hair was usually woven into a braid that hung almost to her waist. But the most striking thing about Lily was her self-confidence. You could tell that Lily was perfectly happy with herself, but without a trace of arrogance. I wondered if I would attain that level of self-confidence by the time I reached fifty. I certainly hoped so.

"What detectives?" Lily asked, wrapping me in a warm, cinnamon-scented hug.

Bobbi Jo and I told Lily about the murder and her connection via the gun and her association with David.

"Dear Goddess, that's terrible," Lily said.

"I don't even want to think about it anymore. Edward told me if they come back that I shouldn't talk to them without our lawyer."

"That's good advice," Lily said. "I hope you plan to take it."

"Are you suggesting I'd do otherwise?" Bobbi Jo asked.

"Well, you've been known to fly off the handle."

"I have not!"

"Not to mention your harebrained ideas," Lily added.

"Yeah, not to mention those," I said, thinking about my previous evening.

"What?" Bobbi Jo asked. "Oh, Skye! Last night! What happened?

"Something happened last night? Besides the murder?" Lily asked.

"It's nothing, Lily." I wasn't really keen on sharing my disastrous attempt at seduction with Lily even if she was one of my best friends.

"You mean it didn't work?" Bobbi Jo asked, her eyes clouded with concern for me.

"What didn't work?" Lily was beginning to sound a little exasperated.

I gave up. I'd never kept anything from Lily and I knew I'd end up telling her the whole story eventually.

"Craig is a cross-dresser." I told Lily about the lingerie and his confession and my attempt to be a supportive wife.

Lily nodded. Nothing ever flustered that woman. "And how did that work out?"

"It didn't. Nothing happened."

Bobbi Jo frowned. "What? What do you mean nothing happened? Craig didn't like the panties?"

"He didn't like anything. The panties. The fact that I'd bought them. The French maid outfit. Nothing."

"It just doesn't make any sense. From my experience with a cross-dresser, he should have been ecstatic."

"Your experience?" Lily asked.

"Bobbi Jo was holding out on us," I said. "Seems her first husband was a cross-dresser and they had incredibly hot sex when he wore panties."

"Oh. And you were thinking the same thing would happen with Craig?"

"That was the plan. But it failed. Or I failed."

"I don't understand it. He can't be a cross-dresser," Bobbi Jo said.

"But he said the lingerie was his," Lily said.

"Obviously it wasn't. I should have known because it wasn't nearly big enough for him."

"So, you think there's another woman?" Lily asked.

"I don't know what to think. But he won't talk about it. He just keeps telling me that there is no other woman and for me to trust him. Although after last night I'm not sure he's talking to me at all."

"Well, how are you supposed to trust him when he won't tell you anything?" Bobbi Jo asked. "What are you going to do now?"

"What *can* I do?"

"You can find out what's up with him, that's what. Obviously there's something that he's not telling you and you have no choice but to find out what it is."

"I have to agree with her," Lily agreed. "After all,

it's affecting you and your marriage."

"I'm not going to spy on him," I said.

"That's not what I meant," Lily explained. "You need to find a way to get him to open up and talk to you."

"Craig? Talk about this? That will take a miracle." I'd spent a lot of years trying to get Craig to talk about his feelings. But, other than surface emotions, nothing. When I'd ask him how he felt about something, I usually got a grunt or possibly an admission that he'd never thought about it. It wasn't that he didn't talk. We talked about current events, television shows, movies, books, people. He just didn't talk about feelings.

"You have to try," Lily insisted. "And if he won't talk, then you'll just have to take matters into your own hands. Normally, I don't approve of prying into someone's secrets, but in this case, I think it's called for."

"I'll get him to talk to me and we'll work this out. It'll be fine." I didn't believe a word of what I was saying, but I didn't want to talk about it any longer.

"I've got to go open the shop," Lily said. Lily owned The Goddess Chalice, a New Age shop on Hawthorne Street.

"I really want to go see David. Skye, will you come with me?" Bobbi Jo asked.

"Sure." It beat going home and confronting last night's failure.

An hour later, we pulled up to David's house laden with a gift basket of fruit, cheese, and wine. David answered the door in a pair of cutoff sweatpants and no shirt. He looked like he'd been crying. He also looked like he could have been on the cover of *Muscle Man* magazine. Or *GQ* if he cleaned up. Tanned legs bulged with muscles I didn't know existed and led to a six-packed torso topped with impressive pecs. A thatch of sandy hair fell across his brilliant blue eyes. I was sure if he smiled his full lips would reveal even, blindingly white teeth. It was almost too much perfection to look at directly at him. Bobbi Jo introduced us and David invited us into the house.

"Sorry about the mess." David closed a pizza box on the coffee table and picked up a stack of body-building magazines from the sofa.

"How are you, David?" Bobbi Jo asked.

"I don't know," he said. "I can't really believe this whole thing." He took a deep breath and shook his head. "I can't stop thinking that it's all my fault."

"Oh, no, darlin'. You can't do that to yourself." Bobbi Jo patted David's shoulder and handed him a tissue from an almost empty box.

"It is, though. All because I didn't feel like going to work last night."

"Now, you can't start thinking that every little thing you did or didn't do led to this," Bobbi Jo said.

"It did. I'd pulled a muscle in my groin and Nat insisted on taking my shift at the gym. I was scheduled to work from two until closing last night. If I'd been the one getting into the car, she'd still be alive."

"You can't know that, David."

"I can't stop thinking about her. She was everything to me. We'd been together for three years, but it was like falling in love every day." Bobbi Jo patted his shoulder.

"Is that a picture of you and Nat?" I asked, pointing to an eight-by-ten framed photo next to the pizza box.

David picked up the picture. "We were on vacation at Yellowstone. She loved that Ironman hoodie. Wore it everywhere. People used to think we were twins when I wore mine. And we were twins. Soul twins."

In the photo, David wore a T-shirt and had an arm around Nat. She looked like an Olympic athlete. Tall and muscular with short blond hair and sparkling green eyes. They looked incredibly happy together. It certainly put my problems into perspective. Craig and I had issues but we could work through them.

I woke up in the guest bedroom again. Following Lily's advice to get Craig to talk about whatever was going on with him, I'd tried everything. I'd asked him every question I could think of. But instead of opening up to me, he'd gotten angry and refused to talk about anything. After accusing me of not trusting him, he'd stormed off to our bedroom. No way was I going to sleep in the same bed with him after that. I lay in bed, reluctant to get up even though it was almost eight. Craig would have left for the office an hour earlier—without his usual breakfast of scrambled eggs, toast, and coffee. That'd show him.

The phone rang and I looked at the caller ID. Bobbi Jo. I didn't really want to talk to anyone, but I was concerned about her after the visit from the cops yesterday. I picked up the phone and mumbled a hoarse greeting.

"Edward," she gasped between sobs.

"What? Is he okay?" Actually, Edward wasn't okay on the best of days. At sixty-two, he had already suffered several strokes and two heart attacks.

"I'm at Mercy Hospital," Bobbi Jo said. "He had another stroke and he's in a coma."

"Oh, sweetie, hang on. I'll be down as soon as I can get there."

"Hurry, Skye."

"Half an hour," I assured her. "I'll be there in half an hour."

I wrote Craig a quick note and stuck it on the refrigerator. Grooming consisted of brushing my teeth and pulling on jeans and a T-shirt. Ten minutes later I was in the Escape with the headset to my cell phone haphazardly placed over my unkempt hair. A glance in the rearview mirror told me that I should have taken a few more minutes to slather some foundation on my face. I punched a speed dial number on my cell phone. Lily would want to know, and Bobbi Jo would need all the support from her friends that she could get.

"Lily? Skye. Bobbi Jo's at the hospital with Edward."

"Holy Goddess! How bad is it?"

"I don't know, but he's in a coma. I'm on my way over there now. Can you come?"

"Of course. Mercy Hospital?"

"Yes."

"At least he'll get the best care there. I'll be along as soon as I can get Jasmine to fill in for me at the shop."

I punched the *end* button and threw the headset to the passenger seat. I'd always thought something like this was coming, even though Bobbi Jo seemed determine to ignore the possibility. Edward had been in poor health for some time. Diabetes, high blood pressure, heart problems. Bobbi Jo had married him when she was only twenty-six. Now, she faced the very real possibility of being a young widow.

I parked my Ford Escape, hoofed across the parking lot at a fast clip, and skidded to a stop at the receptionist's desk. Mercy Hospital's reception area boasted plush purple carpet; a curved, pink-veined marble counter; and a receptionist who should have been a supermodel. I smoothed the wrinkles in my T-shirt and ran a hand through my hair, wincing when I lost a few strands to the prongs in my wedding ring set.

"I'm here to see Bobbi Jo Melrose. Her husband is in intensive care." I waited while the receptionist typed in the name.

"Mrs. Melrose is probably in the ICU visitor lounge if she isn't with her husband. That's on the seventh floor."

I thanked her and took the elevator to the ICU floor and saw a sign for the visitor lounge. Bobbi Jo sat on the edge of a sofa with a paper cup of coffee on the table in front of her. She looked like hell. Her hair was mussed, and there were dark circles under her eyes. She wore a baggy pair of sweatpants and a faded T-shirt. She looked up when I came in, then rose and let me envelop her in a hug.

"How long have you been here?" I asked.

"I don't know. Five or six hours, I guess. Dr. Marcus has been with him for a few hours now."

"You should have called me."

"Well, at first, it was just so confusing. Edward and I were in bed, and suddenly he collapsed and I didn't know what was happening."

I poured a cup of water from the dispenser and

handed it to her. She took a couple of sips and set it down.

"I finally realized he was having a stroke or a heart attack and called 911." Bobbi Jo brushed fresh tears from her eyes. "By the time I could have called you, it was so late, I didn't want to wake you up."

"Oh, sweetie, you know you can wake me up any-time." I wrapped my arms around her again and let her cry for a few minutes. "How's he doing?"

"I don't know. That's the worst part of it. He's had strokes before, but he's never gone into a coma. Our family doctor is with him and he's called in a bunch of specialists. I told him to get the best. I don't care if it takes every penny we have. I can't lose him, Skye."

Just then Dr. Marcus appeared in the doorway. Bobbi Jo jumped up. "How is he? Is he all right? Can I see him now?"

"Not just yet. We have him stabilized and now we need to run some tests."

"Is he still in a coma?" she asked.

"I'm afraid so. We'll have a better idea of his con-dition after all the tests are done. But for now, the best thing you can do is get some rest yourself."

"I'll take her home," I said.

"No. I want to be here in case he wakes up." She shook her head. "When. *When* he wakes up." Then she started crying again.

"You can't do anything right now, Bobbi Jo. The

tests will take some time. Go home and get some rest so you'll be able to see him when he wakes up." Dr. Marcus handed her a small bottle of pills. "These will help you sleep, and I'll call you at home as soon as we know anything."

I called Lily, told her to meet us at Bobbi Jo's house, and hustled Bobbi Jo into the Escape. She'd finally stopped crying. Now she just stared blankly out the window. Again, I was reminded that my problems weren't the worst thing in the world. Craig and I might be having a rough patch right now, but at least he wasn't in the hospital. In a coma.

I'd just gotten Bobbi Jo settled on the sofa and given her one of the pills when the doorbell chimed.

"How's she doing?" Lily asked softly when I opened Bobbi Jo's front door.

"Not good. Edward's still in a coma, and they're running tests."

Lily nodded and handed me a small paper bag. "I brought her some of my herbal tea. It'll help her sleep."

"But the doctor already gave her some pills to do that."

"It won't hurt to give her both. And this won't leave her groggy when she wakes up." Lily waved me toward the kitchen and bustled into the living room to wrap Bobbi Jo in one of her earth-mother embraces.

When I brought the tea to Bobbi Jo, Lily took the cup from me and placed it in Bobbi Jo's hand. "Here, this will help."

"Thanks, Lily. I don't know what I'd do without you two." Bobbi Jo sipped the tea, made a face, and set the cup down. "What's in this?"

"Just some herbs. I blended it myself. It'll help you sleep."

"If I promise to sleep, can I stop drinking it?" Bobbi Jo asked. I muffled a chuckle. Lily's potions worked, but a lot of them tasted worse than castor oil. Lily pushed the cup up to Bobbi's Jo's lips again.

"Let's get you into bed." Lily rose, pulled Bobbi Jo to her feet, and herded her down the hallway and up the stairs. I followed and we got Bobbi Jo undressed and tucked in. She was drifting off when we closed the bedroom door behind us.

"You should go home, Skye. Grant and Kyle have gone fishing, Jasmine is at the shop, and I have nothing better to do than stay here and take care of her."

Grant is Lily's husband and Kyle is her lover. The three of them have been in a poly-amorous relationship for ten years. Grant and Lily had been married for twenty years when she met Kyle. Lily and Kyle fell in love and, being unwilling to cheat on her husband and equally unwilling to ignore her feelings for Kyle, Lily proposed an arrangement. And for the past ten years they have all been in a relationship together. Lily spends half the week with Grant and the other half with Kyle. Kyle and Grant not only love Lily enough to accept this arrangement, they have become best friends. Go figure, because I certainly can't. I can't even manage a relationship with *one* man.

"Thanks. I have a roofer coming over to give us an estimate and I need to be there."

"Take your time."

I waited an hour for the roofer to show up before I noticed the answering machine was blinking. I pushed the *play* button and listened to the man explain that he'd double booked appointments and would have to reschedule. Normally, I'd have been annoyed, but there was so much going on, I was relieved to have a little time to myself. I thought Bobbi Jo would still be sleeping and Lily was there, so I sat down and thought about my own problems.

It was obvious Craig wasn't going to talk to me about whatever he was going through. And if he wouldn't talk, how would I ever know? How could I deal with something if I didn't know what it was? I thought back to my conversation with Lily and Bobbie Jo. Both of them had encouraged me to take matters into my own hands.

I couldn't spy on Craig. Could I? I'd never done that. But I'd never had a reason to before, and I was back to wondering if there was an Amazon goddess in his life. There had to be some reason for that slutty pink thing. Lily, of all people, had told me that she approved of me snooping around to find out what was going on with Craig. It was like getting dispensation from the pope. Who was I to fly in the face of that?

I stood in my living room and considered the situation. Where to start? I knew every inch of this house. There were no secrets here. Not from me. I dusted every single item in the house twice a week. I cleaned everything. I rearranged everything.

I walked through the dining room and into the kitchen. Certainly Craig would never hide anything there. That was my domain. I cooked our meals there; I sat at the breakfast table and scheduled and arranged our lives. No, it had to be somewhere else. I moved on to our bedroom.

The bed was only slightly rumpled on Craig's side, so I straightened the bedding and tossed on the throw pillows. Craig's armoire stood on the wall opposite the bed. Of course I put Craig's clothes away in the armoire, but I'd never really looked through it. Until now, I'd never had a reason to.

I opened the door and scanned the shelves. But they held only the usual items. I pulled open the bottom drawer and riffled through the mismatched socks and sports clothes. I repeated the process on the other drawers but came up with nothing. The only drawer left was the one on top that I couldn't see into. It would be the perfect place to hide something, wouldn't it?

I pulled the occasional chair from across the room and positioned it underneath the drawer. I stepped up on the seat and paused with my hand on the drawer pull. What if I found something I'd rather not know about? But I wanted answers, didn't I? I opened the drawer and looked inside. A box of studs and cuff links for his tuxedo; an old wallet, which was empty; and a collection of ticket stubs, business cards, and match-books from various events we'd attended. I didn't know if I was disappointed or relieved. But I definitely felt guilty.

I returned the chair to the corner and pulled the hamper from the closet. I could do the laundry. At least that was something constructive. I was halfway through sorting the whites and colors when I thought about the den. He used it as a home office when he worked at night or on weekends. I only used it to check my e-mail, play solitaire, and pay the bills. If he was going to hide anything, that's where it would be. I abandoned the laundry and hurried to the den.

Craig kept the home office neat and organized. He even dusted the computer and desktop so I only had to run the vacuum over the carpet once a week. Now I wondered if there was a reason for him cleaning the room. I must have bumped into the desk when I plopped down in the chair, because the screen had been black and then flashed open. But instead of the usual blue background with myriad icons, the screen was filled with a Yahoo e-mail account.

My hand twitched toward the mouse, but I stopped, realizing that this was an e-mail account I'd never seen before. I looked at the top of the page and saw *Welcome, CJW.* Craig James Williams? Who else would it be? I clicked on the in-box icon and the screen blinked and became a log-in screen with the ID *CJW Looking*.

My stomach lurched. What the hell was my husband up to? There was only one way to find out. Log into the e-mail and look around.

Fortunately, Craig was nothing if not predictable. I knew the password he used for everything was *Sheridan* spelled backward. So I typed in *nadirehs* and clicked *okay*. The screen blinked and his in-box appeared with a message from *Sassigrrl*.

My heart pounded and I felt hot all over. So much for all his assurances about not having an affair. This had to be the Amazon goddess.

My eyes flew over the words in the e-mail.

So glad I found your ad . . . can't wait to see you in person . . . sending you a little present . . . look forward to wearing it for you . . . here's a preview.

Son of a bitch! Rat bastard! Lousy, rotten scumbag!

Then I noticed the attachment icon, clicked on it, and waited while the picture opened up. Nothing could have prepared me for the photo of the bubble-gum pink froth with gold lacy ruffles. The same one I'd found under Craig's side of the bed.

With a fully erect penis protruding from the open crotch.

CHAPTER THREE

I stared at the penis for several seconds. Maybe it was more like minutes. Could have been longer. It was a kind of morbid fascination. How often do you see a penis surrounded by pink nylon and gold lace? Finally, I closed the e-mail, grabbed my purse, and left the house.

I started the Escape and sat in the driveway. The problem was I had nowhere to go. I just didn't want to be at home anymore. And I really didn't want to be home when Craig got there. Lily was at Bobbi Jo's and she would be a calming influence. She'd listen and then she would make me believe that it wasn't all that bad.

Then I felt like shit. One of my best friends was going through something terrible and I was all involved with my own problems. Not that they were insignificant. But having your husband in a coma was a bit more serious than a husband having an affair. But this wasn't just an affair. This was another *man*. This went much deeper than just a midlife crisis. If Craig were having an affair with a woman, it could mean that there was something wrong with our marriage. Something that could be fixed. But another man meant something so enormous I was having trouble assimilating it. I needed to talk to someone about it. Someone who would understand. Someone who could help me sort it all out.

I drove to Bobbi Jo's and on the way decided that I wasn't going to talk about it to Lily or Bobbi Jo. My problem could wait until we knew what was happening with Edward. It had only been a couple of hours since I left Bobbi Jo's house, and she was probably still asleep from the herbal tea and the pills the doctor gave her. But I could at least see how she was doing. It was certainly better than thinking about what was happening with my own life.

That's what I intended. But when Lily opened the door, I burst into tears.

"Oh, honey, what's the matter?" Lily put an arm around me and pulled me inside the large foyer. "Come on in and tell me about it."

"H-h-how's Bobbi Jo?" I asked. Then I was sobbing again.

"She's still sleeping. Now come here and tell me what's bothering you." Lily led me into the kitchen, pushed me onto a stool at the breakfast bar, and turned

51

to the sink. She filled a copper kettle with water while I tried to get my emotions under control.

"I'm sorry. I really just wanted to know how Bobbi Jo was doing." My words were somewhere between a sob and a whisper, which annoyed me so much I took a deep breath and willed myself to stop.

Lily nodded as she dropped a tea bag into a cup. "I see." After a few minutes the pot whistled and she poured the water into the cup. More tea. Lily thought everything could be fixed with a cup of tea. I didn't want tea. I wanted this whole mess to just go away.

"You know, you can just use that spigot on the side of the sink. The water from it is almost boiling."

"I know. But there's just something I like about a kettle on the stove." Lily set the tea in front of me. "Now, you want to tell me what the tears are about?"

"Craig left the computer on and there was this e-mail . . ."

"Oh, dear." Lily sat on a stool across from me. "I take it you found something you'd rather have not known?"

"You could say that. There was an e-mail account with the log-in ID, *CJW Looking*. It was open, but I had to use a password anyway. I guess it had timed out. Anyway, it wasn't hard to figure out the password. I mean, it was Craig's and he only uses one password for everything. So I just typed it in and there it was." I was babbling, but I couldn't seem to stop. "It was just awful. I don't know what I thought I'd find, but that wasn't it. No one would ever expect to find anything like that."

"Slow down, Skye." Lily gripped my hand and squeezed hard to stop me. "So, you found a secret e-mail account, and what was there?"

"An e-mail. I thought it was from another woman. It was talking about them getting together. And there was a picture attached and I opened it." Damn, I was sobbing again. I wanted to stop, but it just kept happening.

"The picture was of that sleazy lingerie I found under his side of the bed."

"Oh, no." Lily frowned. "So, Craig really has been having an affair."

"No. I mean, I don't know. The e-mail just said something about the possibility of them getting to-gether. So maybe they haven't even met or anything. Except online."

"Well, then, maybe it was just an idea he was playing with. You know, just for excitement. Maybe nothing even happened."

"That's not it."

"Then what was it?" Lily was beginning to sound a little testy, but if she would just shut up and let me get it all out, she'd know.

"The picture was of a man wearing the lingerie."

"Oh. Are you sure it was a man?"

"Trust me, that was no woman."

"Maybe it was just a really ugly woman."

"With a penis?"

"Oh." Understanding dawned on Lily's face.

"There's a really ugly woman with a penis?" Bobbi Jo asked from the doorway.

"You should still be sleeping, Bobbi Jo." She didn't look much better than she had at the hospital. Her eyes were puffy and her face drawn. There were lines at the corner of her eyes that I'd never seen before.

Bobbi Jo waved a hand and pulled her robe tighter. "I can't sleep any more. Did the doctor call?"

"Not yet," Lily answered. "You want some tea?"

"Coffee. That tea kicked my ass." Bobbi Jo punched a few buttons on the coffeemaker and the thing fed coffee beans into a grinder, ground them, and started the coffee. "Now what's this about an ugly woman with a penis?"

I giggled. Lily chuckled with me. I laughed harder. Bobbi Jo grinned and then started laughing with us. I laughed so hard, I cried.

"Awww, darlin'." Bobbi Jo wrapped an arm around me. "Whatever it is, it can't be that bad." She used the belt on her terry-cloth robe to dab at the tears on my face. "Now, tell me all about it."

Between sobs and hiccups, I told her about the secret e-mail account and the photo of the lingerie with the penis.

"Oh, my gawd! Craig is gay?"

"Not necessarily," Lily said. "He could just be curious, or bisexual."

"I'm not sure that's any better. The fact is that Craig wants to have sex with a man. I don't care if you call it gay, or bisexual, or on the down low. Her marriage is over."

"Well, it's not as bad as all that," Lily interjected.

Bobbi Jo rolled her eyes. "What the hell does that mean, Lily? How could it be any worse? Her husband is having an *affair*. With a *man*. Is there something about that you don't understand?"

"Oh, sit down and have your coffee, Bobbi Jo." Lily poured coffee into a mug and handed it to her. "I understand perfectly well. I'm just saying that Skye has more than one option here."

"I do?" I didn't think I had any choices. Then I realized how incredibly ridiculous that was. Of course I had choices. I just didn't know what any of them might be. Lily looked like she was about to enlighten me. I didn't know if that was comforting or a little scary.

"Well, I'm sure a lot of women would think the only thing to do is to divorce him," Lily said.

"Of course. What else is there to do?"

"She could choose to open her marriage to Craig's lover."

"Lily, I know that your situation works for you." Bobbi Jo held up a hand when Lily started to respond. "And for Grant and Kyle, too. But not everyone wants that sort of—situation."

"It's called polyamory, Bobbi Jo, and I realize that it isn't for everyone. Some people enjoy monogamy. I'm just saying that it's something Skye could possibly consider."

The phone rang, which effectively ended the conversation my friends were having about my marital issues. Bobbi Jo set her coffee cup down so hard the coffee splashed onto the granite-topped counter. Lily picked up the phone, spoke for a moment, and handed it to Bobbi Jo.

"Yes. I see. I'll be there in an hour." She handed the phone back to Lily with a shaky hand.

"Was that the doctor?" I asked.

"He said Edward has come out of the coma. They're still running tests, but they should be done soon."

"Oh, that's great news!" I pulled Bobbi Jo up. "Go take a shower and I'll drive you to the hospital."

"You don't have to do that, Skye. I can drive myself."

"Nonsense. I'm happy to drive you." Because it beat the alternative, which was going home and confronting Craig.

Dr. Marcus met us at the elevator and whisked Bobbi Jo away. I retreated to the ICU waiting room and pondered my own situation while drinking stale coffee.

My mind skittered around actually labeling Craig as bisexual or gay. I'd never been one to label people so I tried to just consider the facts. Obviously Craig was interested in men. From the picture I'd seen I had to assume it wasn't just friendship he was interested in. But that could mean anything from him just wanting to look at pictures to wanting to marry one. My breathing became rapid and shallow. Okay. I'd just think about what Lily had said. She was always the voice of compromise if not reason.

The idea of a polyamory marriage didn't appeal to me. I knew it worked for Lily, but I was definitely one of those people who needed monogamy. Still, I would give it some consideration. What if it would save my marriage? How would it work? Would Craig spend half his time with me and half with the Penis-in-Lingerie? How could he even be attracted to both of us? How would we explain it to our daughter? Or would we keep it a secret from her? A secret from everyone? I didn't like any of the possibilities. I didn't think I could really adjust to it. But the final question that rolled around in my head was the clincher. Could anything save our marriage?

No, polyamory wasn't the answer. At least not to the real question. To my mind, the real question was Craig's sexuality. And until I had the answer to that, I couldn't even begin to think of solutions. Not once in my entire life had I suspected I'd be wondering about my husband's sexuality. After all, Craig was a big, tall, masculine guy. There was nothing the least bit effeminate about him. He wasn't interested in how I decorated the house or what I cooked for dinner. He preferred beer to wine. He watched all kinds of sports. His idea of a great vacation was a backpack and a few thousand acres of wilderness. Craig was a man's man.

That thought struck me as pretty damn funny and I snickered. Then I snorted, which garnered me some strange looks from the other two people in the waiting room. I tried to control myself and sipped at my coffee. The snickers and giggles wouldn't stop and when I snorted coffee through my nose, the couple got up and left. That was good because when Bobbi Jo came in after half an hour, we had the place to ourselves.

"How's Edward?"

"I don't know yet." Bobbi Jo sat down beside me.

"What did Dr. Marcus say?"

"Not a damn thing, the bastard." Bobbi Jo shook her head. "All he would say is that I need to talk to Edward before he can discuss his condition with me. What kind of doctor double-talk is that?" She got up and poured herself a cup of coffee.

"And on top of that, I saw a 'Do Not Resuscitate' order on Edward's chart."

"What?" A cold knot formed in my stomach.

"Oh, I gave the damn doctor hell about that, too. But he said that was Edward's wish and that I needed to talk to him." She slammed the cup down, spilling some coffee onto the counter. "And I would, if they would let me in to see him."

"Calm down, Bobbi Jo. When did they say you could see him?"

"As soon as the last test is done. It should be soon." Bobbi Jo plucked a couple of tissues from the box on the table and blew her nose. "Damn, I hate waiting."

"Oh, look, there he is."

We could see Edward being wheeled into one of the ICU rooms from the elevator. He didn't look good. There were liquid-filled bags hanging on rods, and tubes running all over. His complexion was gray, and I'd have thought he was closer to eighty than sixty-two. Bobbi Jo dropped the tissues and stood up. The nurse saw her and hurried over to the waiting room, holding up a hand to stop her.

"We need to get him settled, Mrs. Melrose," the nurse chirped. "I'll come and get you when he's ready. It'll only be five or ten minutes."

Bobbi Jo nodded and sank down to the sofa, burying

her face in her hands. "This is all my fault, Skye."

"No, Bobbi Jo, it isn't."

"It is!" She burst into tears.

"Now, Bobbi Jo, stop that. You don't want to have puffy eyes and a red nose when you go in to see Edward, do you?" I plucked a few more tissues out of the box and handed them to her.

"You know, Edward and I haven't made love since he had his first heart attack?"

Oh, yes, I knew. We had talked about it at length. Bobbi Jo had told me that it wasn't a big deal to her. Certainly she missed having sex with her husband, but their love was about more than just a physical union. Of course, I'd always thought that of my marriage, too.

"Well, last night, Edward was feeling frisky and wanted to make love. I kept asking him if he was sure. But he just said he wanted one more time with me. Oh, gawd! Now that I think of it, it's like he knew this would happen. If I'd had any idea, I never would have done anything."

"Bobbi Jo, don't do this to yourself. You don't even know exactly what the problem is. It's probably nothing to do with the fact that you made love last night."

"But it had to be. He collapsed right after he— well, you know." Bobbi Jo burst into fresh tears. I was trying to comfort her when Sean approached the sitting area.

"Bobbi Jo? Are you all right?" he asked.

"Oh, Sean, you didn't need to come down here. There isn't anything you can do, really."

"I wanted to be here for you. I'd thought he was feeling better lately. He's been coming into the office more often," Sean said.

Bobbi Jo nodded. "He had more energy. I thought the latest medicine they put him on had really helped his heart condition. But now . . ."

"Don't think the worst, Bobbi Jo. Edward's been through a lot. He'll get through this, too," I said.

The nurse stepped into the sitting area and motioned to Bobbi Jo. I dried her tears and waved her off to see her husband, hoping she'd get some good news.

"This is the last thing Bobbi Jo needs," Sean said. "I mean with the homicide investigation."

I'd pushed that to the back of my mind. So much had happened in the past two days. "I can't believe that detective had the nerve to insinuate something might be going on between Bobbi Jo and her personal trainer. Bobbi Jo and I visited him. David's really torn up about it. He blames himself because Natalie took his shift at the gym because he'd injured himself."

Sean nodded and jingled the change in his pocket. "I remembered that one of the times I called Edward that night, Bobbi Jo answered the phone. So, at least I was able to confirm she was at home."

"I just hope the police believe you. That Detective Spiner was a jerk."

"I need to get back to the office." Sean nodded to me and left.

With Sean gone, I was left alone in the waiting room with more time to consider my situation. Until yesterday my biggest concern had been that I was facing an empty nest when Sheridan left for college in the fall. Some days I couldn't imagine what life would be like without her in the house, and other days I'd think of all the things I could do with my free time. More time to garden, to visit my friends. Maybe I'd even take some classes at the community college. Perhaps get back into photography. Now, I wondered if I would be losing my daughter and my husband both.

Anger flared inside me. How could Craig do something that put our marriage in jeopardy? I didn't even know what he'd done or why. And maybe that was what I was really feeling. Fear that it was all about to change and frustration that there might not be a damn thing I could do about it.

My thoughts were interrupted when Bobbi Jo returned, tears running down her cheeks. I felt a twinge of guilt that I'd been thinking about my problems, which were petty and insignificant compared to what Bobbi Jo was facing. I put my arms around her and listened as she told me about Edward between sobs.

The good news was that Bobbi Jo had not screwed her husband to death. The bad news was that he was dying anyway.

I drove Bobbi Jo home and forced her to drink a cup of Lily's herbal tea in between sips of scotch. She alternately sobbed in anguish at the prospect of his death and railed in anger that he hadn't told her earlier that he was suffering from a terminal form of cancer.

I finally got most of the story, which was that Edward had been diagnosed with cancer a couple of years earlier. It was inoperable and basically untreatable. At least, Edward wasn't willing to go through the treatment they could offer him. He'd only told her about it now because the doctor had informed him that this was probably the end. As in he had maybe a few months to live.

My problems paled in comparison.

Craig looked up from his newspaper and gave me a tentative smile when I walked into the living room. "You look exhausted. How about a glass of wine?"

Oh, great. He was doing the whole there's-nothing-wrong-we'll-just-ignore-that-little-lingerie incident. But I wasn't sure I could handle any confrontations and a glass of wine sounded good, so I nodded.

Craig went to the sideboard in the dining room and poured a glass for me.

"I figured you were still with Bobbi Jo, so I made a sandwich for dinner. How is Edward?"

"He's dying." Saying the words aloud shattered my control. Hot tears rolled down my cheeks and I couldn't stop them. Craig set the wine down and walked over to put his arms around me.

"God, Skye, that's terrible."

He held me while I sobbed and all I could think was how much I'd miss him if we broke up. He had been my rock for so many years. The anger I'd felt before faded away as I stood there with my head against his warm chest, inhaling his unique fragrance, and feeling his strong arms around me.

There's something about living with someone for almost twenty years. Depending on each other for so many things. Weathering the good and the bad together. Even if everything's not perfect, you know that you can depend on that person. Right now, I needed to lean on someone and Craig was there for me. Just like he'd always been. It made the whole lingerie incident seem surreal.

Unfortunately, thinking about that brought me back to the fact that I had to tell him about the e-mail and the picture. Putting it off wouldn't make it any easier on either of us. I pulled away and moved to pick up the glass of wine.

"We need to talk." I might as well have told him we needed to remove one of his testicles. His face screwed into a grimace, then he tried to smile.

"Sure." He went into the kitchen and came out with a beer. "What about?"

"The lingerie." I could tell that he just barely stopped himself from rolling his eyes. "And an e-mail I found on the computer today." I pulled a chair out and sat at the dining room table.

"E-mail?" A flicker of concern shadowed his eyes.

"I found your other e-mail account open on the computer today."

"What e-mail account? You mean the one we both use?" Craig sat down at the table and rolled his beer bottle between his palms.

"No, the *CJW Looking* account." I sipped my wine, giving him time to respond, but he said nothing. I'd learned a long time ago that his first defense was to deny and his second was total silence. "There was an e-mail from *Sassigrrl* with a photo attached."

Craig stopped rolling the beer bottle and stared at the tabletop. "Dear God. I wish you hadn't seen that."

"I didn't think you'd left it open for me to find. But we need to talk about this, Craig."

"There's nothing to talk about."

"Craig, you obviously have some issues about your

sexuality. You need to deal with them." I cleared my throat, which felt unaccountably tight. "*We* need to deal with it."

"I can't believe I've been so stupid." He set his beer down and cradled his head in his hands.

"Listen, I don't think this has to mean the end of our marriage. But we need to get this all out in the open so we can both decide how to handle it."

Silence.

"If you're interested in men, maybe you need to explore that."

"No!"

"But how else are you going to know what you want?" How else was I going to know if my marriage would survive?

"I already know," he mumbled.

"Know what?"

"It was just a curiosity, Skye. I never really intended to go through with anything. When that guy sent me that e-mail and then the lingerie, I realized that it had gone too far."

Now it was my turn to be silent. Mostly because I couldn't think of anything to say. Partly because I wanted him to keep talking. Mostly, I wanted to believe him.

"The reason you found the e-mail account is that I e-mailed him this morning before I went to work. I told him that I didn't want to hear from him again. That it was all a mistake."

"A mistake?"

"The whole thing was just wrong for me. I realize that now. I don't want anything to do with it."

"Just like that?"

"It doesn't mean anything to me. God, Skye, I never meant for anything to come of this. It was just curiosity. It was nothing."

"But these feelings, these desires had to come from somewhere. I mean, I've never been curious about having sex with another woman."

"It's different with men. Men don't look at sex the way women do. It doesn't have to be emotional for us." He took another swig of beer.

"I see." I didn't, but what else was I going to say?

"Let's just forget it ever happened. Chalk it up to a midlife crisis."

This was actually what I'd wanted to hear, wasn't it? That it had all been a mistake. That we could just forget about it and our lives would be normal again. Like it had never happened.

So, why didn't I feel any better?

CHAPTER FOUR

Lily was with a customer when I dropped by The Goddess Chalice to pick up some of the tea she blended for me. The shop was crammed with everything a New Ager might want. Silver jewelry featured goddesses, fairies, pentacles, and Celtic knot work. There were bins of incense, stacks of tarot cards, teas that Lily blended herself, and candles in every size, shape, color, and aroma imaginable. Lily finished with the customer and walked out from around the counter.

"How's Bobbi Jo?"

"About as well as can be expected. She's at the hospital with Edward right now."

"She's there almost all the time, isn't she? I've called her several times over the past few weeks, but I just get her voice mail."

"She wants to spend every minute with him. But she said he might be able to come home later this week, or maybe next. I'm sure they're both looking forward to that. He's been in the hospital for a month now."

I sat in one of the rocking chairs in a corner of the shop while Lily dropped tea bags into cups and poured water over them from a kettle that she kept on a hot plate. "Edward's son, Brian, came in from New York a couple of days ago."

"What's he like?"

"Late thirties. Too good looking to be real. An actor, I understand. I don't think he's ever held a real job. He's staying in the guesthouse. Said he didn't want to impose on Bobbi Jo by staying in the main house."

"Brian is Edward's only child, isn't he?"

"Yes. Bobbi Jo told me that Edward has been supporting him since he moved to New York. Edward doesn't talk about him, and I get the impression that he's disappointed in his son's choice of career."

"Oh, I'm sure Edward wanted a son who would follow in his footsteps and take over the business."

I shrugged. "Whatever he wanted, that's not what he got. I get the feeling that they're not very close. Although Brian says he's going to stay until the end."

"How's Bobbi Jo with that?"

"I haven't really been able to talk to her about any of it. But we're having lunch today. I'm so worried about her, Lily. I don't know how she's going to handle his death. And they still haven't found who killed that woman with Bobbi Jo's gun."

"What a strange coincidence that her gun was stolen

and then used to kill someone she had a connection to."

"I'm not sure the police are buying that it's a coincidence. That Detective Spiner has spoken to Bobbi Jo a couple of times and once he made a snide comment about there being no such thing as a coincidence."

"What a jerk. She doesn't need to deal with that on top of Edward's health. I suppose she'll handle his death the best she can. At least she knows it's coming now." She handed me a cup and took the chair across from me. "I could just strangle Edward for keeping this from her for so long."

"He thought it was best, and maybe it was."

"And what about you?" Lily asked.

"What about me?" I knew what she meant, I just wanted to avoid talking about it.

"You look like hell. Have you and Craig talked anymore?"

The bell over the door jingled and I felt a rush of relief at the interruption. Craig and I hadn't talked any further about his escapade. I'd tried to bring it up a couple of times, but he quietly refused to talk about it and I'd tried to convince myself that everything was fine. I suspected I was in denial, but I wasn't ready for anyone to point that out to me.

"Hey, Mom. Oh, Skye. Hi." Lily's daughter, Jasmine, waved from the door. "I haven't seen you in ages. Did Mom tell you I'm getting married?"

"Of course she did. I can't wait to meet him."

"You'll love him. David is so wonderful. We're really connected, you know? He totally gets me and he's so supportive."

I could only imagine the kind of man who *got* Jasmine. Don't get me wrong—I love the girl. But she is her mother's daughter. Very New Age. Long, flowing, gauzy dresses; flowers in her hair; and lots of silver jewelry. There were rings on almost every finger and a heavy silver pentacle hung around her neck on a velvet string. A Celtic knot design was tattooed around one upper arm and a fairy on her shoulder. Jasmine was truly the love child of Lily and Grant.

"Did she tell you about the wedding? Oh, it's going to be beautiful. I decided to have an all blue wedding. You know, the color blue has exactly the right vibration for a wedding."

"Really?" I didn't even know that colors vibrated.

"Oh, definitely. And it's my personal color, too. And David likes it. But he likes everything I do."

"I remember being excited about my own wedding."

"Was it blue, too?"

"Uh, no. It was very traditional. But I was very excited about planning it. Your wedding is just a couple months away, right?"

"The last Saturday in August." Jasmine nodded energetically. "It was so hard to choose a date."

71

"Oh, I understand. Trying to find a date that most of the family isn't already committed to doing something else is difficult."

"Oh, I didn't think about that. I was trying to find a date where the moon was waxing and Venus was well-aspected for both of us." She leaned forward and put a hand on my knee. "That's very important for the sexual aspects of the marriage."

I wondered how Venus was aspected when Craig and I had taken our vows. Not exceptionally well, I suspected.

"And my wedding planner is fantastic. She's so totally cool." Jasmine waved her hands as she talked. "Let me tell you, it wasn't easy finding one who could see the importance of having the entire wedding blue. But Barbara agreed with me totally."

"You were lucky to find her, then."

"Oh, it wasn't luck. It was a spell. I cast a spell to find the right wedding planner and it worked. Just like the spell I cast to find my one true love, which, of course, is David."

I smiled and nodded. I was so out of my element. The bell jingled again as the door opened to admit another customer.

"Oh, Derek." Lily turned and hurried over to the man. "The tea you wanted is ready. I'm glad you stopped by."

In the space of a few seconds Lily morphed right

before my eyes. One minute she'd been the nurturing earth-mother about to counsel me on my marriage; the next, she was a giddy, flirtatious girl, cooing over the handsome young man who'd just arrived.

"Hi, Lily." The man wrapped his arms around Lily's plump form and lifted her off the ground, then planted a brief kiss on her lips. "How's my girl?"

His girl? The man was at least a dozen years younger than Lily. She placed a hand on his broad shoulder and reached up with the other one to smooth back a lock of chestnut hair that had fallen across his forehead.

"I have to run," Jasmine said. "I just wanted to stop by and say hi." Jasmine gave her mother a kiss and waved at me. "Nice to see you, Derek." She floated out of the shop in a cloud of patchouli.

"Derek, I'd like you to meet one of my best friends." Lily took his hand and pulled him over. "Skye, this is Derek."

Derek and I barely greeted each other before Lily led him over to the counter where she had his special tea stashed. I almost forgot to drink my tea as I watched them. There were soft giggles from Lily, and Derek kept holding earrings and necklaces up to Lily's neck and ears, letting his hands skim along her cheek and neck. I was stunned and watched them shamelessly until Derek finally took his tea and left.

"What the hell was that?" I demanded.

"What?" Lily assumed an air of innocence but I wasn't buying it.

"You were flirting with that man. Outrageously. Who is he?"

"He's a friend. Although I wouldn't mind if he were more than that." Lily giggled.

"I gathered that much. Lily, are you having an affair with him?"

"Heavens, no! I would never cheat on Grant and Kyle."

"You just said you wouldn't mind if he were more than a friend."

"Well, yes, I did. But I would never do anything unless Grant and Kyle agreed."

"This is too much for me. I can't imagine having a husband and a lover and wanting another one."

"So, Craig satisfies every one of your needs?" Lily asked.

That stopped me in my tracks. I didn't answer Lily but the minute she asked the question, my mind had screamed *NO!* In fact, I couldn't think of any need that Craig was satisfying lately. Worse, I wasn't even sure what my needs were. I was saved from thinking about it any further by the chirp of my cell phone. I dug it out of my bag and flipped it open.

"Skye?"

"Oh, Bobbi Jo. Am I late for lunch?" I glanced at

my watch. Eleven thirty. I wasn't supposed to meet her for an hour.

"It's Edward." Her voice was almost a whisper. "He's gone."

Edward's doctor had asked Bobbi Jo if he could perform an autopsy. The cancer that had killed him was rare and little was known about it. Bobbi Jo had agreed, of course, hoping they would discover something that would help someone else with the same disease. Brian had argued against it, saying he didn't like the idea of his father's body being desecrated. But Bobbi Jo had stood her ground, insisting that Edward would want to do anything that would help someone else. The doctor scheduled the autopsy for the following week, so Bobbi Jo had delayed the memorial service until the weekend following the autopsy.

The next week was a blur of exhausting activity. I spent as much time as possible with Bobbi Jo. I helped her pick out an urn for Edward's ashes on Tuesday. I arranged for a caterer for the reception that would take place after the memorial service on Wednesday. I held her hand while she listened to the reading of Edward's will on Friday. I answered her phone and relayed messages of condolence. I kept a list of everyone who sent flowers and cards. Mostly, I listened to her cry. And on Saturday, I answered her door when the detective came by.

"Is Mrs. Melrose in?"

"Detective Madison, right?" I asked.

A shadow darkened his light blue eyes and he ran a hand through his short black hair. "Right. We met when I was investigating the Natalie Turner homicide."

"Where's the other detective?"

"Detective Spiner is busy with another case. Why?"

"I didn't care for his attitude last time."

"I see. I'd like to speak to Mrs. Melrose."

"I'm sorry, she isn't receiving visitors right now. May I give her a message?"

"I'm afraid not. I have to see her."

"What's this about?" I could tell from the stubborn look on his handsome face that he wasn't going to tell me. "Her husband just passed away a few days ago. If this can wait—"

"This pertains to his death."

"Oh, I see." I opened the door wider and motioned him to follow me. "Have a seat. I'll get her." What the hell could this be about? I slid open the screen door to the patio. Bobbi Jo was sitting under the shade of an umbrella. The glass of iced tea I'd made for her was untouched, the ice cubes almost melted. The fashion magazine on the table hadn't been opened.

"Bobbi Jo? There's someone here to see you."

"I don't want to see anyone."

"I know, sweetie, but it's Detective Madison from the police bureau."

"Tell him his timing sucks and if he wants to talk to me again about that murder, he needs to make an appointment with my lawyer."

"I think you need to talk to him. He said it's about Edward."

Bobbi Jo looked up, perplexed. "Edward?"

"Let's just go talk to him. I'll stay with you."

"Okay."

She'd been like this since Edward's death. Just going through the motions. I was worried about her, and I didn't think the detective was going to make her grieving process any better.

"You wanted to see me?" Bobbi Jo asked.

"Mrs. Melrose. I'm sorry to bother you at a time like this."

"Please have a seat." Bobbi Jo gestured to a chair as she sat on the sofa. I sat next to her and held her cold hand.

"Mrs. Melrose, I've just received the results of your husband's autopsy."

"I don't understand. Why would you be informed about that?"

"Normally I wouldn't. But the autopsy revealed that your husband didn't die from the cancer."

"Then what did he die from? A heart attack? Another stroke?"

"He died from an overdose of a beta-blocker. That's a drug often given to patients suffering from heart problems."

Bobbi Jo nodded. "Edward routinely took a beta-blocker. He'd been taking it for several months. It seemed to be helping."

"Do you have that medicine here?"

"Of course."

"Could I see it?" He stood up.

"I'll get it," I volunteered. "Is it in the bath-room?"

"In the right-hand drawer," Bobbi Jo said.

"I'm sorry, I don't want anyone else handling the bottle. If you'll just show me where they are?"

Bobbi Jo nodded, stood, and led the way to the bathroom. I tagged along and watched from the doorway while he used a tissue to drop the bottle into a plastic bag. He held the bag up and looked intently at the transparent amber bottle. We all trooped back to the front room.

"When did you get this filled?" he asked.

"A few days before Edward went into the hospital. Why?"

"There're only about a dozen pills in here. The label says the prescription was for sixty pills."

"The bottle was almost full. Edward hadn't taken more than a few of them." She looked confused. I was probably starting to look a little pissed off. Was the detective suggesting something? Like Bobbi Jo had overdosed Edward?

"Your husband received a massive dose of this drug, which caused his death."

Bobbi Jo gasped. "Are you saying my husband was murdered?"

"We ruled out the possibility of suicide since your husband didn't have access to the pills. Unless someone assisted him."

"Edward would have seen suicide as cowardly."

"Are you suggesting that someone assisted Edward to commit suicide by giving him the pills?" I asked.

Detective Madison turned his attention to me. "No, I'm not. Although that is a possibility, we believe that Mr. Melrose was murdered."

"Who would want to kill Edward?" Bobbi Jo asked.

"That's what I plan to find out." He set the baggie down on the coffee table and flipped a page in his small notebook. "Who would have had access to those pills?"

"I suppose anyone who was in the house. Myself, of course, and Brian, Edward's son. He's been staying here for a few weeks, since Edward first went to the hospital."

"Me." Both of them looked at me. "Well, I mean, I've visited, so I suppose I had access to them."

"Your name?"

"Skye Williams." Detective Madison scribbled in his notebook.

"Anyone else?"

"We had a small gathering a week before Edward went into the hospital. I could get you a list of everyone who was here," Bobbi Jo offered.

"I'd appreciate that. What about anyone who was here after he went into the hospital and before he died?"

"My friend, Lily was here. His assistant, Sean Castleton, came by a few times. And Jimmy McLaughlin, his business partner. I believe Jimmy's secretary, Irene, dropped off some papers once. But I don't think she left the living room."

I watched Detective Madison write the names in his notebook while something nagged at the back of my mind.

"You aren't sure?"

Bobbi Jo thought for a moment. "No, I'm sure. I asked her to come in, but she was in a hurry to meet someone for lunch."

Detective Madison made another note, then put the pill bottle in his pocket.

"They're pills," I blurted out.

"What?" Detective Madison looked up.

"The beta-blocker is a pill. Wouldn't Edward have thought it was strange that someone wanted him to take a handful of pills?"

Detective Madison raised his eyebrows. "Good point, but the pills could have been crushed and mixed in with something."

Bobbi Jo's eyes glistened with unshed tears. "Edward was so doped up, he hardly knew what was happening a lot of the time."

"Oh." How sad that her last days with him had been marred by that. I reached over and grasped her hand.

"I'm sorry to have bothered you, Mrs. Melrose. And I'm very sorry for your loss." Detective Madison stood. "If you think of anything else, please call me."

I walked him to the door and stepped outside. "Have you found the person who murdered Natalie Turner?"

"No. We've pretty much hit a dead end."

"You mean you've closed the case unsolved?" I asked.

"Is that what you want to hear?"

"Excuse me?"

"You seem very concerned about it."

"Of course I'm concerned about it. It bothers Bobbi Jo that it was her gun that killed the woman."

"She should be concerned. It doesn't help that her husband was murdered, too."

"But Sean told me he remembered that Bobbi Jo answered the phone once that night he called Edward. It proves she was at home and couldn't have murdered Natalie Turner. Not that she had any reason to."

"Yeah, I remember Mr. Castleton's conveniently remembering that. Nice alibi for your friend."

"You don't believe him?" Detective Madison might be one of the best-looking men I'd ever seen, but he was starting to piss me off.

"Castleton was her husband's assistant. That gives him a reason to manufacture an alibi for his boss's wife."

"Good-bye, Detective Madison." I would have slammed the door in his face but I didn't want to upset Bobbi Jo. I walked into the great room. Bobbi Jo was curled on the sofa sobbing. How was she ever going to get through the funeral?

I stood in the walk-in closet I shared with Craig and stared at my clothes. So far, staring had not created the perfect outfit for the memorial service. I had three black dresses. A cocktail dress that was entirely inappropriate for a funeral. A simple sheath that would be perfect, but it had been a little tight for almost a year. And one that was just plain ugly. I looked at the rest of my side of the closet. It was a wall of beige with an occasional spot of sage green or soft blue peeking out. When had my clothes become so boring? When had *I* become so boring?

I pulled out the dress that was tight. My pants had felt looser the last couple of weeks. The situation with Craig seemed to have created an overload of nervous energy and I'd been using it to clean out the garage and closets, and working extra hard in the yard in the mornings. In the afternoons, I went to Bobbi Jo's and we usually swam for an hour. Maybe something good had come of all that activity. I carried the dress into the bedroom and laid it on the bed.

Craig was still in the bathroom, but the door was open. He'd made a feeble attempt to get out of the memorial service, pleading an overdue project at work. I'd compromised by telling him he could leave after we got to the reception. I didn't think Bobbi Jo would care, or even notice, if he was there or not. I wondered if Detective Madison would attend. In the movies, detectives always went to the funeral. Didn't they say the murderer always went to the funeral, too? Or was that just if they knew the victim?

I sat on the bed and pulled on black stockings. "That detective bothered me. He had an attitude."

"I think they have to have an attitude. It's part

of the job description." Craig leaned out of the bathroom, his face covered in lather.

"He almost accused Bobbi Jo of killing Edward. And he still suspects her of the other murder."

"He's just eliminating suspects. After all, she inherited a lot of money."

"Well, what about Brian? He got a bundle, too."

"Wasn't he told not to leave town? That sounds so corny."

"He wasn't happy about it, either. Evidently he wants to audition for a new play and staying here is cramping his style."

"I don't think Brian *has* any style," Craig said.

"It's just doesn't make any sense. Edward was going to die in a few months anyway. Bobbi Jo and Brian would have gotten the inheritance then."

Brian had thrown a fit when the will had been read. Evidently Edward had changed his will and hadn't informed Brian that his inheritance would be in the form of a trust fund. Still, he was set for life, since the trust fund would give him half a million a year until he died. Bobbi Jo received the bulk of Edward's estate. About thirty million dollars. Most of it was invested and would earn her well over a million a year. Edward's attorney had called Bobbi Jo to let her know that Detective Madison had requested a copy of Edward's will.

"Then it had to be someone else," Craig said.

"Who? The only people in his room were Bobbi Jo and Brian and the hospital staff." Actually, I wasn't sure about that. There could have been other people who had been allowed to visit Edward.

"I'm sure they'll figure it out."

I slipped the black dress over my head just as Craig came into the bedroom.

"It would help if they'd find whoever killed that woman with Bobbi Jo's gun. Could you zip me up?"

"Sure." Craig moved behind me and zipped the dress. I looked in the mirrored closet door and realized I'd lost quite a few pounds. The dress skimmed over my hips and tummy, where before I'd had to clench my stomach muscles into a knot to avoid looking pregnant.

"I've lost some weight. This used to be tight on me."

Craig glanced at my reflection for a fraction of a second. "Really?"

Men! Or was it just Craig? He'd never been one for compliments, but surely he could see the difference, if he looked. Maybe that was it. Craig never really looked at me anymore. I pushed the feelings aside and finished dressing. This wasn't the time to think about what I looked like or if Craig ever looked at me. My focus had to be on Bobbi Jo today.

We were both silent on the short drive to the memorial

service. I'd offered to drive Bobbi Jo, but she had insisted on driving herself. I wasn't sure that was a good idea, and I planned on driving her home after the service.

Edward had left Bobbi Jo explicit instructions about his memorial service, and she'd made sure everything was exactly the way he'd wanted. The eulogy would be given by Jimmy McLaughlin, his friend and business partner.

I sat on one side of Bobbi Jo, Brian on the other. Sean Castleton and Jimmy McLaughlin had taken the seats across the aisle from us. Even though Craig hated funerals, he'd promised to sit in the back of the room, although when I turned around, I didn't see him. I suspected he'd slipped out as soon as I was seated. The only people in the back row were Detective Madison and another man who was obviously a cop.

At the end of the eulogy a recording of "Spirit in the Sky" was played.

"Edward always liked that song for funerals." Bobbi Jo gripped my hand. "He was anything but religious, but he said it sounded like the kind of song you'd want to usher you into the presence of a higher being."

"Come on. I'll drive you back to the house."

"You don't have to, Skye. I'm fine. Really."

"I know. But I want to."

Learning that someone had murdered Edward had lifted the fog Bobbi Jo had been in. She wanted the killer found. The fact that the police considered her a suspect didn't appear to bother her at all. She carried Edward's urn in her lap as I drove back to her house. Brian was behind us and turned off the main driveway to the guesthouse in the back. When we went inside, she placed the urn on the mantle in the front room.

"This is where he said he wanted to be. He told me to take his urn home so he could watch over me." A half laugh gurgled in her throat. "He said not to put it in the bedroom, though. Said he was going to try to be an angel and he didn't want to test himself by watching me in bed." A tear ran down her cheek and she wiped it away. "Damn, I'm gonna miss that man."

I gave her a fierce hug. "I know. We all will. Why don't you go rest for a few minutes?"

"I can't. Everyone is going to be here soon."

"That's what I'm here for. Go lie down and I'll check on the food."

"No, I should help you," Bobbi Jo protested.

"No way. How often do I get the run of your kitchen?" I wasn't completely kidding. Bobbi Jo had everything in her kitchen. Wolff stove, Sub-zero fridge, yards of granite counters, a beautiful island with a sink and disposal. The only thing she didn't have was Emeril. Not that she couldn't afford him.

Lily arrived with Grant and Kyle a few minutes later. I put them to work setting out all the food the caterer had dropped off earlier. When the food was

LIZ WOLFE

set up and the bar stocked, I sent Lily to get Bobbi Jo
ready to greet her guests.

"Hey, how long do I have to stay?"

I turned to see Craig standing in the doorway
of the kitchen. He looked like a little boy forced to
entertain guests after going to church on Sunday. It
was such a normal married moment that I felt a tug at
my heart. I'd moved back into our bedroom after our
last talk. We still hadn't made love, but Craig would
frequently cuddle with me. I tried to ignore the feeling
of desperation that accompanied the snuggling along
with the strained air between us most of the time.
Craig still refused to talk about the lingerie and I'd
given up asking about it. Oh, I knew I was avoiding it.
But I kept hoping that it really had just been a curiosity
on Craig's part. Something that would just fade away
with time.

"Just half an hour?" I asked. "Go make some
drinks for people, talk a little? Then you can go home
and work on your project."

"You'll call me when you're ready to come home?"

"Sure, but I'll probably be here for hours. I thought
I might even stay the night with Bobbi Jo. Is that all
right with you?"

"Of course. I'm sure she could use a friend right
now." He walked across the kitchen, put an arm
around me, and kissed the top of my head.

That was the Craig I loved. "Go." I waved him out.

The next six hours were a blur of conversation and activity. Bobbi Jo greeted the guests as they arrived and Lily and I made sure one of us was with her most of the time. Craig held out for at least an hour before he begged off. I couldn't blame him. I knew how much he hated anything to do with funerals.

Brian stood in front of the huge marble fireplace and talked to whomever approached him. He looked sad and dispirited and went to the guesthouse before most of the guests had left. I suspected that Bobbi Jo needed rest more than the condolences of her guests and set about approaching each one with a gentle hint that it was time to leave. I carried a tray of shrimp to a young man Brian had been talking to earlier. I didn't recognize him and he'd been standing alone at the fireplace since Brian left.

"Shrimp?" I asked, offering the platter.

"Sure, thanks. These look great." He piled half a dozen of the shrimp onto his plate.

"Were you close to Edward?" I asked.

"Actually I got closer to Edward than was probably good for me."

"Excuse me?"

He laughed and waved a shrimp. "Sorry. Funerals make me nervous."

"That's understandable. How did you know Edward?"

I asked.

"He took over my company. About three months ago. Took the damn thing right out from under me." He popped the shrimp in his mouth and dropped the tail on his plate. "Matt Nichols. What's your name?"

"Skye Williams." I shook his limp, slightly greasy hand. "When did you sell your company to Edward?"

"Oh, no. I didn't sell it. Refused to." He grinned and swilled more of whatever alcoholic concoction was in his glass. "He *took* it. All by him—oops"—he put his hand over his mouth to cover a burp—"self. Gotta hand it to the man. He went out with a bang."

"Did you drive here?" I asked.

"Huh?"

"I think maybe you need to take a cab home."

"Okay. Whatever you say. I think I took a cab here."

"Perfect." I waved Lily over. "Lily can you call a cab for Matt?" I gave Lily a look and she picked up on it.

"Come here, Matt. I'll take care of everything." She put her arm around Matt and threw me a wink. Another disaster avoided.

I made the rounds with the platter of shrimp, relieved that the problem was resolved. Lily would pour Matt into a cab and make sure he had the cash to pay for it. As I passed the shrimp around and delivered a gentle reminder that Bobbi Jo was exhausted, I wondered what Matt had meant about Edward taking his company. Did the police know that Edward had taken Matt's company? Had they questioned him? Matt was so drunk I really couldn't tell if he was angry about it. Seemed like a reasonable response to losing your business to someone. I tucked the information away for future use, because I was still more than a little pissed that the police considered Bobbi Jo a suspect.

Gradually, everyone left. Jimmy McLaughlin and Sean stayed until the end and seemed reluctant to leave even then. I was just glad that it was over.

"Looks like we're about done." Lily carried a load of dishes into the kitchen.

"How's Bobbi Jo?" I asked.

"She's holding up. The last of the guests are leaving. She's saying good-bye."

"I was thinking about staying with her tonight."

"I don't think she'll let you, but it can't hurt to ask. Go talk to her."

"Talk to who?" Bobbi Jo asked as she carried in another stack of dishes.

"You," I said, turning to her. She was pale and her hands shook as she set the dishes down. "Why don't I stay here tonight? Just in case you need something."

"No. Really, Skye, I appreciate it. But tonight I think I'd rather be alone. I haven't finished saying

91

good-bye to him yet."

"It's important to say all your good-byes," Lily said. "Skye, you want a ride home?"

"Will you call me if you need anything?" I asked Bobbi Jo.

"I will. I promise."

"Come on, Skye." Lily took my hand and pulled me along. I was reluctant to leave Bobbi Jo. I knew she had to be fragile right now. Hurting. Alone and lonely.

"There's nothing you can do," Lily assured me. "Some things people just have to do for themselves."

I let Lily pull me out of the house. I was totally exhausted and had to admit I probably wouldn't have been of any real help to Bobbi Jo. But it was hard to leave her. I settled in the backseat next to Lily with Grant and Kyle in the front. As we drove to my house, Grant and Kyle talked softly. It was obvious just from their tone that the two men were close friends and I was amazed again at how this relationship worked for the three of them. Each of them had a strong underlying friendship with the other two. They accepted each other's flaws and quirks and loved each other in spite of them. Or, perhaps because of them.

Surely, Craig and I could work out our situation. We'd been friends for two years before we'd even started dating, and I'd always thought our marriage was based on mutual respect and genuine love for each other. We just had to get back to that friendship and go forward from there.

"Thanks for the ride," I said as we pulled into the driveway. The lights were out in the house and I was happy that Craig had already gone to bed because even a normal conversation seemed like too much effort right now.

"I'll call you tomorrow." Lily waved.

I checked the alarm pad and was surprised that Craig hadn't set the alarm. I pulled my keys out and opened the door, flicking on the light as I entered. I remembered that Craig was working on a project for work. He must still be in his office. I looked down the hallway to the den, but the door was open and the lights were off. He was probably working in the bedroom on his laptop. I hated to spoil his fun, but there was no way I was going to try to sleep listening to him tap on the keys. I climbed the stairs and turned on the hallway light just as our bedroom door opened.

It wasn't so much that Craig was naked that shocked me—it was that he was fully aroused, and wearing a condom.

My stomach churned a flash of white-hot heat up into my chest and onto my face. The tops of my ears burned with the intensity of it. I walked past him to the bedroom door.

"Skye, don't," Craig pleaded in a hoarse voice.

I ignored him and turned the doorknob, pushing the door open.

"Skye, please don't."

The man in our bed couldn't have been past his mid twenties. His chest was hairless and he had longish blond hair. One arm was thrown up over his eyes. He was wearing the pink and gold lacy piece of discount crap.

CHAPTER FIVE

I am a total chickenshit."

"Where the hell did that come from?" Bobbi Jo set two halves of a toasted bagel, a small tub of cream cheese, and a jar of blackberry jam on the counter.

"I'm sitting here waiting to make sure Craig has left the house before I go back to get some clothes. I know I'll have to talk to him eventually."

"Well, of course, you'll talk to him. But that doesn't mean you have to do it until you're ready. No sense in letting him call all the shots. I'm still shocked about all this, Skye. I mean, the cross-dressing was one thing, but sex with a man?"

"*Shocked* is definitely the word for it."

"And the guy was just lying there in your bed with that thing on?"

"Please." I held up my hand to stop her. "I don't want to think about it. Why is that when it happens in your own bed, it seems worse?"

"I think it's a girl thing. I don't think men care

about that part, and that's why they don't think anything about bringing their mistress home when the wife is away. Have you made an appointment yet?"

"An appointment?" I asked.

"With your doctor. You need to get in right away."

"My doctor? What for?"

"Darlin', your husband has been having sex with a man. And with you."

The breath left my body and I didn't seem capable of inhaling. Why hadn't I thought of the repercussions to my own health? Oh, right, I'd foolishly been preoccupied with my emotional well-being.

"He was wearing a condom," I said.

"That time. Skye, you can't know that he was safe every time. Hell, you don't even know how many times he's done this. Call your doctor."

I pulled my cell phone from my pocket and punched in my doctor's number, trying to remember the last time Craig and I had made love. Three months? No, it had been cold because I'd been wearing flannel pajamas, so it had to have been at least five, maybe six. Had Craig and I really not made love for six months? It seemed like a very long time, but I was sure that was right. A few minutes later I had an appointment for that afternoon. The receptionist had tried to get me to tell her exactly why it was an emergency, but I'd gotten by with mumbling something about the possibility of being exposed to an STD. I closed the phone and looked at the clock.

"He must be gone by now."

"I'll call and see if he answers." Bobbi Jo picked up the phone and punched in the number. After a few seconds she shook her head and hung up. "Went to voice mail. Let's go."

"You don't have to go with me, Bobbi Jo. I'm just going to pick up a few things and come back."

"I know. But we're girlfriends. Girlfriends stick together. Besides, I need something to do."

Bitterness roiled through me as I drove to my house. *My* house? Then why was I the one packing up and leaving? Because Craig wouldn't. He'd stay there, hoping that it would all blow over or disappear or something. I wasn't much for confrontation myself, but this I couldn't ignore.

I'd never expected my marriage to end. I knew that over the years Craig and I had settled into an uneventful relationship. To be honest, it had always been more comfortable than exciting. I wondered if I was more upset about losing Craig or about losing the life I'd become so comfortable with. Still, I hated what he'd done. I hated the deceit. I hated not knowing how long it had been going on. I hated not knowing why or how it had happened. I hated thinking that somehow it was ultimately my fault.

I pushed the button on the garage door opener and breathed a little easier when I saw Craig's car was gone. I pulled into the garage and closed the door. The neighbors didn't need to watch me loading my stuff into the Escape. Not that they would say anything. At least not to me. Our neighborhood was filled with people who thought they had too much class to interfere. But they sure talked to each other about what went on.

"What do you want me to do?" Bobbi Jo asked.

"There're some suitcases in the closet in the guest room."

"I'll get 'em." Bobbi Jo left me in the living room and headed up the stairs.

I walked over to the built-in bookshelves flanking the fireplace and picked up a framed picture of Sheridan. It was a photo I'd taken last summer while we were at the beach. Her long, dark hair blew out behind her and she held a shell to her ear. Was I doing the right thing by leaving? Maybe there were other options, but I needed to leave for a while. I needed to be away from Craig to think it all through.

"What all do you want me to pack?" Bobbi Jo asked from the top of the stairs.

"Just enough to last a week or two." I went to Craig's office to get the bills that needed to be paid and an extra checkbook.

I grabbed the bills from the wooden holder where I kept them and opened the bottom drawer of the desk for a checkbook. When I pulled it out, the edge caught on a folder and lifted it from the drawer, spilling the contents on the floor. Craig's pay stubs. He was so careful to file them in chronological order. He'd have a fit to find them on the floor. I laid the bills down and picked up the check stubs, trying to keep them in order. What did I care if he was upset? I was upset about a lot more than some papers being out of order. I stuffed them back in the folder without straightening them. One fell out and I picked it up.

What was this? The amount on his pay stub didn't match the amount that was deposited to our joint checking account every two weeks. There was a five-hundred-dollar difference. I looked at the stub closer. Under direct deposit there were two listings. One was the amount regularly deposited into our account, the other was the five hundred dollars deposited to a different account.

Son of a bitch!

I pulled the drawer open farther and felt around the back. Nothing. If he had another account, then he had to have a checkbook for it. I stood in the center of the room and looked around. The room was almost bare with only the desk and chair and a small loveseat under the window. I opened the closet door. Winter coats hung from the rod with mismatched luggage on the floor, and boxes on the shelf above. In the corner was a small, camouflage-print duffle bag. Craig had used it as a gym bag until I'd bought him a new one. I reached up, pulled the bag down, and opened it.

Checkbook and register. Condoms. K-Y Jelly. Several cocktail napkins with email addresses and phone numbers scrawled on the back. My hands shook with anger.

I turned one of the cocktail napkins over. *Meat Packers Union 69* was printed in neon-colored blue and green. What the hell was that? I opened the checkbook. The first check was numbered one hundred. The check register was unused except for the initial deposit. Two thousand dollars, dated three years earlier.

"Hey, I got pretty much everything you'll need for a week." Bobbi Jo set one of the suitcases down.

I stuffed everything back in the duffle bag and shoved it back on the shelf.

"Here." I handed Bobbi Jo one of the suitcases from the closet floor and grabbed the other two. "I'm taking everything I can pack."

Bobbi Jo lifted her eyebrows but took the suitcase and went back upstairs. I picked up the bills and shuffled through them looking for the two credit cards that I used. I stuffed them into a pocket and tossed the bills on the desk. Let Craig figure out how to pay the damn bills himself.

We filled the luggage with my clothes, lugged it all to the garage, and tossed it in the back of the SUV. I went back to the den and grabbed my camera bag, then stopped in the kitchen to get the bowl I'd gotten from my great-grandmother and the expensive set of knives in the solid maple knife block. I pulled the magnet Sheridan had made in kindergarten off the refrigerator and looked around the room. There was so much of me in the kitchen. I wanted to take the Waterford crystal and the good china. I wanted my food processor and marble rolling pin.

Stuff. It was just stuff. Besides, I could get it later. Right now, I just wanted to get out. I trudged to the garage, threw everything into the backseat, and climbed into the Escape.

Next stop—the bank.

"What happened to you?" Bobbi Jo's eyes were wide. "I've never seen you like this."

I told her about the contents of the camouflage bag. "He's been seeing men for at least three years and he was having five hundred dollars a paycheck put into that secret bank account."

"But you do all the banking. How could you not know?"

"Because I was a stupid, trusting wife, that's how. I never looked at his pay stubs." I pulled into the bank's parking lot and dug the checkbook out of my bag. "I'll be right back."

I stood behind the only other person in line and opened my checkbook. The register showed just over nine thousand dollars. The next clerk smiled and motioned me to her counter.

"How may I help you?"

"I'd like a cashier's check in the amount of nine thousand dollars," I said. I pulled out my bank card and identification.

The clerk took the cards, punched the information into her computer, and smiled. "Who would you like that made out to, Mrs. Williams?"

"Myself."

A few seconds later a machine spit out a cashier's check and the clerk handed it to me. "Will there be anything else?"

"Yes, I'd like to take my name off this account."

"You would?"

"Yes. Please."

The clerk disappeared for a moment, then came back and handed me a form. "Just fill this out and sign it. Will you be opening another account?"

"Of course." Did she think I was going to stuff the money under my mattress or put it in the freezer?

"I'll get one of our new account representatives for you."

I didn't want an account at the same bank that Craig used. I didn't want to be reminded of him every time I wrote a check. "I don't have time for that just now. I'll open a new account later." At a different bank.

"Fine. I'll take care of this for you, Mrs. Williams."

"Thank you." I hurried back to the parking lot and got into the Escape. "Where do you bank, Bobbi Jo?"

"First National. Why?"

"Where's the closest branch?"

"The one off Hadden Parkway. Why?"

"I need to open a checking account. I thought it might be best if I don't have the account at Craig's bank." Screw Craig. He could use the money in his secret account. Plus the money in our—his—savings account. The money invested in the stock market. He could cash in his 401K for all I cared. It's not like I'd be using it when he retired.

I drove to the bank and this time Bobbi Jo accompanied me inside. The bank manager came out and pulled Bobbi Jo into his office while I filled out the forms for a new account, using Bobbi Jo's address. I turned over the cashier's check with only a little twinge, showed my ID, received my book of temporary checks, and thanked the clerk.

"Oh, I'll need a credit card, too." I had two credit cards in my name, but they were tied to the bank account

I shared with Craig.

"One moment." The clerk punched some information into his computer and smiled at me. His phone rang and he picked it up, spoke briefly, then hung up and turned back to his computer.

"We can offer you a Platinum card with no annual fee and a ten-thousand-dollar limit. Will that be all right with you?"

"Yes, thank you." Frankly, I was surprised. I knew my credit was good, but ten thousand dollars was more than I'd expected. I'd been thinking more in the three- to five-thousand-dollar range. The clerk handed me a folder stuffed with papers that had spewed from his printer.

"There you are. You should receive a debit card and the credit card within a week."

Bobbi Jo emerged from the manager's office holding some papers as I finished with the clerk.

"All set?" she asked. I nodded and we returned to the car. Bobbi Jo fastened her seat belt and turned to me. "Did they give you a decent credit card?"

"How do you know I asked for a credit card?"

"I told the manager that you were a friend of mine and I'd appreciate it if he could take care of you."

I narrowed my eyes at her.

"Well, what's the point of having money if you don't use it? Or at least the influence it gives you.

They're terrified I'll move my accounts to another bank." Bobbi Jo laughed. "Like one bank is better than the next."

"What are those papers?"

"Stuff from our safe-deposit box. I didn't even remember that we had one." She looked at the folded papers. "He had an insurance policy on Jimmy in case something happened to him. Ten million dollars."

"Ten million? That's a lot."

"It was to protect the business. I certainly don't need them now." Bobbi Jo dropped the papers into the back of the Escape.

I thought ten million dollars was a hell of a motive for murder.

"The bank treated me very well. Thanks."

"So, what exactly did you just do?"

"I took most of the money out of our joint account and opened an account for myself."

"That's my girl!"

"Now, I need to find a place to live."

"Don't be silly. You'll stay with me."

"I can stay with you for a while, but I need my own place. Sheridan needs a home. And I need to provide it for her."

"Sheridan's at that performing arts school for the rest of the summer and then she's going to college. She won't mind staying at my place for a while. You can take your time finding a place. Meanwhile, you'll stay with me."

No, she certainly wouldn't mind staying at Bobbi Jo's. Between the swimming pool and the luxurious guest rooms with the big screen televisions and stereo systems, not to mention the billiard room, the screening room, and maid service, Sheridan would be happy to spend some time there. Then my stomach churned.

"Oh, God. I have to talk to Sheridan."

"What did the doctor say?" Bobbi Jo asked.

"I'm probably fine. He did something called a rapid test for HIV and it was negative. But he wanted to make sure so he ordered a DNA test, too. He'll call me with the results when they come in."

"Oh, darlin', I'm so sorry you have to go through this."

"Yeah, me, too. Remember when having an STD just meant taking antibiotics?"

We let the conversation drop, probably because it was an uncomfortable subject. The fact that I had to be tested for HIV along with a host of less serious STDs made me angry all over again. I also felt concerned for Craig. I didn't know how often he'd had gay sex or if he'd been safe about it. Then I was pissed that I was worrying about him. I didn't want to care. I wanted to just wipe him from my memory, but I knew that wasn't going to happen. Annoyed with my depressing thoughts, I pulled a notebook and pen from my bag.

"What's that?" Bobbi Jo pointed to the list I was writing.

"A list of stuff I need to do." I added another item to the list as Bobbi Jo looked over my shoulder.

"Find a place to live. Get a job. Talk to Sheridan. Get a lawyer. Divide stuff with Craig." Bobbi Jo pulled a bottle of sauvignon blanc from the refrigerator. "Sounds like you need a drink."

"I won't argue with that. I really appreciate this, you know."

Bobbi Jo handed me a glass of wine and smiled. "What? Letting you stay here?"

"You have enough to deal with right now." The wine was delicious, and I felt the tight muscles at the base of my neck relax.

"That's just it." Bobbi Jo picked up the wine bottle and waved for me to follow her into the front room. "I don't have nearly enough to deal with. Edward is gone. My life pretty much revolved around him. Oh, I had my own friends, like you and Lily. But for the most part, Edward was my life. Don't get me wrong. That's exactly how I wanted it. I loved Edward being the center of my universe."

"It must be so hard for you."

"I'd just about prepared myself for Edward's death. But I thought I'd have a few months with him." She set the wine bottle down so hard I thought it might break. "Who the hell wanted him dead, Skye?"

"I can't imagine anyone wanting Edward dead." Then I remembered Matt. "Do you know Matt Nichols? He was at the house after the memorial service."

"I met him once when Edward was trying to buy out his company. Seemed like a nice man."

"He said something about Edward taking his company. He specifically said that Edward didn't buy it but took it."

"He did? I don't remember much about the deal. Edward didn't talk much about his business. Said it was boring."

"Matt was pretty drunk that day. Maybe it was just that he was having some regrets about the deal."

"I'll mention it to the detective. He told me to call him if I thought of anything that might help them." Bobbi Jo set her wine glass down. "Anyway, now that the memorial service is over and all the business stuff has been handled, I have nothing to do. You, on the other hand, have way too much to do. The least you can do is let me help."

Leave it to Bobbi Jo to make it sound like I was doing her a favor by letting her help. "If I could, I'd let you do all of it."

"Overwhelming, huh?"

"Pretty much. I guess I need to figure out what to do next. And I think that means talking to Sheridan."

"Is she rehearsing for the show at school all weekend?"

"No, the rehearsal is just Saturday. She didn't think it was worth the trip to come home for a few hours on Sunday."

"Then call her and tell her you'll pick her up on Sunday morning. The sooner you take care of it, the better you'll feel. Then we can start on the next thing."

There were a lot of next things to choose from, but I knew Bobbi Jo was right. I really couldn't concentrate on anything until I'd talked to Sheridan. Waiting until she came home the following weekend would just be too long.

"Which leaves us with tomorrow." Before I could say anything, the phone rang. Bobbi Jo looked at the caller ID. "It's Craig."

I'd have to talk to him sooner or later. I nodded and Bobbi Jo handed me the phone.

"Hello?"

"Skye, I've been trying to call you all day. You didn't answer your cell phone."

"I was busy."

"I can see that. All your clothes are gone."

"Yes. I'm staying here for a while. But I'll be looking for a place of my own soon."

"Skye, it doesn't have to be like this. We can work this out."

I sighed loud enough that he could hear me. "It's not something *we* can work out, Craig. It's something *you* need to deal with."

"I don't want to lose you."

"Craig, don't you think it's a little late for that? I mean, being curious about something is one thing, but finding you and some guy in our bed is pretty final. At least for me." I paused but Craig didn't say anything. "I think the time we could have worked anything out passed about three years ago when you opened up the checking account you never told me about." I forced myself to wait through the full minute of silence before Craig responded.

"I don't really know what to say about that."

"You could start by telling me why you felt it necessary to hide money from me." There was a longer silence during which I gathered Craig wasn't quite ready to discuss the hidden account.

"I don't know what I'll do without you. You know, I never meant to hurt you."

Why do people say that? *I never meant to hurt you.* The fact was, Craig probably didn't set out to hurt me. The problem was that he didn't do anything to ensure that he wouldn't hurt me. I didn't want to say any of that to him. He sounded scared and fragile. I knew I probably shouldn't care, but I did.

"I think we both have to find new lives for ourselves now. I'm not saying that we can't still be friends. Someday. But I'm going to need some time to deal with your betrayal."

"I feel like such an ass."

I couldn't bring myself to argue with that.

"What are you going to tell Sheridan?"

What, indeed? Certainly not that I'd found her father in bed with a man. "I'm going to tell her that we've grown apart and have some issues that we can't resolve. That's all."

"I should tell her." Craig's voice was barely a hoarse whisper.

"Tell her that you had an affair? Craig, I don't think she needs to hear that. What good would possibly come of it?"

"No. Not about the affair. About my sexuality. She's going to find out sooner or later and I'd prefer that she hear it from me."

"Not yet, Craig. I think you need to come to terms with it before you say anything to her."

"You're right. I mean, I was just experimenting. A lot of men experiment. It doesn't mean anything." Craig's voice sounded high and edgy. "I mean, I know it was wrong to not tell you. But . . ."

I had no answer for that. I had no idea if it was even true. I hadn't considered that Craig would want to stay married. Could he have just been experimenting? And if that's all it was, could we save our marriage? Something deep inside me said no. It wasn't just experimenting, and there was no going back. There was just something fundamentally *wrong* about having to get an HIV test when you were married.

"I guess you're right," he said. "She doesn't need to know anything right now."

"Craig, I'm going to see her on Sunday. I'll tell her that we're separating."

"Will she be home next weekend?"

"I don't know. But she might want to stay here with me."

"Of course, anything she wants." Craig cleared his throat. "What about you? You'll need some money."

"I took some money out of our checking account today." I couldn't bring myself to let him find out how much when checks started to bounce. "Actually, I took out most of it."

"That's not a problem."

"I have to go now. I'll talk to you after I see Sheridan." I didn't wait for Craig to say good-bye before I hung up the phone. Bobbi Jo came back in and I realized I hadn't even known that she'd left the room.

"You okay?" she asked.

"You got any more wine?" I finished the wine in my glass just as Brian knocked on the kitchen door.

Bobbi Jo pushed the wine bottle toward me and waved at Brian to come in. "Hey, Brian, you want some wine?"

"No, thanks." Brian shuffled his feet, looking around the kitchen. "I didn't realize you had a visitor. I'll come back another time."

"Don't be silly, Brian. It's just Skye. And she's going to be here for a while. Did you want something?"

Brian didn't say anything so I took the initiative. "I need to call Sheridan, so I'll do that from my room." It was obvious that Brian wanted to say something to Bobbi Jo but was uncomfortable saying it in front of me.

I was a little relieved that Sheridan didn't answer her cell phone and left a message that I'd be there on Sunday morning for a visit. I knew she wouldn't question it. I'd driven up before just to spend some time with her. That made me feel a little guilty. She would think I was just coming to visit with her and then I'd end up laying this bomb on her. I refused to think about how I was going to scar her for life and returned to the kitchen to find Bobbi Jo staring at the back door.

"Hey, where's Brian?"

She turned to look at me. "I guess the son of a bitch went back to the guesthouse."

"Okay. What happened?"

"He just marched his scrawny ass in here to tell me that he's contesting the will."

"Contesting the will?"

"Didn't I just say that?" Bobbi Jo demanded. "The little bastard thinks I somehow influenced his father into setting up the trust fund for him."

"Maybe it's just an initial reaction. Maybe the lawyer can explain it to him."

"I don't really care if he explains it or not. I had to argue for months with Edward about what he was leaving Brian. If I hadn't, Brian wouldn't have half of what he's got now. Edward was determined to leave Brian a pittance because he'd wanted his son to follow in his footsteps. For God's sake! It took me forever to convince Edward that there was nothing wrong with Brian being an actor and that it didn't mean that Brian didn't love him just because he didn't want to be in the same business as Edward."

"It's probably just a delayed reaction to his father's death."

"Well, I'm having a delayed reaction to him being a pain in the ass, which he's been ever since Edward and I got married. I swear to God, Skye, if he pushes this, I just might have to give him a wake-up call."

CHAPTER SIX

I left Portland at seven on Sunday morning. Bobbi Jo had offered to come with me, but I'd decided against it because I wasn't sure Sheridan would be comfortable hearing this with Bobbi Jo there. I pulled up at her dorm less than two hours later. I opened the front door to the dorm and saw Sheridan at the top of the stairs.

"Hey, Mom!" Sheridan hiked her backpack over a shoulder and rushed down the stairs. She gave me a hug and smacked her lips against my cheek.

"Have you lost weight? Your jeans look loose."

"No, they're just old. Trust me, I eat like a horse, Mom." Sheridan closed the door behind us. "So, what's up? Why did you want to see me today? Or is this just part of the empty-nest thing?"

"Let's have breakfast. You haven't eaten yet, have you?"

"Sounds great. There's a pancake house just down the street."

She looked so happy. How was I going to tell

her? Even without any details, she would be devastated. What a great mother I was. Take my kid out to breakfast and rip her world apart. Sheridan was still chattering and I tried to listen to her as I pulled into the restaurant parking lot.

"The show is going to be great. This is the first time I get to sing a solo. You and Dad will be there, right? It's the second week of August. I forget the exact date, but I'll e-mail it to you later."

"Of course we'll be there. Have we ever missed one of your performances?"

"Well, Dad has, but not you."

We settled into a booth and ordered breakfast. I let Sheridan continue chattering until the waitress brought my coffee and Sheridan's hot chocolate and orange juice.

"So spill," Sheridan said, stirring the whipped cream into her chocolate. "I can tell you have something to tell me."

I didn't feel ready to tell her, but I knew I'd never be ready. "Your father and I—well, we've . . ."

"You've what? Mom, you're acting really nervous. Just spit it out."

"It's no act. I *am* really nervous. I never thought I'd have to do this." My voice broke and I picked up my coffee, trying to cover it.

"What? Are you guys getting a divorce or

something?"

She looked at me for a moment then put her spoon down. "Oh."

"We've separated." I waited for her reaction. Sheridan's expression didn't change so much as it just disappeared. There was no emotion on her face. No surprise, no hurt, no anger. None of the things I'd expected.

"What happened?"

"We've just grown apart." It sounded lame even to me.

"Grown apart? How?"

"It isn't important, Sheridan."

"Yes, Mom, it *is* important."

"It's just that some things have come up over the past few months." It had only been a few weeks, but months sounded better to me somehow. "We've discovered that we want different things out of life." Actually, wasn't the problem that we both wanted the same *thing*?

The waitress placed our plates before us and Sheridan spread butter over her French toast and topped it with a generous amount of syrup. I'd ordered fruit and cottage cheese and I didn't think I'd even be able to eat that. Sheridan popped a bite of food into her mouth and chewed for a moment.

"Like what kind of things?" she asked.

"We just have different interests."

"You seem to be awfully calm about it."

"Really? I've been a bundle of nerves thinking about telling you."

"Yeah, but you aren't like coming apart at the seams over the divorce."

"I suppose not. Somehow, it feels like this has been coming for a while." Guilt twinged through me as I remembered some thoughts I'd had in the past few years when Craig and I had been through some rough patches. Thoughts about what it would be like not to be married to him.

"Does this mean that Dad is coming out of the closet?"

My fork clattered to the table.

"*What?*" I immediately realized that I'd almost shouted and lowered my voice. "What are you talking about, Sheridan?"

Sheridan paled and looked like she might cry. "I thought you knew. I mean, how could you not know after living with him for so long?" How, indeed? I'd asked myself that very question a couple hundred times.

"I, uh, I shouldn't have said anything."

I felt like someone had ripped my heart out. How could my lovely, innocent daughter know about her father? What had she seen in him that I hadn't?

"Look, Mom, I thought you knew. I never would have said anything. God, I feel like such an idiot." She wiped at her eyes with her napkin.

"Honey, it's all right. I'm just surprised that you had any idea. How did you find out?"

"It was last year. You guys were having a cocktail party for some people from Dad's office and I was hiding out in the den, chatting with some of my friends online. They all got off-line and I was just looking at stuff on the computer."

"What kind of stuff?"

"I wasn't snooping. I was just bored and waiting for someone to log on that I could talk to. So, I did a search on picture files and started looking at them."

"What did you find?"

"Some gay porn." She shrugged. "You know, naked guys with hard-ons and then guys screwing each other and stuff like that. I didn't think you'd be interested in that kind of stuff and that only left Dad."

"Dear God." I was going to kill Craig.

"But that wasn't the only thing."

"What else?"

"Remember when Tony came over a few months ago with his older brother, Steve?"

"Yes."

"Well, Steve is gay, and he told Tony that he was sure Dad was gay, too. So, Tony told me, because he thought it was something I should know."

"How could Steve tell?"

Sheridan grinned. "Tony said that Steve told him gay men have a kind of *gaydar* and they just know when another guy is gay."

I wondered who else knew about Craig's sexuality. Sheridan knew; her friends knew. Yet, I hadn't figured it out in two decades of marriage.

Sheridan pushed her food around on the plate for a moment. "So, that's why you guys are breaking up, isn't it?"

"Well, yes, it is. I wasn't going to tell you because I didn't think it concerned you. Besides, it's your father's place to tell you when, or if, he decides to."

"I'm sorry, Mom. I should have told you last year."

"No." I reached across the table and squeezed her hand and then had to force myself to let go of it. I wanted to hold on to her forever. "It wasn't your responsibility. In fact, you never should have known. I'm furious that your father had pictures like that on the computer where you could see them."

"Well, he had them kind of hidden. I mean, if I hadn't done a search, I'd never have just come across them. So are you going to tell Dad?"

"What? That you saw the pictures or that you know about his sexuality?"

"Either, I guess."

I wondered how I could yell at Craig about Sheridan seeing the pictures if I didn't tell him. And I really wanted to scream at him about it. I wanted to scream at him about a lot of things. And I wanted to never talk to him again.

"Mom, really, it wasn't that big a deal. It's not like I've never seen a penis before."

Did I want to know where she'd seen a penis? No, definitely not. At least not right now.

"I don't want Dad to feel uncomfortable about me knowing he's gay or about the porn."

I didn't care if Craig felt uncomfortable. But I cared about how Sheridan felt. "I'm still angry he exposed you to that, but I don't think it would help him to know. He wanted to tell you about his sexuality, but I thought he should wait."

"Okay."

"But maybe that's wrong."

"Why?"

"You shouldn't have to feel like you have to keep a secret until he decides to tell you. You shouldn't be put in the position of pretending not to know."

"Mom, I've been in that position for a while already."

"You shouldn't have to be going through any of this."

Sheridan smiled at me and lifted a shoulder. "Neither should you."

I'd taken Detective Madison's card from Bobbi Jo's before I left. I didn't want her to know that I was going to talk to him. Not that I was hiding anything. I just thought the less often she had to hear about it or think about it, the better. I punched his number into my cell phone when I was about an hour from Portland.

"Scott Madison."

"Detective Madison, this is Skye Williams."

"Yes?"

"I'd like to discuss something with you. Could you see me today?"

"Is this about the case?"

"Yes. I have something I want to ask you about."

"I can come to your house. Just give me the address," he said.

"I'm staying with Bobbi Jo and I'd rather not meet there."

"Okay. How about Java Java on Fifth Street?"

"I'll be there in an hour."

He was sitting in the back of the coffee shop when I entered. He already had a cup of coffee and a plate on the table. I stopped to order a double Americano and a tuna sandwich, and took the coffee to his table.

"Mrs. Williams." He stood while I placed my coffee on the table and sat down.

"Please call me Skye." I was becoming increasingly uncomfortable with being called Mrs. Williams. It felt like a lie now.

"Call me Scott. Nice to see you again." I wondered if he used that disarming smile to get information from people.

"Thank you. I'm sorry I asked you to come out on a Sunday."

"No problem. I live close by."

I pulled the insurance papers from my bag and held them out. Scott took them, accidentally brushing his hand against mine. "This is an insurance policy on Jimmy McLaughlin. Edward Melrose was the beneficiary." I waited while the waiter placed my sandwich on the table. Scott picked up the papers and looked at them.

"They were in a safe-deposit box that Bobbi Jo had forgotten about."

"And?"

"Bobbi Jo said that the policy was to protect the business in case something happened to Jimmy. I thought that Jimmy probably had a similar policy on Edward."

"He did. We already knew about the policies."

"So Jimmy got ten million dollars when Edward died?"

"Yes. Actually, he'll get it if he isn't the one who murdered Mr. Melrose."

"You suspect he did it?"

"It's very common for business partners to have life insurance policies on each other."

"But the policy is payable to Jimmy personally, right? This one states that the money would have been paid to Edward rather than to the business."

"Yes, Mr. McLaughlin is the direct beneficiary, not the business."

"Doesn't that make him a suspect?" Getting information out of the man was impossible.

"Business partners are usually on our short list of suspects in a homicide. Especially with an insurance policy like this," he said.

"I see. Well, I'm sorry I wasted your time. I just thought you might not know about it."

"Skye, I'm not out to prove Mrs. Melrose murdered her husband."

I didn't comment but I wanted to believe him.

"The hospital records show that in addition to Mrs. Melrose and Brian Melrose, Mr. Melrose also was visited by his assistant, Sean Castleton; his partner, Jimmy McLaughlin; and his ex-wife, Charlotte Melrose. Plus anyone on the hospital staff would have had access to him. There are a lot of people who had the opportunity to kill him."

"And they all had access to the beta-blocker?" I wanted to find something that would convince him that that Bobbi Jo couldn't have killed her husband.

"Anyone in the hospital could have gotten their hands on the drug. In fact, almost anyone who wanted it could have gotten it from somewhere. You can probably buy it on the Internet."

"So, it comes down to who had access to Edward and who wanted him dead?"

"Motive and opportunity."

"Did Matt Nichols visit Edward in the hospital?" I asked.

"His name wasn't on the list. Why?"

"He was at the reception after the memorial service. He said something about Edward taking his company out from under him because he wouldn't sell it. But I guess if he didn't visit Edward, he's not much of a suspect."

"Just because he wasn't on the list doesn't mean he couldn't have gotten into the room. I'll check him out."

"That's very nice of you," I said.

"It's my job to find out who killed him. Frankly, I don't think Mrs. Melrose did it."

Relief poured through me. "You don't?"

"She knew he was dying in a few months, and

there's no indication that she had a reason for wanting him dead sooner."

I bristled a bit, but told myself that the man was a cop. It wasn't his job to speak softly or to care about my feelings.

"Besides, my gut tells me she didn't do it." He held up a hand. "But she's still a suspect until I find out who did it."

"I see. What about Natalie Turner's murder?"

"Again, she's still a suspect, but I don't see any motive there, either."

"Detective Spiner seemed to think Bobbi Jo was fooling around with David. I can assure you that wasn't the case."

"Noted," he said.

"You don't believe me?"

"It's not a matter of believing you or not. Detective Spiner is working an angle, that's all."

"An angle?"

"Look, Skye, I don't want to insult your friend. It's just that Spiner thought it was possible that Bobbi Jo was having an affair with Pearson and killed Natalie Turner to get her out of the way. When Edward Melrose was murdered, he thought she might have gotten rid of her husband in order to be with Pearson."

I was so angry I felt like I might explode. "That's a total lie. How can he even think that about Bobbi Jo?

She loved Edward. He was the center of her world." Scott held his hands up like he might need to fight me off. I wasn't sure he wouldn't.

"Calm down. It's just a theory, and there's no concrete evidence to support it."

"Well, he needs to come up with a theory that doesn't involve Bobbi Jo."

"You're really something, you know that?"

"I am?"

"Yeah. I mean, usually when someone is a suspect in a murder case, their friends just kind of fade away. But you didn't. In fact, you've pushed me to think about the evidence. You've questioned everything."

"Of course. Bobbi Jo is my best friend. I'd do anything for her."

"Exactly. You're loyal. Fiercely loyal."

"I don't know if I'd say fiercely, but yes, I'm loyal. That's a big part of friendship."

"I find that very attractive. It makes you a good friend. I hope your friends are as good to you."

"They are. I don't have a lot of friends, but the ones I have are loyal."

"Are you married?"

"Excuse me?"

He pointed to my hand. "There's a tan line where you'd wear a wedding band. So, I figure you're either recently divorced or you forgot to put your wedding ring on." He grinned. "I don't know many women who forget to wear their wedding rings."

"You don't miss much, do you? I'm recently separated."

"I think I'm supposed to say I'm sorry, but I'd be lying." I felt a little rush. Maybe it was just having a man flirt with me. My face felt hot and I was sure I was blushing.

Scott reached over and put his hand over mine. "Don't worry so much about your friend. As I said, I don't think she did it."

"I still want to throttle Craig," I told Bobbi Jo as we dined on chicken Caesar salads by her pool.

"Oh, darlin', I don't blame you a bit. I would have wanted to kill him before this." Bobbi Jo put her fork down and leaned back. "But the reality is, this hasn't caused any damage to Sheridan."

"She's only eighteen."

"And eighteen-year-olds today know way more than we did when we were that age."

"I suspect they know more than I do now."

"So, there's really nothing to be gained by killing him. Unless there's an insurance policy involved. Then we might want to reconsider."

"Bobbie Jo!" Still, I laughed. She could always make me laugh. Even now. With my marriage in ruins and her husband gone forever.

"I know. It's a crude thing to say, what with Edward's murder and all. I guess I just have a crude side to me. I was raised in a trailer in the middle of Nowhere, Texas. I imagine that's where it comes from." It was really good to hear her laugh again.

"They'll find who killed him, Bobbi Jo."

"Well, enough about serious stuff. Let's talk about something fun."

"Shoot."

"I've come to a decision."

"Sounds serious."

"Well, it's not. It's anything *but* serious." She reached over and lifted a bottle of wine out of a terra-cotta wine cooler and pulled the cork out. I pushed our empty wineglasses toward her. Something told me I'd need the wine before too long.

"So, what's the big decision?"

"I'm going to start dating."

"Dating?"

"Sure. Edward told me that he wanted me to get back out there. He wanted me to enjoy life to the fullest. And that he'd be damned pissed if I didn't find someone else."

"But do you think you're ready for a relationship?"

"Hell, no, darlin'. I'm not interested in a relationship. I had that with Edward. I'm interested in sex."

"Sex."

"Yeah. Hot, sweaty, steamy, scream-till-you-lose-your-voice sex."

"Without a relationship." I was beginning to sound stupid, even to myself.

"I had the relationship of my life with Edward. He was everything I could have wished for. Except for the sex. Not that the sex wasn't great. It was. Really, *really* great. It's just that once Edward had that first heart attack, the sex kind of died."

"I know, Bobbi Jo. But—"

"You can't talk me out of it, Skye. I've made up my mind." She leaned forward. "Just think about it. It really makes sense. I got all the love I could need for several lifetimes from Edward. Now, all I need is sex."

Before I could answer, Lily walked out to the patio. I breathed a sigh of relief. Maybe Lily could talk some sense into her.

"Hi," Lily said. "Oh, good, you have wine."

Bobbi Jo plucked another glass from the cart, filled it with wine, and passed it to Lily. "What's up with you?"

"Later. What are you guys doing?"

"Well, we talked about killing Craig," Bobbi Jo said. "But I talked Skye out of it."

"That bad?" Lily asked.

"Sheridan already knew her father is gay. Evidently she found some gay porn pictures on his computer and a friend of hers told her that his older brother, who is gay, was sure that Craig was gay, too. Something about gaydar."

"Makes sense," Lily agreed. "How are you doing with all this?"

"Oh, I'll be just fine. As soon as I find a place to live and get a job and figure out why my daughter is so much more savvy than I am about just about everything." I picked up my wineglass and waved it in Bobbi Jo's direction. "You should ask her what she's planning."

"Oh, Bobbi Jo, that's great. That you're making plans, I mean. It's not easy to get back into life after a partner has moved on. The sooner you put your life back together and move on, the better."

"Oh, she's planning to get back into it." I laughed and realized that I was definitely feeling the wine. I didn't care. In fact, it felt good to relax, even if it was chemically induced. "Go ahead, Bobbi Jo. Tell her."

Bobbi Jo graced me with a glare, then giggled. "I'm going to start dating again."

"Really?" Lily asked. "Do you think you're really ready for that?"

"Oh, she's ready, all right. But what she isn't telling

you is that it's not really dating she's after. She just wants to have sex."

"Well, there's nothing wrong with sex. But something tells me this is more than dating." She held her glass out for a refill. "Or different."

"Oh, yeah, it's different," I said.

"So, how different is it?" Lily asked.

"It's not that big a deal. It's just that I've had the love of a lifetime with Edward."

"Several lifetimes," I interjected.

"Yes. Several lifetimes." Bobbi Jo glared at me again. "Anyway, I realize that I'll never have that with another man. But I'm not ready to give up companionship."

"Certainly not," Lily agreed.

"All I really need is sex. And my memories of Edward."

"Bobbi Jo, I don't think that's what you really want, is it?"

"Of course it is. It's perfect. I'm calling it my Man-a-Week plan."

"Man-a-Week?" Lily asked.

"I figure having a different man each week will keep it fresh and interesting," Bobbi Jo said.

"And I thought I had problems." Lily laughed and shook her head.

"What kind of problems?" I asked. They had to

be easier than what Bobbi Jo and I were dealing with. Maybe Lily had something we could actually do something about.

"Well, I met this really nice man. Skye, you met him in the shop a couple of weeks ago. His name is Derek."

"I remember. I didn't get to talk to him much, though."

"We've developed a definite affection for each other."

"Are you kidding, Lily? You already have a husband and a lover." Bobbi Jo laughed and pointed at me. "And you think I'm nuts?"

We'd been friends too long for Lily to take offense at Bobbi Jo's words.

"Oh, I don't expect you to understand. I've never thought polyamory was for everyone. But it works for me. And for Grant and Kyle, too."

"But a third man?" I really couldn't even imagine how tangled that would be. "How can you divide yourself between three men?"

"It doesn't really feel like I'm dividing myself," Lily said. "And over the years Grant and Kyle and I have worked out a kind of schedule."

"You mean for sex?" Bobbi Jo asked.

"For having time with each other, although that also includes time for sex."

LIZ WOLFE

"So, how's that work? Like you have Mondays, Wednesdays, and Fridays with one guy and the rest of the week with the other?" Bobbi Jo asked.

"Something like that. But we don't have specific days. I usually spend a few nights with each of them."

"Just how often *do* you have sex?" I asked. I'd known about Lily's polyamory relationship since I'd met her, but somehow I'd never considered just how often she was having sex.

"It varies, but it's probably about five times a week, sometimes more."

"Five times a week?" I sat back stunned. Craig and I had never had sex more than twice a week. And that was only in the months following our wedding. Of course, it might have been different if I'd been married to a heterosexual man.

"And just how are you going to fit another man into that?" Bobbi Jo asked.

"Well, relationships aren't just about sex. Besides, Grant and Kyle aren't sure about it."

"I guess they would have an opinion about it," I said.

"They aren't completely opposed to it. But they've grown comfortable with just the three of us," Lily said. "Anyway, I should probably forget about it until after Jasmine's wedding. That's my other problem."

"I thought everything was all settled for her wedding." Jasmine hadn't seemed the least bit distressed when I'd talked to her in Lily's shop.

"It was until her wedding planner decided to run off with David's father."

"Oh, my gawd! She didn't!"

"I'm afraid she did. David's mother, Claire, is not taking it well," Lily said.

"I imagine not, but what is Jasmine going to do without the wedding planner?" I asked.

"I have no idea. The woman returned most of the fee, but the wedding's less than two months away. There isn't a wedding planner in town who will take over at this point."

"But, surely, everything's already planned, isn't it? I mean the caterer, the flowers, all that stuff?" I asked.

"I think so. But that woman was so ditzy, I'm not sure. Jasmine is at home now going through the folders."

"That poor baby." Bobbi Jo shook her head. "Weddings can be a bitch. I was a bridesmaid more times than I care to remember. That's one of the reasons Edward and I didn't have a big wedding."

"I remember planning my wedding. Craig and I were engaged for exactly one year because my mother insisted on it. I couldn't wait to get married."

"Did you have a big wedding?" Bobbi Jo asked.

"Big enough. I think about a hundred guests. And I didn't even have enough sense to have a wedding planner."

"You did it all yourself?" Lily asked.

"Well, that's not such a big deal for someone like you," Bobbi Jo said. "You're the queen of organization. I've seen you throw together a cocktail party in twenty-four hours."

"Maybe you could help Jasmine," Lily suggested.

"Oh, I don't know, Lily. Weddings are different now."

"But you said you wanted a job. Jasmine can pay you the fee that the wedding planner returned."

"I'd never take money from Jasmine."

"Well, if you want to do it for free, that's your choice," Lily said.

"Looks like you're recruited, Skye," Bobbi Jo said.

"Okay. I'll help her pull everything together. If the wedding planner has already arranged everything, then it's just a matter of keeping everything on schedule. But you two have to help out, too."

"Sure, sounds like fun," Bobbi Jo said.

"This could turn into a career for you," Lily said.

Somehow I didn't think a bitter divorcée would make a great wedding planner. And I was definitely in the bitter stage. But it was only two months and I really did feel bad for Jasmine. I knew she had her heart set on a special wedding day. Besides, what could go wrong?

"Now that the wedding issue is settled, let's get

back to this plan of yours, Bobbi Jo," Lily said.

"What about it?"

"Aside from the fact that it's just a bad idea, aren't you concerned about what might happen?"

"What could happen? I'm an adult. I know how to be careful."

"What about that stalker you had?"

"Oh, gawd, that was years ago."

I shuddered. Almost ten years earlier, some maniac had been stalking Bobbi Jo. He'd called her at home, often several times a day. He'd followed her when she went shopping. Edward had hired a bodyguard for her. It had gone on for over a year but the police had never been able to do anything about it.

"John Templeton got twenty years in a Louisiana prison for raping that poor girl. I'll never hear from him again."

"But something like that could happen again," I said.

"Believe me, darlin', something like that only happens once in a lifetime. Besides, it's not like I'm going to go to the sleaziest bars in town to pick up men. I'm going to pick and choose from the best men in Portland."

I thought Bobbi Jo's plan had disaster written all over it, but it was obvious she wasn't going to listen to me or Lily. All we could do was be there for her when it fell apart.

CHAPTER SEVEN

"Skye! Thank the Goddess you're here." Jasmine jumped up from the kitchen table and wrapped her arms around me. "I can't thank you enough for doing this."

"Hey, what are friends for?" I gave her a hug and sat at the table, carefully moving one of the stacks of papers.

"Well, I don't know if you're going to be calling me a friend for long. This is a mess. I mean, I thought Barbara had a lot more done."

"It can't be that bad. We'll figure it out."

"You want some coffee?"

"Oh, I'd love some. I only had one cup before I left Bobbi Jo's." Jasmine fussed with the coffeemaker while I tried to sort some of the papers. There didn't appear to be any order to the piles of paper. "I'll be right back. I have to get something from my car."

I trotted out to the car, grabbed a large plastic crate, and was back at the table as Jasmine was pouring the coffee.

"This will help." I set the crate on the floor next to my chair and took a cup of coffee from her. "Now, we need to go through all this paper and get it organized."

"How? It's just a mess. She didn't have anything together. I went through all the folders and everything was just jumbled up."

"Sit," I commanded. "And relax. It's just a matter of going through it one piece at a time." I picked up a sheet of paper. "Catering estimate. Anything to do with catering goes in this folder." I pulled a folder from the crate and labeled it.

"Okay. Here's one for flowers." Jasmine handed me another paper. "And this one, too. This one's for the bridesmaids' dresses." Jasmine kept handing papers to me and I filed them away. By lunchtime, we'd gotten through the piles of paper.

"See? It really isn't that hard." I didn't tell her that we'd just done the easy part. I wasn't even sure everything had been ordered, which could be a disaster. Who was I kidding? It would absolutely be a disaster.

"You are so totally organized, Skye. I'm amazed." She laughed. "Organization isn't exactly my strong point." Jasmine leaned over. "I'll bet you're a Virgo. Virgo is a very organized sign."

"You're good. My birthday is September tenth."

I stuffed the last folder into the case. "I'll take this stuff with me and go through everything, then we'll get together in a couple of days and see where we are. How does that sound?"

"Great. I can't tell you how relieved I am. I've been spending so much time making my wedding gown that I kind of let this part slide."

"You're making your own gown? I'm impressed." My own sewing skills were pretty much limited to replacing buttons.

"All I have left to do is the hem."

"Would you like me to pin it up for you?"

"No, thanks. I mean, I'm sure you're capable of doing it. I'm just being a control freak about it. I want to do all of it myself. That way if anything is wrong, I only have myself to blame."

"I see. Well, if you change your mind, let me know." I remembered being more than a little obsessive about certain aspects of my own wedding. Maybe I should have paid a little more attention to my choice of the groom.

"Actually, I could use your help. Will you put the gown on so I can pin up the hem?"

"Doesn't it need to be pinned up while you're wearing it?"

"We're the same height," Jasmine said. "It'll only take a few minutes." Jasmine grabbed my hand and dragged me down the hallway to her bedroom. She pulled the ice-blue wedding gown from the closet, laid it on the bed, and left me alone to change. I stripped out of my jeans and shirt, toed off my sandals, and looked in the full-length mirror.

At forty-two, my figure was still boyish. Small breasts, slim hips. I'd hoped that having Sheridan would fill out my hips and breasts but, except for the six months I was breast-feeding, it hadn't worked. Still, I'd always been comfortable with my body. More so, now that I'd lost the extra pounds I'd been carrying for a couple of years. Sure, I wasn't voluptuous. I'd never had cleavage. Or hips that swiveled in an enticing manner. And I was okay with that.

Now as I looked at my lack of breasts and hips, I wondered if that was part of what had attracted Craig. Did my lack of feminine attributes allow him to pretend he was really with a man? I shuddered at the thought that my marriage had been such a sham.

Then I laughed at myself. I didn't know what exactly was going on with Craig. But surely he hadn't married me because I was less womanly than someone else. Besides, if that had been his intention, it had obviously failed since we were never very sexually active. It wasn't my lack of breasts and hips. No doubt it was the lack of a penis that was a problem for Craig.

I pushed the disturbing thoughts aside and stepped into the dress. Holding the skirt off the floor, I walked back to the kitchen.

"You look beautiful," Jasmine gushed as she pulled the zipper up. Well, of course. This was her wedding dress. She'd think a dog looked beautiful in it. The satin was tightly fitted around my torso, flaring out to a full skirt at the hips, with long tapered sleeves that ended in points over my hands. Then there was the gaping neckline that my small breasts had no hope of filling out. Luckily no one but Jasmine would see me in it. Still, it was a beautiful gown and I felt extremely feminine. And that felt good.

"Come in here." Jasmine pulled me into the sunroom off the kitchen. "There's more room." She guided me up onto a small step stool. "Stay right there. I just have to get my pins." Jasmine trotted through the kitchen and down the hall.

I stood perched on the tiny stool hoping it wouldn't take long because I could hardly breathe. The sliding door opened behind me, and I tottered around to find a man covered in dirt and sweat holding two pots with blue mums.

"Stop!" I held up my right index finger in the universal sign to halt. Jasmine would kill me if any dirt got on her wedding gown.

"Okay, okay." The man backed up a couple of steps and let his gaze move from my head to the floor and back. "You're very tall."

I glanced down. The gown fell almost to the floor,

covering the footstool. "I'm standing on a stool."

The man nodded and grinned at me, causing little lines to appear at the corners of his green eyes. Which were dancing with amusement. He leaned against the doorjamb and gestured toward me with one of the pots. "So, what's with the dress?"

"Jasmine has to hem it. What's with the plants?"

"I need to know if they're the right color."

"They're blue. What color should they be?"

"Blue."

"Well, there you go." I leaned over to look through the kitchen, hoping to see Jasmine. The top of the gown fell forward and I grabbed for it and straightened up.

"But are they right shade of blue?"

"How many shades are there?"

"I don't know, but there must be hundreds of shades of blue."

"No, I mean how many shades of blue are available in the mums?"

"Oh, Max, they're beautiful. Just the right shade of blue." Jasmine returned, put her box of pins down, and clapped her hands like a little girl. It was kind of sweet seeing her so excited about her wedding.

"But will they still be blooming for the wedding?" she asked.

"No. I'm putting these in my garden. I'll get the

ones for the wedding a week before the big event."

"Oh, Max, this is Skye Williams. Skye, Max Harrison. He's our next-door neighbor, and he's making the yard and garden perfect for my wedding reception."

Max grinned. "I'd offer to shake hands, but I'm dirty."

"Nice to meet you, Max." I gave him a little finger wave.

"Yeah. I need to get these in the ground. I'll see you around." Max left with his blue mums.

"He's cute, huh?" Jasmine picked up her pins and settled on the floor in front of me.

"I suppose. But are you supposed to be noticing cute men right before your wedding?"

"No, silly. I meant for you. Mom told me that you and Craig are getting a divorce. If you think he's cute, I could tell him and you guys could go out."

"No!" I tried to take a deep breath, but the dress prevented that. "I mean, I don't think I'm really ready to date just yet."

"Oh, well, when you're ready you should really consider Max. He's a sweetheart." Jasmine motioned me to turn a bit. "And he's a writer. So, you know, he's smart."

"What does he write?"

"Fantasy, I think. Maybe it's science fiction." Jasmine shrugged and motioned me to turn again.

"So, what are you going to do? I mean, you didn't work before, did you?"

"No, I didn't work. Although I think the politically correct phrase is that I didn't work outside the home."

"I know what you mean. It's a lot of work to run a house and rear children. That's what I want to do."

"You'll make a wonderful mother." A little ditzy, but wonderful.

"I plan to." Jasmine stood up and moved a few yards away. "Turn around." I turned slowly while she examined the hem for evenness. "So, are you going to get a job? Although I would think that after being married for so long, he'll probably have to give you enough alimony to live on."

The word *alimony* reminded me that I was supposed to see an attorney at three. Bobbi Jo had made the appointment, insisting that waiting was not an option. I knew she was probably right, but somehow I felt disloyal to Craig.

"I have to run, Jasmine. But I'll call you in a couple of days and we'll go over the details."

"Any time that's good for you. I can't thank you enough for doing all this, Skye."

"No problem. We just have to get the plans organized." I stepped down from the stool and ran on tiptoes down the hall to the bedroom. I shucked the dress off and placed it carefully on the padded satin hanger, then pulled on my jeans and shirt and rammed my feet into my sandals. I had an hour to drive back to Bobbi Jo's, change clothes, and get to the offices of Munson, Tate, and Stanford.

I hadn't had time to apply any makeup but at least I was wearing a suit and heels when I walked into the law offices in downtown Portland. Andrew Stanford only kept me waiting ten minutes past our appointment and apologized nicely for the delay. He was nattily dressed in an expensive suit, his nails were manicured, and his feet were shod in soft Italian leather.

He looked totally gay to me.

"You're thinking about a divorce?" he asked as I settled in the chair across from his enormous rosewood desk.

"No."

"I'm sorry. I have a note here that you wanted to see me about a divorce."

"Yes, I do."

"But you said no."

"Oh, I'm sorry. I meant that I'm not *thinking* about a divorce. I want one. Definitely. I want one."

"Ah. Good. No, I mean—not that it's good to get a divorce. It's—" He took a deep breath and smiled.

"I'm glad we understand one another. Tell me about the situation."

"The situation?"

"Why do you want the divorce?"

"Oh." What could I say? I didn't really think it was my place to out Craig by telling everyone that I'd caught him in bed with another man. "Do I have to have a reason?"

"No. You only have to state that there has been an irreconcilable and permanent breakdown of the marriage."

"That's it," I agreed.

"However, if there are issues of child custody, the past and present personal conduct of each party will be taken into consideration by the judge." He leaned forward and smiled gently. "What I'm saying is that if your husband fights you about the custody of any children, we can use his personal conduct to convince the judge to rule in our favor."

"We only have one child. She's eighteen, so there won't be any issues with custody. I'm sure Craig and I will be able to agree about everything."

"I understand. A lot of couples set out with the best of intentions." Mr. Stanford shrugged and lifted his hands palms up. "But occasionally, it doesn't work out. Often, one party will begin to feel he or she is being taken advantage of and want to change the agreement. It's my job to make sure your best interests are served in the agreement."

"I understand. Craig and I are still amicable. I can't imagine we'll have any problem working everything out." My voice sounded stiff and formal, which I supposed was normal since I felt stiff and formal. I hadn't really considered how involved getting a divorce would be. It seemed overwhelming, and I just wanted it done and over with.

"Good. It's always best when both parties can agree to terms. Now, how much spousal support do you want?"

"I don't want any, but I realize I'll need financial help until I can get a job and support myself. I haven't worked during most of our marriage."

"We'll ask for half of the value of the house, half of any stocks, retirement benefits, that sort of thing. Also medical coverage for you and your daughter." Mr. Stanford made notes on a legal pad as he talked. "Did you want to keep the house?"

"No. I've already moved out."

"Oh, I see. I wish you'd contacted me earlier. You could have stayed in the house."

I almost shuddered at the thought of staying in the house where Craig and I had played out our farce of a marriage.

"The next step will be for me to draw up a petition

of our requests and present them to your husband's attorney. Do you know who it is?"

"This has all been very sudden. I don't know if he's even contacted anyone."

"No problem. I can find out."

"How long will this take?"

"The actual dissolution will occur ninety days after we file the petition, unless your husband contests. If that happens, I'm afraid it could be drawn out for a while."

"I see. I'm sure Craig won't contest anything."

"That would make the process smoother and quicker," Mr. Stanford agreed. "I know this is a lot to take in, so why don't you take a few days to consider your options, then we'll meet again?"

"That would be fine."

"I would advise you to consider your stand on spousal support very carefully. You were married for twenty years and you haven't worked outside the home for most of that time. Finding a position that will afford you the same lifestyle you're accustomed to could take some time." Mr. Stanford stood and moved to show me to the door. "There's no reason you shouldn't be able to live as you do now. Your husband owes you that."

That thought made me sick. I didn't want to depend on Craig for money. I wanted to make my own way. But doing what? At least I had a college degree, though it was rather ancient. Up until a couple of days ago I had cooked meals, cleaned the house, done the laundry, paid the bills, organized our lives, and took care of our daughter. How did that experience translate into a career?

Not well at all.

I was still pondering my lack of career options when I got back to Bobbi Jo's house. She had left me a note that she would be out until six. It was only four thirty. I stood in the kitchen wondering what I should do. The problem was, I didn't have anything to do. This wasn't my house so there was nothing I could clean or organize. I didn't even know if there was anything I could cook for dinner. I opened the refrigerator to find a salad already made and a pan of lasagna ready to go into the oven, courtesy of Bobbi Jo's part-time housekeeper. I was debating what else I could do when my cell phone chirped.

I pulled it out and looked at the number. Craig. I walked back to the living room, sank down on a chair, and flipped open the phone. "Hello?"

"Hi, Skye. I just wanted to know how it went with Sheridan."

"Well, you know Sheridan. She was fine. I don't think she was happy about it, but she understood."

"What did you tell her?"

"Just that we've decided we're better as friends than as partners."

"What did she say?"

"Exactly?" I'd never lied to Craig about anything that I could remember. Certainly not about Sheridan.

"Don't you remember?"

How could I forget? "Not exactly. But she isn't upset about it."

"Not at all?"

"You know Sheridan. She's very mature."

There was a long pause. "I'm really sorry about this."

I stifled a sigh. "Craig, it's not like you chose this."

"I thought we'd be together forever. I still remember when I first met you the summer before your senior year in high school. God, you were so damn spunky. I think I fell in love with how you always had something funny to say."

"You did?"

"I was always amazed that you dated me. I was the nerdy, computer geek, and you were the popular girl."

"Me? Popular? I always thought I was too much of a smart-ass to be popular."

Craig laughed. "Yeah, there was that. Still, I was surprised you went out with me. I don't think I really believed you'd married me until our first anniversary."

"Why?"

"We were so different. We never really had much in common."

"Oh, I don't know. We both like sex with men."

151

"Now, that's something you would have said back then." Craig laughed.

"Back then? Did I change that much?"

"I suppose we both did." There was an incredible sadness in his voice and I didn't want to talk to him like this any longer.

"I met with an attorney today."

"I see."

"You should probably get an attorney, too."

"That won't be necessary, Skye. I'll agree to anything you want." He sighed heavily. "God, I'm such a loser. You deserve better than this."

"Craig, you know that isn't true." I wasn't sure I really believed that. Not that I thought of him as a loser, but I was hoping I deserved better.

"It is true. I'm an ass. I can't believe I did this to you." There was a muffled noise. Was he crying? "I wish there was something I could say to make it right."

I'd complained for years that Craig never wanted to talk to me when we had a problem. Now, he did. But this wasn't something that could be fixed by talking. There was nothing he could say that would erase what had happened. Nothing would change his attraction to men. There wasn't even anything I could do that would make this easier for him. My own emotions were bouncing all over the place. I hurt for Craig; I hurt for myself. I didn't want to be married to him anymore, but I resented losing my husband and the life I'd built. The house phone brought me out of my thoughts.

"I need to get the other phone."

"Sure. I understand. I'll talk to you later."

I ran into the great room and grabbed the phone. "Melrose residence."

"Bobbi Jo?" a woman's voice asked.

"Bobbi Jo isn't home right now. This is Skye."

"Oh, yes. I met you at Edward's funeral," she said. "This is Charlotte Melrose. Would you tell Bobbi Jo that I called? I just wanted to see how she's holding up."

I wasn't quite sure what to say to her. Charlotte and Bobbi Jo had always been on friendly terms. That alone was incredible to me, especially since Edward and Bobbi Jo had gotten together shortly after Charlotte and Edward's divorce. Fortunately, before I had to come up with some polite chatter, Bobbi Jo opened the front door, laden with shopping bags.

"Oh, hold on a sec, Charlotte. Bobbi Jo just came in."

Bobbi Jo dropped her packages in the entryway and took the phone from me. While she was talking, I moved her packages into the great room. I poured myself a tall glass of iced tea and squeezed in a wedge of lemon. By the time I returned to the great room, Bobbi Jo was saying good-bye to Charlotte.

"Charlotte's so nice to call and check on me,"

Bobbi Jo said.

"I guess it's good to be friends with the ex, huh?"

"Oh, Charlotte never minded that Edward remarried. She said all they ever did was argue, so it was nice that Edward found someone he could get along with. Of course, Charlotte was out dating every man within a fifty-mile radius before the ink was dry on the divorce papers, so I guess she didn't much care what Edward did."

"Hasn't she remarried now?"

"Not exactly. She's been living with a guy for a couple of years. A *younger* guy. I think she's about thirteen years older than him."

"Nice," I said.

"He's got a design business of some kind. I know it was real touch and go for a while. Charlotte was telling me a couple months ago that his business might go under because it was undercapitalized."

"I guess the five million she inherited from Edward must have come in handy, then."

"Absolutely. She was just telling me that the business is back on its feet now."

"That's convenient," I mumbled.

"Skye! What are you thinking?"

"Well, it's just that his business needed money, and then when Edward died, he had all the money he needed from Charlotte."

"I don't even want to think about what you're implying."

"I know. It's an awful thought, but I don't like that the police still consider you a suspect, either."

"Oh, that's nothing." Bobbi Jo waved her hand in dismissal. "They'll find the murderer soon, and it won't be me or Charlotte." She kicked off her high-heeled sandals and sat on the sofa, reaching for the shopping bags. "Look at what I got today." She started plowing through the bags, pulling out clothes, shoes, makeup, and lingerie.

"Did you leave anything for the other shoppers?"

"Very funny." She wrinkled up her nose and stuck her tongue out at me. "I'm going out tonight. You should come, too."

"Where?"

"To the Union Bay."

"I'd rather die." The Union Bay was a trendy bar and club frequented by the thirty- and fortysomething crowd. I'd been there a couple of times with Craig but it really wasn't my kind of place. Aside from the occasional couple, most of the patrons were single and looking. I wasn't single—yet. And I was definitely not looking.

"Why are you going there?"

"To pick up a guy." Bobbi Jo pulled a short black skirt from one of the bags and held it up. "Do you think this is too short?"

"Not for sunbathing."

"Skye, it's what all the girls are wearing this season. And look at the cute top I got to go with it." She pulled out a blouse with fluffy sheer sleeves and a low neckline.

"This is just wrong, Bobbi Jo." The conversation with Craig had left me edgy, and I knew I was sounding a little bitchy.

"Is not." Bobbi Jo folded the clothes and stuffed them back into the bags. "Look at this purse. Isn't it great?" She dangled an embroidered silk bag before me.

"It's great. But, really, Bobbi Jo. I think this whole idea of meaningless sex is just a way to avoid the reality of your life right now."

"You're wrong. I've given this a lot of thought." She stood up and fussed with wrapping tissue paper around the purse. "I could never find another man like Edward. So, why even try? I'd just be hurt and disappointed. This way, I'm not. I know exactly what to expect."

"Basically, you're going after the one thing that you didn't have with Edward." I rose from the chair. There was no point in arguing with Bobbi Jo about this, but I hated to see her do something so irresponsible.

"You wouldn't understand, Skye." Her voice held an edge of anger, an undercurrent of sadness. "You haven't lost your husband."

All the anger, frustration, and grief bubbled to the surface. I most certainly *had* lost my husband. To another man. To another lifestyle.

"Haven't I? I've lost my husband and learned that my entire marriage has been a lie."

We stood a few feet apart, staring into each other's stark, grief-stricken faces. I immediately regretted my words. Bobbi Jo and I had never fought or even sniped at each other in all the time that we'd been friends.

"Oh, gawd, Skye, I'm so sorry." She wrapped her arms around me and hugged me fiercely.

"No, I'm sorry." What kind of lousy friend was I?

"I'm such a bitch."

"No, you aren't. Having a gay husband isn't the same as having a dead husband."

"Might as well be." Bobbi Jo sniffled and wiped away her tears.

"I can't argue with that." We both started laughing.

"Gawd, I don't know what's wrong with me. Must be PMSing. I'm either laughing like a maniac or crying over a stupid television commercial."

"You don't usually have PMS," I reminded her.

"Well, maybe it's menopause. Although I'm only thirty-eight and I think that's a little young."

"I think it's part of the grief process. Edward has only been gone for a few weeks. And the circumstances haven't made it any easier on you."

"Well, if this is because I'm missing Edward, it really sucks." Bobbi Jo wiped at her eyes again. "Because that means it's going to go on for a very long time."

I wrapped my arms around her. She definitely had the tougher situation. At least I could get mad at Craig for breaking up our marriage and changing our lives—even if it didn't make it right. Bobbi Jo could only grieve for the love she had lost.

CHAPTER EIGHT

B obbi Jo had insisted on continuing with her plan
and had gone to the Union Bay. I'd heard her
come home after midnight and she was still in
bed at ten. Whether with a hangover or regret, I didn't
know. Hopefully not with someone she'd brought
home. I was more than a little worried about how Scott
Madison might view her activity. Would he think she
was being the merry widow? Glad to be rid of her elderly,
sick husband and eager to hit the town? God, I hoped
not. Maybe I should talk to him about it. Explain the
situation. Not that there was a way to explain Bobbi Jo.

I dropped a bagel into the toaster and opened the
yellow pages to the employment agency section. There
were a lot to choose from. I made a list from the larg-
est ads and started making phone calls. In less than an
hour, I had three appointments for that afternoon. I
luxuriated in the glow of achievement until I realized
I didn't have a résumé. I wasn't even sure what I could
put on a résumé.

The doorbell saved me from having to consider that problem for the moment. I opened the door and my stomach did a nervous flip.

"Hi, Scott. If you're here to see Bobbi Jo, she's still in bed."

"No, I need to see Brian. Is he around?"

"He's staying in the guesthouse. Come in and I'll call him on the intercom." Scott waited in the living room while I went to the kitchen and buzzed the intercom connecting the two houses.

"Brian, it's Skye. Detective Madison is here. He wants to talk to you."

"About what?"

What was I, his secretary? "I don't know. Can you come over?"

"Yeah. Give me a minute to get dressed. I was still asleep."

I returned to the living room. Scott was still standing where I'd left him. "Brian has to get dressed. Can I get you some coffee?"

"No, thanks. How have you been?"

"Fine, and you?" I sat on the sofa. "Do you have any more leads on who killed Edward?"

"Nothing new really."

"Then what are you doing? Sorry, I didn't mean that to sound like you aren't doing your job. I just wondered what was happening with the investigation."

"It's all right." He smiled and I felt a little more at ease. "This is the nonglamorous part of the job. Paperwork and legwork."

"I don't understand. Shortly after Edward was admitted to the hospital, it was no secret that he was going to die in a few months. Why wouldn't they have just waited for nature to take its course?"

"Actually, that element pretty much narrows our list of suspects."

"How?"

"Since everyone knew Edward was dying anyway, the killer had to be someone who didn't want to wait the few months it would take for the cancer to kill him. Someone who had a reason for wanting him dead immediately."

"Well, that leaves Bobbi Jo out. She had no reason for wanting Edward to die sooner rather than later."

"Do you know anything about the cancer that Edward had?"

"Not really," I admitted.

"I spoke to Dr. Marcus and he told me that Edward would have suffered a lot in the coming months. The cancer becomes incredibly painful in the final stages. He also told me that Mrs. Melrose was aware of that."

"Bobbi Jo wouldn't have killed Edward, even to save him from suffering." He was back to accusing her again—and just when I was starting to like him.

"I'm just explaining why she's still on the suspect list."

Brian's entrance kept me from saying some things I would probably have regretted later. How could Scott stand there and even suggest that Bobbi Jo would have killed Edward for any reason?

"Detective Madison." Brian nodded and gestured toward a chair. "Have a seat."

Scott nodded and sat in the chair, pulling out his small notebook and a pen. He flipped through a few pages, then glanced up at me. I guessed I was supposed to give them some privacy.

"I'll be in the kitchen if you need anything." Of course, that didn't mean I couldn't listen to their conversation. Bobbi Jo had a right to know what was happening in the investigation and as her best friend, I had an obligation to eavesdrop. Fortunately both men had strong voices so I could hear them just fine as long as I kept quiet.

"I understand you had an argument with your father the day before he was killed."

"I don't know what you're talking about, Detective."

"According to one of the ICU nurses, the two of you were arguing about your career as an actor."

"Oh, that. It was nothing. Dad didn't like the fact that I'd rather be an actor than take his place in the business. It's an argument we've had on several occasions." Brian sounded tense.

"Did he threaten to cut you out of his will altogether the other times, too?" Scott asked.

"What exactly are you getting at, Detective Madison?"

"What I'm getting at is that your father threatened to change his will less than twenty-four hours before he was murdered. So, is it just a coincidence that he was killed before he could change his will?"

"You son of a bitch! I didn't kill my father."

"As I said before, don't plan on leaving town anytime soon."

I jumped when Brian stalked through the kitchen and slammed out the back door. Evidently the conversation was over. I walked back to the front room. Scott stood and tucked his little notebook into his pocket.

"You can tell Mrs. Melrose that we're continuing the investigation."

"She doesn't have any plans to leave town, either, in case you're interested." I leveled a glare at him, but he seemed impervious to it. I might have closed the door just a little harder than was absolutely necessary when I showed him out.

"Who was that?" Bobbi Jo asked from behind me.

"Detective Madison." I was concerned at the dark circles under her eyes, the pallor of her skin. "Are you all right?" I followed her into the kitchen.

163

"I'll live. I'm just not sure how happy I am about it." She splashed coffee into a cup, added a liberal amount of cream, and slumped onto the stool across from me.

"Hangover?"

"I hardly drank anything. Ordered a Bloody Mary but it made me sick to my stomach, so I switched to virgin Marys."

"Maybe you're coming down with something."

"Puked when I got home, then puked again this morning. Must be the flu." She took a sip of coffee, made a face, and set it down. "Even coffee doesn't taste good."

"Try some juice," I suggested.

"Why was Detective Madison here? Did he have any news?"

"Not really." I told her about his conversation with Brian.

"Gawd, I wish they'd hurry up and find out who really killed Edward. I know Brian is kind of selfish and spoiled, but he wouldn't murder anyone. Brian might have argued with Edward about him changing his will, but he'd never kill him. Brian loved his father."

I didn't know Brian at all, but he struck me as shallow and self-involved. I didn't think he was capable of really loving anyone but himself. Was it possible that he had killed Edward before the will could be changed?

"Did he say anything else about the investigation?"

"No. Just that it was continuing." I wasn't about to tell her that she was still a prime suspect. Or that Scott thought she might have euthanized her husband. "Mind if I use your computer? I need to write a résumé."

"Knock yourself out, darlin'. I'm going to go stand in a hot shower until I feel better."

I settled in front of the computer, hoping that Bobbi Jo would take her illness as a sign that her plan to screw her way through the grieving process wasn't going to work. Half an hour later, all I had on the page was my name and Bobbi Jo's address.

"How's it going?" Bobbi Jo curled up in the over-stuffed chair next to the computer desk.

"It's not." I pushed back from the keyboard. "The only thing I have to put on a résumé is that I was a housewife and mother. Before that, I had a string of part-time jobs while I went to college."

"You're just looking at it wrong." Bobbi Jo leaned over and looked at the résumé template. "Tell them what you can do, what you have done, instead of telling them where you did it."

"Really?"

"Sure. Who says you have to set it up that way? Let me do it."

I stood and looked over her shoulder as she typed.

She filled the page with my *skills and abilities* and my *practical experience*. My eyes skimmed over the words.

Arranged lavish buffets, cocktails, and sit-down dinners for groups of ten to forty, including menu preparation, food and drink preparation, food service, and cleanup, often under intense deadlines. That was true. Craig had been fond of inviting clients and co-workers to dinner with little advance notice. Once, he'd called me at ten in the morning to advise me that he'd invited a couple dozen co-workers for drinks and hors d'oeuvres at six. It wouldn't have been such a problem if Sheridan hadn't been home from school with the flu.

Taught primary education to a small group of children, including preparing lesson plans, selecting materials, and individualizing lessons for each child, and reporting status to parents. I'd homeschooled Sheridan for several years. In the beginning, it was to be a group effort with two other women in the neighborhood who had three children between them. But it had quickly degenerated into a situation in which I did the teaching and the other two women played tennis and went shopping. The following year, I'd homeschooled Sheridan alone.

Residential interior design, including faux painting techniques, wallpaper installation, furniture and accessory selection, and reorganizing rooms for maximum efficiency, beauty, and traffic flow. I'd decorated three different homes while I'd been married to Craig.

Personal shopping for men and women, from execu-tives to children, including selecting seasonal wardrobes and working within tight budgets. That must be about the fact that I'd bought all of the clothes for Craig, Sheridan, and myself for years.

"Now, what about hobbies?" Bobbi Jo asked.

"Hobbies?"

"Yeah, you know. Stuff you do for fun?"

"I know what a hobby is. Let's see. Well, I like to take pictures. I even had a setup for developing black and whites. And for a while, I was really into the whole scrapbooking thing." That was something else I'd need to get from the house. All the scrapbooks I'd made while Sheridan was growing up. And the boxes and boxes of photos.

"Perfect!" Bobbi Jo started typing again.

Photography, including developing, framing, and artistic presentation.

"Wow. It looks like I can do anything."

"Just have to put the right spin on it. Now, what are you going to wear to the interview?"

Ack! I only had two hours until I had to be at the first appointment. The problem was, I'd only brought one suit with me when I'd run from the house I shared with Craig.

"Shit! I don't have anything to wear to the inter-view but that awful suit I wore to the lawyer's office."

"Darlin', you have nothing to worry about." Bobbi Jo rose and waved for me to follow her. I obediently traipsed down the hall after her. "Now, you want to look powerful, but not overwhelming." Bobbi Jo walked into the enormous master suite and opened French doors to a walk-in closet. Lights came on automatically as soon as she entered.

"Damn. This is as big as my bedroom." I looked at all the rods holding clothes, the shelves with rows of shoes and purses, the built-in drawers that must have held panties, bras, hosiery, and lingerie.

"It's bigger than your bedroom," Bobbi Jo said. "Now, you don't want a real strict suit look. I think that would be too much. But you want something that says suit without actually being a suit."

I barely heard her. Bobbi Jo had the equivalent of the Neiman-Marcus Misses Department in her closet. How did she ever decide what to wear? She riffled through a section of her wardrobe and pulled out a plastic hanger bag.

"This will be perfect. The skirt is really short on me so it'll be just right on you."

I peeked at the label and grinned. Jean Paul Gaultier. I was about to go from frump to fabulous.

I collapsed on Bobbi Jo's sofa and took stock of the damage.

The crisp linen skirt and silk blouse had become a mass of wrinkles and the curls Bobbi Jo had coaxed into my hair were nothing but limp tangles clumped together by Bobbi Jo's expensive hair spray.

"You look like you been rode hard and put up wet." Bobbi Jo sauntered into the room patting her hand over a yawn. Her hair and clothes were rumpled, and there was a slight indentation on one cheek.

"Did you take a nap?"

"I just couldn't keep my eyes open." She padded into the kitchen and returned with two glasses of grapefruit juice.

"You never nap."

"I know, but for some reason, I was just so sleepy. Almost fell asleep watching *Dr. Phil*. But how did the interviews go?"

"Rotten. Worse than rotten. One place offered me some temp work as a receptionist."

"Oh, no." Bobbi Jo's eyes sparkled with tears.

"It's not that bad, Bobbi Jo. Certainly nothing to cry about."

"I'm just in the strangest mood today. I started crying when a Kodak commercial came on the TV."

It seemed to me that the loss of her husband was finally catching up with her. I hoped this meant that her Man-a-Week plan was coming to an end.

"I know you're disappointed about the interviews, Skye."

"Oh, I'll get over it. It was just my first foray into corporate America anyway. All three of them suggested that I improve my computer skills and that's just for clerical jobs. Evidently a bachelor's degree in liberal arts doesn't mean much, especially when it's a couple of decades old. About the only thing I'm qualified to do is to ask 'do you want fries with that' and 'would you like to go large for thirty-nine cents.'"

"You'll find something," Bobbi Jo assured me. "It's not like you need to have a job immediately. You should take some time and see what you want to do."

"I know, but I really want to start supporting myself as soon as I can. I don't like the idea of living off Craig."

"I don't know why not. You spent nineteen years keeping his house, raising your daughter, and making his life as easy as possible. You deserve something for that."

The doorbell rang before I could argue with her. Not that I had much of an argument anyway.

"That's Lily. I thought we could all have dinner tonight," Bobbi Jo called over her shoulder as she opened the door. At least she wasn't going out tonight.

"I could use some wine," Lily announced.

"Sure thing, darlin'." Bobbi Jo headed for the kitchen while Lily joined me in the living room.

"You look like hell, Skye."

"Gee, thanks." I lifted my head from its resting position on the back of the sofa and glared at her.

"Well, it's true. And what's with the dressy outfit?"

"It's nice, huh? It was better looking before I had three interviews and discovered I'm barely qualified for a temporary receptionist position and just over minimum wage."

"Ouch. I'm sorry."

"It's all right. What's up with you?"

"Nothing good." Lily took the wine that Bobbi Jo brought her. "Grant and Kyle are still hesitant to bring Derek into our relationship."

"You have to respect that. It's got to be difficult to think about bringing another person into a relationship that has been strong and steady for a long time."

Lily frowned at me. When Bobbi Jo nodded her agreement, Lily included her in the frown. "Derek has decided that he wants a relationship with just me. He says that he loves me and can't bear to be without me and won't even consider a relationship that includes anyone else."

"Sounds like it's more of a disappointment than a problem," Bobbi said. When Lily didn't reply, I sat up and leaned toward her.

"It's just that I've—well, I've fallen in love with Derek. I don't know if I can just let him go."

"Now, *I* need a glass of wine. You want one, Skye?"

"Lily, are you saying that you'd leave Grant and Kyle for Derek?"

"Don't answer until I get back." Bobbi Jo hurried to the kitchen.

"I don't know. He's all I can think about."

"I said to wait for me," Bobbi Jo called.

Lily avoided looking me in the eye.

"So, does he mean that much to you?" Bobbi Jo set our wine glasses on the table.

"I don't know what to do. I love Derek so much. He's everything I've ever wanted in a partner. I'm not sure I can walk away from that."

"Not sure? Are you serious? You're going to leave Grant and Kyle?"

Lily pulled her shoulders back and looked up. "I'm saying I'm considering it. I've never felt anything like this for anyone. If I don't do something about it, I'll never know what could have been."

"You have totally lost your mind," Bobbi Jo said.

"Me? What about your Man-a-Week plan?" Lily shot back.

"That's different. You're talking about hurting two men who love you very much just to take a chance on someone you've known how long? A month?" Bobbi Jo took a healthy gulp of her wine and made a face.

"Gawd, what is wrong with this stuff?"

"Mine tastes fine," I said. "Maybe it's that flu that made you sick last night and this morning."

"The flu doesn't make wine taste bad. What do you mean sick?" Lily asked.

"Oh, I went out last night and had a Bloody Mary and it made me sick. I puked last night and then again this morning. It's probably the flu. Which might not be so bad because evidently I've put on some weight."

"Where?" I asked. Bobbi Jo looked as slender as ever, although she was wearing a loose T-shirt over her shorts.

"The shirt that matches these shorts wouldn't even button up."

"Oh. Are they tender, too?" Lily asked. "And do you feel weepy sometimes?"

"How did you know that?" Bobbi Jo asked.

"I had that flu twice." Lily looked at me and snickered. "Skye had it once, too."

"It takes a long time to get over it." I nodded and tried to keep from laughing.

"How long?" Bobbi Jo looked stricken and I snorted.

"Nine months usually. Although I'd guess from your symptoms that you've only got another seven months to go," I said.

"What the hell does that mean?"

"Honey, you're pregnant." Lily smiled at her.

"No-o-o-o-o!" Bobbi Jo jumped up from her chair. "That's not possible. Edward and I tried for years. Besides I haven't had sex in—" She gasped and clapped her hand over her mouth.

"I guess it was a little parting gift," I said.

Bobbi Jo sank back down in her chair. "Oh, my gawd!"

"Are you all right?" I asked.

"But it still can't be true," Bobbi Jo protested.

"I don't know of anything else that makes you puke and your breasts swell at the same time. I was just like you with the alcohol, too. Couldn't stomach it even before I suspected I was pregnant."

"You need to take a test." I got up and grabbed my purse. "I'll go get one at the drugstore."

It seemed like all our lives were in turmoil. Bobbi Jo might be pregnant, much to her surprise, and right after her husband had been murdered. My soon-to-be-ex-husband was gay. Lily had two husbands that she was considering leaving for a younger man. How had our lives become so complicated? And when? At least the pregnancy test would provide one solid answer. Of course, then Bobbi Jo would have another decision to make. Geez, would it never end?

I shook off the question and viewed the selection of pregnancy tests. Pregnancy must be popular because there were a lot of tests to choose from. Back when I'd gotten pregnant we still went to the doctor for a test. I wasn't even sure how they worked. I reached for one to read the box but it was wedged in. I pulled and the container of condoms next to it fell to the floor. I quickly put the container back on the shelf and started picking up the condoms. With both hands full of condom packets, I started putting them back in the bin. I fumbled, dropping most of them again and stooped to pick them up thinking perhaps Lily should have run this errand.

"Planning on partying this weekend?"

I turned to see one of the most gorgeous men in the world kneeling beside me, gathering up handfuls of condoms. Sandy blond hair, sparkling green eyes with a couple of laugh lines at the corners. Dimples on either side of a breathtaking smile. Well-formed chest and broad shoulders in a crisp white T-shirt. Beautiful, muscular tanned legs in khaki shorts. Perfectly formed feet in Birkenstock sandals.

"I knocked these over."

"Ah. Just tidying up, then." He picked up the last of the condom packets and we both stood.

"Actually, I came in for this." I threw a handful of condoms back into the container and pulled the pregnancy test off the counter, my other hand still full of condom packets.

He replaced the condoms he'd picked up. "I see. Well, good luck, whichever way it goes."

I tried to think of an answer but was interrupted by a short, slender man who hurried across the aisle.

"Oh, there you are, Paul." He laid a possessive hand on Paul's arm. "We need to run if we're going to catch the movie."

Paul smiled and nodded, then turned to walk off with the other man. I stood there with my mouth hanging open. A young woman across the aisle smiled at me, looked at the two men walking away, and then shrugged.

He was gay.

How could I not see that? What the hell was wrong with me? Maybe instead of gaydar, I had some unusual affliction that prevented me from recognizing sexual identity when everyone around me could.

"Can I help you with anything?"

"What?" I turned to look at an elderly gentleman in a white jacket with a blue embroidered patch on the breast pocket.

"What?" He held a hand up to his ear.

"Did you want something?" I raised my voice so he could hear me.

"That's what I was asking you," he yelled.

"Oh. I'm just trying to decide on which one."

"Depends."

"On what?"

"When was your last period?" he almost shouted. "And how long after that did you have intercourse?"

"I don't know."

"How can you not know when you had intercourse?"

"It's for a friend." I really wished he'd stop yelling. People in the main aisle were staring at us.

"Take this one. It costs more, but it'll give results even if you're just a day late."

"Thanks," I mumbled, grabbed the box, and headed for the checkout stand. I paid for the test and rushed back to Bobbi Jo's house.

I held the box up as I entered the living room. "I got it!"

Lily grabbed the box from my hand. "Oh, this one is good. Jasmine always uses it when she's late." She opened the box and pulled out the test stick. "She wants to start a family right away."

"I can't believe I'm doing this," Bobbi Jo grumbled, taking the test wand from Lily. "It just isn't possible for me to be pregnant."

Lily rolled her eyes at me. "Just go pee on the stick, Bobbi Jo."

Bobbi Jo walked down the hall to the bathroom

and Lily and I sat down to wait. After a few minutes, I stood up.

"How long does it take? I didn't have time to read the box."

"Five minutes." Lily glanced at her watch. "One minute to go."

I paced the length of the living room a couple of times and looked at Lily again. Lily looked at her watch and stood up.

"Time's up."

CHAPTER NINE

A re you sure you should have left Bobbi Jo alone today?" Lily asked, setting a glass of iced tea on the table.

"She went to see the doctor. Can you believe she's pregnant? She still isn't convinced. Said the test was probably wrong."

"How do you think she'll handle it?" Lily poured a glass of tea for herself and sat at the table. "She's always said she didn't have an overwhelming desire for children."

"I think that might have been because she never got pregnant. She and Edward tried until he had his first heart attack."

"Still, having a baby with the man you love is one thing. Having his baby after he's dead is another."

"She was bouncing between being sure the test result was wrong and hoping it was true. I think it's the best thing that could happen to her."

"Well, it sure puts a stop to her Man-a-Week

plan," Lily agreed.

"What kind of plan is that?" Jasmine asked from the hallway.

"You don't want to know," I told her. "But it looks like Bobbi Jo is pregnant."

"Oh, that is so wonderful!" Jasmine jumped up and down and clapped her hands. "I hope I get pregnant soon, too."

Dear God, was I ever that young? That hopeful? I wondered what marriage would hold for her. Hopefully not the same as it had held for me. I pulled my thoughts back to Jasmine's wedding.

"I went through all the paperwork Barbara left."

"Cool. Is everything just about done?" Jasmine asked.

I wished. "Not exactly. There were a few things that seem to be missing. Did you choose a caterer yet?" I pulled out the folder holding all the bids from the caterers.

"Oh, sure. We did that a few months back. Moveable Feast is the one we chose."

I flipped through the folder and pulled out the bid sheet from Moveable Feast. "Let's give them a call to confirm the order. Is this the buffet you decided on?" I handed the sheet to Jasmine and opened my cell phone.

"That's it. I chose a cold buffet because I thought

it'd be hot in August. Gazpacho for soup. Caesar salad. Tabbouleh, pasta primavera, with eggless pasta and tofu for the vegans. Salmon aspic. Cold ham, turkey, and roast beef. Breads. And little individual cheesecakes for dessert. And the wedding cake, of course." She had the whole menu memorized. I just hoped the caterer had the order. There should have been a confirmation of the order in the mess of paperwork Barbara had left behind.

"Hello, I want to check on an order for a cold buffet for a wedding reception in August." I was put on hold while the woman found the right person. "Yes. The Hargrove-Taylor wedding on August twenty-six." I could hear paper being shuffled while the woman mumbled to herself.

"No, I'm sorry. There's no order for that wedding. I see that we sent a bid for a cold buffet, but I never heard back from the wedding planner."

"What?" I felt a little sick. It was way late to be looking for a caterer. "Are you sure?"

"Positive."

"Well, could you still do it?"

"Let me check the calendar."

I crossed my fingers and gave Jasmine a hopeful smile.

"I'm afraid we're already booked for that date."

"I see. Thank you, anyway." I closed the phone and tried to smile at Jasmine who looked like she might cry at any moment. "They don't have the order, and they're booked for that date now."

"Oh, no."

"It's all right. We'll call some of the other caterers. Someone is bound to be open for August twenty-six, and your menu isn't complicated." Lily picked up her iced tea and excused herself, mumbling something about why she'd insisted on a wedding planner. I resisted the urge to call her a coward and punched in the number of the next caterer. After a long string of refusals due to other obligations, Jasmine's lower lip was trembling over a puckered chin. I gave her an encouraging smile and punched in the number for another caterer

"Hey, Jasmine. Why the long face?" Max asked from the sunroom door.

"My wedding's ruined!" Jasmine wailed.

"Oh, it can't be totally ruined." Max hurried across the sunroom and wrapped his arms around Jasmine. That's all it took for Jasmine to let loose the flood of tears she'd been holding back. I prayed the next caterer would be available. A few minutes later, I hung up the phone disappointed. Jasmine was standing with an arm around Max, wiping tears from her cheeks and looking at me hopefully.

"Well, that was only six caterers. There are a lot of caterers in Portland. I'm sure we'll find someone who's available."

"Maybe Vince could do it," Max suggested. Jasmine and I both looked at him with interest.

"Who's Vince?" I asked.

"Friend of mine. He does catering on the side, so his prices are reasonable."

"It's a pretty big reception," I pointed out, afraid to hope this could be the answer to a very big problem. "Over a hundred people."

"A hundred and thirty seven," Jasmine supplied. "At last count."

"I could ask him, anyway."

"Is he good?"

"He's great. He's catering a little get-together at my house this weekend. Why don't you come and you can judge for yourself?"

I glanced at Jasmine, who was nodding her head enthusiastically. It wasn't like I had other plans. "What night?"

"Saturday. Around seven."

"I'll be there," I said with as much enthusiasm as I could muster. "How should I dress?"

"Anyway you like." Max grinned at me. "Everyone else will be kind of elegant casual."

"Fine." Whatever the hell that meant.

"It means just about anything," Bobbi Jo said. "Who's going to be at this little soiree?"

"I have no idea. Does it make a difference?"

"Yeah, a little. Elegant casual means a lot of different things to a lot of different people."

"Hold on." I pulled out my cell phone and punched the speed dial number for Jasmine. "Hi, Jasmine. Listen, do you know who's coming to this party at Max's?"

"Not really. Let me ask Mom."

I held while she asked Lily. There was some chatter that I couldn't really understand, then Jasmine told me to hold on a sec. Finally Lily came on the line.

"Call him and ask. Usually his parties are for other writers and people in publishing, but it could just be a bunch of his friends. Not that his friends are shabby or anything." She rattled off Max's phone number and I repeated it, gesturing for Bobbi Jo to write the number down.

"Call him," Bobbi Jo ordered.

"How do you even know what she said?"

"I could hear it was Lily and it's what she'd tell you to do. Call him."

"Fine." I punched in the number she handed to me. "Hi, Max, it's Skye."

"Skye! Nice to hear from you."

"Thanks." I hesitated. He sounded really happy to hear from me, which was nice. Really nice. Craig had never sounded that happy to hear from me. Bet he sounded happy to hear from his sissy lover though. "I just wanted a little clarification on the dress code for your party."

"Just wear whatever you feel comfortable in."

"That would be my sweats." I laughed. "I think Elegant casual demands a little more than that."

"You probably look great in sweats." I blushed at the compliment.

"I just wanted to make sure I'm dressed appropriately. What exactly did you mean by elegant casual?" I saw Bobbi Jo making huge arm gestures at me. I interpreted them as best I could. "Who will be there? Is it a business thing?"

"Kind of. There's a writer's conference in town, and I'm having my writer's group and some of the publishers, authors, agents, and editors over." He paused. "It's not a big deal, really. You'll see everything from jeans to suits. Does that help?"

"Sure. Thanks. I look forward to it." I closed the phone.

"What did he say?"

"Anything from jeans to suits. It's a bunch of writers, editors, agents, people like that."

"We gotta go shopping," Bobbi Jo declared.

"You just went shopping." I pointed to the three large shopping bags on the living room floor.

"*You* have to go shopping. And I'm going with you."

"Why? It's a business thing. I'll just wear one of the dresses I have."

"Which shade of beige?"

"They aren't all beige."

"Right. I think there's a taupe dress that's especially lovely on you."

"Bitch."

"Whatever. You need to look sharp."

"Sharp?" I wasn't the sharp type. I was the soft edges type. "Maybe I can just borrow something from you. What did you buy today?"

"Maternity clothes."

I didn't know if Bobbi Jo was happy about her unplanned pregnancy or not. She'd wanted a baby early in her marriage but had resigned herself to being childless. Now with Edward gone, did she want to have this baby alone?

"I've never been so happy. It's a miracle"

We held hands and danced around like six-year-olds. We squealed. We giggled. We laughed until we cried.

"The doctor confirmed it?"

"He did a blood test and a pelvic. I'm definitely

pregnant. And everything looks fine to him. I was worried, you know, about being able to carry to term, because of those earlier miscarriages, but he said everything looks perfect to him. I've got these gawdawful huge pink pills to take—prenatal vitamins. And he said to get some exercise every day and no drinking. Not that I can, 'cause it makes me sick as a dog. And lots of veggies and fruit. And lean meat and milk. He says I'm about eight weeks pregnant. Like I didn't know that. I mean, I know the exact moment I got pregnant." Bobbi Jo stopped jabbering and tears filled her eyes.

"Don't think like that, Bobbi Jo. Edward would be so happy. He *is* so happy. You know he's watching over you."

"Hell of a going-away present, isn't it?" Bobbi Jo plucked a tissue from a silver box and blew her nose. "I wanted to give Edward a baby for so long and then I just gave up the idea because he couldn't—well, you know."

"You only wanted to have a baby for Edward?" Oh, this couldn't be good.

"Well, I guess I did. I mean, he wanted to have a baby and anything he wanted sounded good to me." Bobbi Jo blew her nose again and took a deep breath. "Oh, gawd! I'm going to have a baby all alone!"

"No, honey. Not alone. You have me and you have Lily. Lily knows everything there is to know about having a baby. It's really wonderful. You're going to be so happy."

"I am?" She sniffled a little. "When? 'Cause right now, I don't know what I feel, but I'm pretty sure it's not happy."

I took her hand and dragged her over to the sofa. I had no idea what to say to her. Did she not want to have the baby? Did she want an abortion? "You want something to drink?"

"Yeah, I'd like a damn martini, but I can't have one!"

"How about some juice? Or milk?" Milk would be good. Didn't milk make you sleepy?

"Tomato juice," Bobbi Jo said. "It'll be like a Bloody Mary. Or maybe some cranberry juice. That'd be like a Cape Cod."

I hustled into the kitchen and poured a large glass of tomato juice for Bobbi Jo. I squeezed a wedge of lemon into it, added a dash of Worcestershire sauce, and a touch of Tabasco. It didn't look much like a Bloody Mary so I rummaged in the vegetable bin and stuck a stalk of celery in the glass. I snagged a Dr. Pepper for myself. That was another thing Bobbi Jo would have to give up, so I might as well help her out by drinking one.

"Here." I handed her the virgin Bloody Mary and settled on the sofa next to her. "So, show me the new clothes." Bobbi Jo giggled and pulled over one of the shopping bags. She'd bought five outfits. Cadeau, Liz Lange, Mommy Chic.

"When I was pregnant with Sheridan, I just wore Craig's shirts and left my jeans unbuttoned."

"The whole time?"

"Afraid so. No, that's not true. I had one dress that I wore everywhere the last few months."

"One dress?"

"I know, it sounds like your worst nightmare." Bobbi Jo saw everything in life as a shopping opportunity. "But it was no big deal. I was young and in love and starting my life." I put the clothes back in the shopping bags. "You know, you aren't even going to show for a while. By the time you need maternity clothes, it'll be cold."

"Oh, I hope I show right away. I want everyone to know I'm pregnant."

"I guess this puts a stop to your Man-a-Week plan."

"Not completely."

"What? Are you nuts? Have you lost your mind?" I took a deep breath to calm myself. "Bobbi Jo, you can't go out and pick up men for casual sex while you're pregnant."

"I'm not." She smiled in a way that was somehow wicked. I was certain I didn't want to know, but I couldn't stop myself from asking.

"What does that mean?"

"I'm transferring the plan to you."

"I don't want the plan."

"You know, you should go out with Detective Madison."

"Please."

"What? He's cute."

"I'm not even divorced yet. And I'm too busy with the wedding to think about a social life. Jasmine's wedding planner left everything in a shambles."

"I have an idea. I'll ask Sean to help with the wedding."

"Sean?"

"You met him. Edward's executive assistant."

"I remember him."

"He's just all torn up about Edward's death and now he doesn't have very much to do at work. Jimmy promised me that he'd find a place for him in the company, but it might take a little time."

"You think he'd know what to do?"

"Oh, I'm sure of it, darlin'. He used to set up conferences and events for Edward and Jimmy all the time. You know, he's been such a sweetheart. He's been calling me a couple of times a day just to see how I am."

That sounded a little extreme for her husband's assistant. But I'd noticed that he seemed very concerned about Bobbi Jo at the hospital, too. Maybe he had a crush on the late boss's wife.

I pulled up to the curb in front of Max's house at seven fifteen. He'd said seven and I'd tried to be fashionably late, but I suffer from terminal punctuality. There were no cars in front of his house so I could only assume I was so far from not fashionably late that I was early. I told myself that it didn't matter. I wasn't here socially. I was here to check out his friend the caterer. Arriving earlier was better, actually. I could nip in, check out the caterer, and duck out. I certainly didn't need to sit around talking to his writer/editor/agent/publisher friends.

Bobbi Jo had taken me shopping. She'd insisted on buying the outfit for me. I was going to wear a pair of nice beige linen pants with a cream-colored blouse that would have been perfect with a string of pearls. But, no. Bobbi Jo was determined that I carry on with her Man-a-Week plan, and that I be properly dressed for it. I wasn't about to do her Man-a-Week plan, but I mollified her by letting her pick out the outfit.

Not that there was anything wrong with it. Actually, it was really, really nice. And it cost a lot more than I would have spent on an outfit. She'd chosen midnight blue crinkle-pleated pants with a matching spaghetti-strap top and a diaphanous kimono jacket in a silver, blue, and white print. I felt very elegant even with all the gel she'd mushed into my hair.

I gingerly patted my stiff hair and stared at my toes while I waited for Max to answer the door.

"Skye! I'm glad you're early."

Damn. I knew I should have waited longer. "Didn't you say seven?"

"Sure. But that's because I wanted you to be early." He stepped back and motioned me into the room. "So you can meet Vincent."

"Vincent?"

"The friend who's starting a catering business. Come on. I'll introduce you. Nice outfit." Max's eyes skimmed the length of my body and I felt a flush of pleasure.

I couldn't remember the last time Craig complimented me on my clothing. Maybe I should go shopping with Bobbi Jo more often.

"Vince, this is Skye. She's the one looking for a caterer for a wedding. Skye, Vince."

I held out my hand, then realized that his were wrist deep in a huge bowl of pâté. He shrugged and laughed. "Nice to meet you. We can shake hands later."

Vince lifted the glob of pâté from the bowl and slapped it onto a platter covered with waxed paper. I was relieved to see he was wearing latex gloves.

"How many people? And what kind of food?" As Vince talked, he began sculpting the lump of pâté.

"About a hundred fifty guests, and Jasmine would like a cold buffet. Would that be a problem for you?" Vince's hands moved confidently over the pâté, forming a rectangle, smoothing lumps, slicing off parts and then smoothing them back on.

"Oh, love, nothing will be a problem. Just let Vince take care of it. I'm thinking a lovely antipasto display, and a selection of dips—fresh hummus, a creamy spinach. I've got a wonderful recipe for mango salsa. It's just to die for."

I stepped back to avoid the spatter of pâté from Vince's hands as he waved them around. He returned to the pâté sculpture while he rattled off more menu suggestions. With a few more strokes, the pile of pâté took on the form of an open book. Vince carefully sliced indentations into the edges to resemble pages, then picked up a large carrot and cut it in half. He deftly cut a thin curl off the carrot, nicked the ends into two points, and placed it on the sculpture, forming a perfect bookmark.

"I could provide a cold buffet for a hundred and fifty, with servers, for twenty-five a head. That doesn't include desserts or beverages."

I was sold. Vince could certainly perform miracles

with food, and he was well within Jasmine's budget. He opened the refrigerator and added the pâté sculpture to the incredible amount of food already stacked on the shelves.

"Did you do all that here?"

"Oh, no. Most of it I made at home. I have a much larger kitchen than Max, although his is rather nice, in a homey way. So what do you think about the wedding?"

"Done. Can we get together next week and go over the details?"

"Absolutely, love. Now you two need to get the hell out of my way so I can finish everything." Vince pulled off the latex gloves, tossed them into the trash, and waved us out of the kitchen.

"Would you like a drink?" Max put a hand under my elbow and guided me out of the kitchen and back to the living room. The house was larger than I'd originally thought. The living room took up most of the first floor. The kitchen was closed off, accessible by a swinging door, the dining room occupied one end of the space and the opposite end held a neatly arranged office area.

"No, I'm driving. Water would be nice, though."

"But you're not driving for a while, right?"

"Actually, I need to get home soon. In case Bobbi Jo needs something."

"Right. You've been staying with her since you left your husband."

"How did you know that?"

"Oh, sorry. Lily talks a lot." Max busied himself with pouring water into a glass and adding ice cubes.

"Yes, she certainly does." I laughed, noticing the faint blush on his cheeks. "Don't worry about it. You can't help knowing everything when Lily's involved. Did she tell you Bobbi Jo is pregnant?"

"Quite a shock, from what I understand." Max poured himself a glass of white wine and handed me the water.

"Especially to her." I took the glass and smiled at him. "I just feel like I need to be there for her right now."

"I understand. But surely she can do without you for a couple of hours. There're some of the guests now." Max set his wineglass down and walked to the double front doors, throwing them both open.

A small group entered, laughing, talking, kissing Max on both cheeks. If it hadn't been for the super cool outfit Bobbi Jo had talked me into, I would have felt like a frumpy, middle-aged housewife. But I didn't and it felt pretty good. Maybe I'd take Bobbi Jo shopping with me more often.

I chatted with Max's guests if they approached me, but mostly I watched. I couldn't tell the writers from the editors from the agents from the publishers from the ones who were just friends of his. Not that it mattered. But I noticed that a lot of them appeared to be gay. There were two women who had their arms around each other most of the time. One had bright blue hair plastered to her head with gel, the other had black hair with neon red spikes. Both wore leather pants, skintight tank tops with no bras, and lots of jewelry. There were several men in *elegant casual* outfits that probably cost more than my entire wardrobe. I was definitely out of my element. But at least I didn't look it.

"Sure you don't want something stronger than water?" Max asked after shouldering his way through a group. I was still positioned next to the bar.

"No, thank you. I really have to be going soon."

"Why? Bobbi Jo is probably fine without you."

"I know, but—"

"How thoughtless of me. You probably aren't really ready for socializing, are you? My partner left me about three years ago. We'd been together for five years and I had no idea it was coming."

"Oh." That explained a lot. Max was gay.

Max reached over and squeezed my hand. "It gets better. It really does. Just takes a while."

"This has been great and I really appreciate you introducing me to Vince. He's going to save me by catering this wedding. But I need to get going."

"You sure? Vince hasn't even brought out any of his masterpieces yet." Max leaned over and whispered, "He likes to save the good stuff for later."

"I have a lot to do tomorrow. Don't tell Jasmine, but her wedding plans are in shambles."

"Cross my heart." Max made a cross over his chest. "Come on. I'll see you out."

"No, really. Stay with your guests. I'm parked almost at your front door."

Max insisted on walking me to the door, opened it, and waited until I was in my car before he closed it. Nice guy. Maybe all the nice guys were gay. I chastised myself for the negative thought all the way back to Bobbi Jo's house. I hated being bitter and suspicious. No, I hated Craig for *making* me bitter and suspicious.

The house was mostly dark when I pulled into the driveway. I opened the front door and only a couple of small lights were on in the living room. Sheridan had come home from school, as promised, but she'd decided to spend the night with a friend. I walked into the kitchen to get a glass of wine before I turned in for the night.

"Hey, come join me out here," Bobbi Jo called from the patio.

I took my wine out to the patio. Bobbi Jo was reclining in one of her chaises, sipping fruit juice. The patio was dark except for the lights in and around the pool and the two candles she'd lit on the table next to her.

"How was it?"

"Weird. Strange. I felt totally out of place."

"You just need to get out more, darlin'."

"Or stay in more. It was a very hip crowd. I think over half of them were gay."

"That's not possible."

"Why?"

"I don't know. It just doesn't seem possible.."

"You weren't there. I swear, Vince, the caterer, was gay, then all these people showed up. There was a lesbian couple, so many gay guys, I couldn't count them. Even Max is gay."

"No!"

"Truth."

"Lily never mentioned him being gay."

"Why would she?" I asked.

"Why wouldn't she?"

"Whatever."

"I just think that you're going through a phase. You think every man you meet is gay."

I set my wineglass down and thought about that for a moment. I picked up the amber glass globe that held a lit candle and moved it under my chin, hoping it cast an eerie light on my face. "I see gay people everywhere," I said in a hoarse whisper. Bobbi Jo laughed and waved her hand at me.

"Sometimes they don't even know they're gay."

"Oh, gawd! You are too much, Skye. But I still say it's just an overreaction."

Was it? I didn't think so.

CHAPTER TEN

By Wednesday, the Blue Wedding was under control. Bobbi Jo's enormous dining room table held a variety of plastic bins with color-coded folders containing schedules, contact lists, pictures, estimates, confirmations, and notes. I knew exactly when everything would happen, where it would happen, who had to be there, what it would cost, and who was doing it. I took a moment to sit back and admire my handiwork. Mine and Sean's, to be truthful.

"Oh, excuse me. I need to take this." Sean glanced at his cell phone display. "It's Mr. McLaughlin."

I watched Sean from the dining room. He was short and slender and always immaculately dressed. He'd been delighted to help when Bobbi Jo had asked him. We'd spent the last two days going through every scrap of paper and making phone calls. He was a whiz at getting things organized, and he wasn't afraid to use his position at McLaughlin-Melrose Corp. to persuade people to do his bidding.

I still thought he had a crush on Bobbi Jo. His eyes followed her when she was in the room, and if she was out of the room, he found a reason to go find her. He'd seemed almost angry when he'd heard about Bobbi Jo's pregnancy, but he'd covered his reaction before she realized it. I supposed it was understandable that he wouldn't be thrilled to discover her pregnancy if he had a crush on her, but there was something about his reaction that bothered me. Maybe it was because he was a smarmy little creep.

I watched him standing at the kitchen window and knew he was watching Bobbi Jo on the patio while he talked on the phone. I didn't think she had any idea that he was suffering from puppy love. Maybe I should point it out to her.

"This investigation has everyone on edge," he said when he came back.

"Yes, it does."

"Mr. McLaughlin wanted to know where some of the financial records were about a takeover deal he and Edward were working on. Evidently that detective looked into some of the finances of the business and thinks that Mr. McLaughlin had a motive to kill Edward." Sean rubbed at a small white spot on his left cheekbone.

"Really?"

"They'd been working on buying out this small company for months. But MMC Industries didn't have the cash flow to purchase them outright. Edward wasn't really involved in much of it, and I think Mr. McLaughlin was trying to get financing for the buy-out. I guess the detective figured that was motive for him to kill Edward."

"How much money was involved?"

"About eight million. That's not a lot, but MMC has been a little overextended because of a deal that went sour last year." His finger moved to rub the little scar again.

"I see." That insurance policy would come in handy to Jimmy right now.

"Sean, did you know Edward's first wife?"

"Charlotte? Sure. She and Edward were friends. He even helped her boyfriend out when his design firm was in trouble a few months ago."

"How nice of him. What kind of help?"

"Edward helped him write up a business plan so he could get a loan. Saved his ass. Karl got the loan, expanded the business. He's doing great now. Just got written up in *Northwest People* as one of Portland's most successful businessmen."

That pretty much cleared Charlotte and her boyfriend of any motive for murdering Edward.

"I think that pretty much covers everything," Sean said, closing a folder.

"Yes, it does. I really appreciate all your help with

this." A car horn honked, and I walked into the living room to pull aside the drapes.

A bright red Mini Cooper with a white roof sat in the driveway. Sheridan tooted the horn again and got out of the car. I opened the door and walked out to meet her.

"Which one of your rich friends loaned you this?"

Sheridan paused to wipe a smudge from the side mirror, then grinned at me. "It's mine. Isn't it great?"

"Yours?"

"Dad just gave it to me."

"*Your* dad?" Craig and I had discussed getting Sheridan a car. I'd been for it and he'd been against it. Of course, I'd been thinking more of an older, reliable, ugly car that would take her where she needed to go while not encouraging her friends to suggest joyrides. Not this shiny new Mini Cooper for her to zip around in. Craig had insisted that Sheridan should earn the money for her own car if she wanted one. He didn't mind her borrowing mine after she got her license, but he insisted that buying her own car would give her a sense of responsibility. I always suspected that he wasn't crazy about the sense of independence and freedom she'd get from having her own wheels.

"Isn't it beautiful?" Sheridan admired the shiny red and white car.

"Sheridan, I'm astounded."

"Oh, I know Dad only did it because he feels guilty about the divorce."

She knew that? When had my little girl grown up? When had she become mature enough to figure out motives? Especially parental motives. Not that Craig had any claim to subtlety.

"But I think I should enjoy it while it lasts. He'll settle down soon and it'll be back to me begging for everything."

Now she could predict his future actions. Probably with a great deal of accuracy, too. "Has he talked to you?"

"About being gay? Yeah. We discussed it last weekend. It's cool. I think he was relieved that I didn't freak out on him. Like half the guys I know aren't gay. I'm into performing arts, after all."

"No doubt. Did you tell him you already knew?"

"Are you kidding, Mom? No way. For one thing, it would have just made him feel bad, and for another, there's more guilt involved if I don't."

"You are a mercenary and manipulative child." I put my arm around her and squeezed, unable to keep the grin off my face.

"Yeah, I'm proud of me, too," Sheridan joked but returned the hug. My cell phone chirped and I released her to answer it.

"Hi, Jasmine. I just went over all the plans. Everything

is set. We're totally organized."

"Wedding favors," Jasmine wailed.

"What about them?" I searched my mind for some memory of wedding favors and came up blank.

"I just remembered that we don't have any. How could I have overlooked wedding favors?"

"Stay calm, Jasmine. We'll think of something." I had no idea what. The wedding was less than two weeks away. Not enough time to order anything personalized, but surely we could come up with something.

"Can you come over?"

"I'll be there soon." I closed the cell phone. "I need to go over to Jasmine's. Evidently she forgot to do anything about wedding favors."

"Cool. I'll drive you. I haven't seen Jasmine in a long time." Sheridan jumped in the car and started the engine. I ran inside to get my bag and master folder.

"Sean, I have to go over to Jasmine's. Evidently she forgot about wedding favors. Do you want to come and meet her?"

"Oh, no, thanks. I have some things I need to take care of. I can meet her later."

"Okay. Tell Bobbi Jo I'll be back in a while."

"Sure."

I tucked the folder into my bag and headed out to the car. Sheridan turned the music down and put the car into gear. She was a competent driver, and I had to give Craig credit for that. I'd been useless at teaching her to drive, but Craig had excelled at it and spent a lot of hours in the car with her, making sure she would be a cautious and responsible driver.

I felt tears well in my eyes. Anger and resentment fought their way through me, vying for top position. How dare Craig ruin our lives this way? We'd had a really, really good life and he'd ruined it all. He'd wasted almost twenty years of my life and made Sheridan a child of divorce. And even if she could joke about it, I still believed it had to hurt her. I glanced at my beautiful, talented, intelligent daughter. She seemed to be handling it fairly well. A new car could soothe a lot of ragged emotions in an eighteen-year-old. I let the anger storm for a few more minutes and finally had to admit that Sheridan was fine. She wasn't harboring any resentment toward her father. Why would she? She'd known about him for some time now.

No, the problem was me. Rather, my reaction to the situation. It was my life that had been turned upside down. I was the one who didn't have a clue what my future held, had no idea how I would support myself, where I would live, who I would grow old with. I'd devoted myself to Craig and Sheridan and our home, secure in the knowledge that Craig and I would grow old together. We'd babysit our grandchildren, travel together after he retired, and eventually settle into our old age wrapped in the warmth of shared memories. Now none of that would happen, and I had no dream to replace it with.

The past few weeks, I'd been keeping myself busy. Between the wedding plans and Bobbi Jo's pregnancy and worrying about the murder investigation, I'd managed to keep my emotions tamped down. I'd kept the fear and anger at bay. Now everything was bubbling to the surface. Sheridan continued to chatter about her life at school while I tried to sort through my emotions. Was I really angry at Craig? Or was I just afraid of being on my own? I didn't really blame him. Maybe for marrying me in the first place. But it's not like he could choose his sexual identity. He couldn't stop being gay in order to make my life easier. No, the sad fact was that I was just feeling sorry for myself.

"Mom?"

I looked over at Sheridan, surprised to find we were parked in front of Lily's house. "Oh, sorry, I was just thinking about the wedding plans."

"You know, it's really cool that you're doing this for Jasmine. Besides, it'll give you practice for when you do my wedding."

"I hope that doesn't happen for a long time."

"Mom!"

"You're only eighteen, Sheridan. Why would you even be thinking about marriage?" I stopped halfway up the walkway and clutched her arm. "Is there something you need to tell me?"

Sheridan laughed, and if I didn't know better I'd have thought she was enjoying torturing me. "Well, there is this guy I've gotten to know in the play." She must have interpreted the look of horror on my face accurately. "Relax, Mom. We haven't even gone out yet. You know, it's kind of natural for girls to think about their wedding."

"I know. I just don't like to think that you'd get married before you finish your education and have a little time to enjoy yourself."

"You got married at nineteen."

I lifted an eyebrow. "Exactly."

Jasmine opened the door and hurried us into the sunroom, jabbering excitedly all the way. Max was standing there holding a champagne flute.

"Hi, Max. This is my daughter, Sheridan."

They greeted each other while Jasmine continued to chatter behind us. I decided I'd better find out what she was talking about and turned my attention to her.

"So, then Max tells me that he has the perfect solution for the wedding favors."

Max held up the champagne flute and I could see that it was filled with candle wax.

"Isn't it lovely?" Jasmine asked. "And he said we could add some flowers to the candle wax and make the wax blue so it'll go with the rest of the wedding. Then every guest will have a candle to take home with them."

I took the glass that Max held out and looked at it. "It's a fine idea. I think adding some flowers would be nice and we can tie a ribbon around each one." The candle was very nice and it seemed a logical and simple solution to Jasmine's latest panic. I looked up at Max. "Do you know anything about making candles?"

"Actually, I made this one. For my sister's wedding. I could use some help, though. We'll need a lot of them."

"I can help," Sheridan offered. "I'm not due back at school until Sunday."

"I knew I had a kid for a reason." I grinned at Sheridan. "What all do we need?" I asked Max.

"A champagne flute for each guest, candle wax, wicks, ribbons, and the flowers."

"I can get the champagne flutes from a wholesaler that mom uses," Jasmine offered.

"Sheridan, if I give you a list of items, can you get the candle-making supplies and the ribbons at the craft store?" Max asked.

"Sure. I have a car now." Sheridan beamed.

"Then you and I will pick up the flowers at the Flower Mart," Max said to me. He sat down to write out a detailed list for Sheridan while Jasmine called her mother about the wholesaler.

"Okay, Mom. Thanks. Tell them I'll be there in half an hour. Oh, hold on, there's another call coming through." Jasmine clicked over to the other call and listened. I watched as her face crumpled. Tears streamed down her cheeks and her lower lip trembled. She sniffled and nodded while she listened.

Dread crawled up my spine. This could not be good news. Jasmine hung up the phone, evidently forgetting that her mother was still holding the line for her.

"The band just cancelled. My wedding's ruined."

"You're amazing." I stopped inside the Flower Mart and looked at the rows and rows of flowers.

"I'm very pleased that you recognize that"—Max grinned at me—"but I have to admit that I didn't invent the Flower Mart; I just knew where it was."

"No, I mean the way you calmed Jasmine down. I had no idea what to do."

"She's always been a bit excitable. I've known Jasmine for a long time. Since she was about three."

"You've lived next door that long?"

"No. My aunt owned the house. I visited her a lot. Then when she died a couple of years ago, she left me the house."

"So, do you really know a band that can step in and play at her wedding?"

"Of course I do. Some old friends. They do a few gigs now and then. Mostly hard rock, but they can play anything. We just have to give them a list of songs that she wants."

"I can see the list now. 'Blue Bayou,' 'Blue Monday,' maybe 'Lady Blue.'"

"'Don't It Make Your Brown Eyes Blue.'" Max frowned. "I don't think the band actually plays the blues, though."

"Maybe we could just get them to wear blue outfits?"

"Only if that means blue jeans and T-shirts." He laughed at my expression. "Don't worry, the guys will dress appropriately, but I can't promise blue."

"I'm just glad she didn't want blue food."

Max took my hand and tugged me down an aisle that featured dried flowers and greenery. "I know she wants some mistletoe in the candles and the best vendor is down here."

We'd already picked up lavender, lemon blossoms, pansies, rosemary, and freesia. Each of them had some special meaning, none of which I really cared about, which was good since I also couldn't remember them.

"What do the pansies mean again?" I asked Max.

"Thought. And the rosemary is remembrance,

freesia is trust, lavender is loyalty, and mistletoe is for fertility. Jasmine, of course, is amiability."

"How do you remember all that?"

"I worked for a florist for a while. That's how I know about the Flower Mart." He pulled me over to a small booth. Every kind of dried flower imaginable hung in bunches and clumps from every available spot. A short, skinny man hunched over a work counter littered with clippings, floral wire, and spools of ribbons.

"Hey, Antonio!" Max called.

The little man turned from his work, a big smile creasing his face. "Max! Where you been?" He shook Max's hand and clapped him on the shoulder. "Ah, you been a busy boy, no?" Antonio waggled his bushy eyebrows and beamed at me.

"Antonio, I'd like you to meet Skye. She needs some mistletoe."

"Ah, no! Woman this beautiful? I bet the boys all line up to kiss you."

I laughed, hoping it covered the fact that I was blushing. "It's not for me. We're making wedding favors."

"Ah. Good, good." Antonio nodded his head, then winked at me. "About time someone made an honest man of him."

"Oh, no, it's not our wedding!" Obviously he didn't know Max very well.

"It's for a friend of ours," Max explained. "Oh, come on, Antonio. You can't be that disappointed."

"Breaks my heart." Antonio patted his chest. "But at least you kiss the lady, yes?" Antonio pointed to the beam over our head. We looked up to see a massive bunch of mistletoe.

Antonio laughed. "Means you gotta kiss the young man, you know? Like at Christmastime."

"I thought that was only for Christmas," I said.

"No, it for alla time, now you kiss." Antonio gestured to the mistletoe. "You no kiss, you anger the gods and your friend's marriage fail. You want that on your head?"

"Not me," Max said. "How about you?" Max slowly lowered his lips to mine. I was expecting a brief peck, but his lips settled gently on mine and I felt his arm move to my back, pulling me closer. His mouth moved softly over mine, and I felt myself lean into him a bit before I came to my senses and pulled away. What the hell was I doing kissing a gay man? Wasn't it enough that I was divorcing one? I considered the possibility that I might have some fatal flaw when it came to choosing men. I tried to step away from Max, but he kept his arm draped over my shoulder.

"That good enough for you, Antonio?"

"You should be asking the lady if it was any good."

I smiled, purchased the mistletoe, thanked Antonio, and hustled back to Max's car, all the while trying not to appear like I was rushing.

"You okay?" Max asked.

"Sure. I'm fine. I just have so much to do, you know."

"Don't forget, the candle making is tomorrow." Max loaded our purchases into the car.

Damn. I'd forgotten I'd promised to help with the candle making. Maybe I could come up with an excuse to get out of it.

"Might as well get it done. One less thing for Jasmine to worry over. And don't forget the band rehearsal is Sunday afternoon."

"Who could forget that?" I spent the ride back to Lily's house wondering if there would be any way to get out of both events. By the time we arrived, I'd resigned myself to attending at least one.

"Hey, Mom. You ready to go?" Sheridan and Jasmine were on the front porch, evidently waiting for us to return.

"Sure."

"Max, all the candle supplies are in the sunroom with the champagne flutes." Sheridan opened her car door. "See you tomorrow."

I climbed in the car, relieved at her reminder that she would be there for the candle making, too. Then

I wondered why I felt that way. It wasn't like I was afraid to be alone with Max. Just because he'd kissed me didn't mean he was going to come on to me. It was a joke. He was gay. God! When had I become so up-tight? I needed to loosen up some.

"Mom, I need to talk to you about something," Sheridan said as she pulled away from the curb.

"Sure, honey. What?"

Sheridan took a deep breath. "I've been accepted by Mario Lauria as a student."

"I didn't know you'd applied. Sheridan, that's wonderful!" Mario Lauria was a famous voice teacher. Sheridan had dreamed of studying with him for years. He was also very expensive and I had no idea how I would pay for the lessons, but I would. I'd find a way.

"What about college?"

"I'll stay here and go to Portland Community College. I think it's better anyway because I don't even know what I want to major in."

"You think your father will be all right with this?" Craig had pushed her to enroll at UC Santa Cruz, his alma mater.

"I already told him. I think he's a little disap-pointed about me not going to UC, but he's fine with it. He's even paying for the lessons."

"More guilt payment?" I felt a little guilty myself at the relief that Craig would be footing the bill.

"Probably. Don't worry, Mom, I'm not going to take advantage of Dad. Did you know he's dating?"

Craig was dating? That felt strange. And annoying. How could he just wipe away our marriage and start dating? "No, I didn't know. Have you met the man? I assume it is a man?"

"Yeah. He's okay, I guess. I mean, I don't have anything against gays, you know. But it feels a little weird having your father date a guy."

"I know what you mean. Feels a little weird to me, too."

"Who would have ever thought we'd be having this conversation?" Sheridan laughed and I felt like I could just about burst with pride. How could I think my marriage to Craig was wasted when I'd produced this beautiful young woman?

"Dad asked if I wanted to live with him, but I really think he needs his own space right now."

"I think you're right. Don't worry about it. I'll find us a place to live by then. Do you have any preferences about where you'd like to live? Close to the school?"

Sheridan proceeded to give me her ideas about what a cool place to live would be like until we arrived back at Bobbi Jo's. Bobbi Jo was lounging on the patio with a fruit smoothie.

"Hey, y'all. Lily is coming over for dinner. I'm

going to burn some chicken on the grill. Lily promised she'd bring everything else."

"Great. I could use some food. Especially food prepared by someone else." I took a chair across from Bobbie Jo. "Sheridan just told me she's been accepted by Mario Lauria."

"That girl's going to be a star. Maybe a Broadway musical, or have a song in the Top Forty."

"First, I want her to go to college."

"You can't live her life for her, Skye. Let her make her own choices."

"Easier said than done. You'll find out for yourself soon enough."

Bobbi Jo patted her tummy. "I can hardly wait." The doorbell rang and Sheridan yelled that she'd get it. "That's probably Lily. I'll light the grill if you'll get the chicken out of the fridge. It's marinating in a bowl."

"Hi, Skye." Lily set a stack of three plastic bowls on the counter. "Coleslaw, fruit salad, and a green salad. Do you have salad dressing? I didn't think to bring any."

"In the door of the fridge." I took the chicken out to Bobbi Jo and returned for tongs.

"I can't thank you enough for helping Jasmine with her wedding. I probably would have killed her by now." Lily set three bottles of dressing on the counter.

"She's not that bad, Lily. She's just excited and

wants everything to be perfect."

"Well, she'll get over it as soon as she gets married."

"Sounds like you're having issues."

"Same old shit." Lily poured herself a glass of wine. "I swear, if I'd known men were so impossible, I'd have considered becoming a lesbian."

"If I had two husbands and was considering a third, I'd have myself committed."

Sheridan danced into the kitchen. "What's for dinner? I'm starved."

"Take those plates and the silverware to the patio. It'll be ready soon," I told her.

Lily followed her with the bowls, then came back for serving spoons and her wine. I poured myself a glass of wine, grabbed the napkins, a loaf of French bread, and a knife, and joined the others.

"Do I have time for a quick swim?" Sheridan asked Bobbi Jo.

"Chicken should be ready in about ten minutes."

"I'll wait then. It'll take me almost that long to go upstairs and change."

"We have an eight-foot privacy fence. Just shuck off your clothes and jump in. There's a robe in the pool house when you're done."

"Really?" Sheridan giggled.

"Edward and I used to swim nekkid all the time."

We were all silent for a moment at the mention of

Edward. I was torn between wanting to ask Bobbi Jo if she'd heard anything from Scott and not wanting to bring it up at all.

"I talked to that detective today," Bobbi Jo said.

"Is there any news?" I asked.

"It sounded like he thinks Jimmy is the prime suspect now." Bobbi Jo laughed. "Can you imagine that? Edward and Jimmy have been friends forever. He'd never do anything to hurt Edward."

Bobbi Jo turned the chicken and waved the tongs toward the pool, seemingly having forgotten about the investigation. "You know the difference between being nude and being nekkid?"

"I shudder to wonder." I was still thinking about Jimmy McLaughlin and the money he needed for the buyout he was attempting. I hated to think that Edward's longtime friend might have killed him, but I was happy that Bobbi Jo was no longer the number-one suspect.

"Nude is when you don't have any clothes on. Nekkid is when you don't have any clothes on and you're up to something."

"I've never swum in the nude before," Sheridan said.

"That's a relief." My comment garnered me a giggle from Sheridan as she stripped off her shorts and T-shirt. She hesitated at her bra and panties, but just for a moment.

The three of us watched as Sheridan ran to the pool and dove in. She swam half the length of the pool underwater, then surfaced, pushing her long, dark hair off her face.

"Were we ever that beautiful and vivacious?" Lily asked.

"Probably. We've just forgotten about it." I watched Sheridan as she swam across the pool with swift, strong strokes.

"I think that's the beauty of getting older," Bobbi Jo offered. "We have memory loss so we forget just how great we felt and looked when we were young."

"I guess so. Now, we're consumed with just keeping our bodies together. Never mind how they look." Lily smoothed her long gauze dress over her plump belly and thighs. "I went to the dermatologist last week and he bitched at me about sun spots on my arms and legs. Told me the skin on my limbs should look just like the skin on my belly."

"What? It should have stretch marks?" I asked.

Lily laughed and poured herself another glass of wine. I held my glass out, ready for a refill.

"I can't wait to have stretch marks," Bobbi Jo said.

"Only a woman pregnant for the first time could say that with a straight face," Lily said.

I had to agree with her. But I knew I wouldn't give up the joy of having a child just to have a smooth tummy and firmer breasts. Neither would Lily.

Bobbi Jo placed the chicken on a plate and carried it to the table. I called Sheridan out of the pool and we all gathered for dinner. I hadn't eaten lunch and the two glasses of wine were making my brain a little fuzzy, but that was okay.

"Sheridan's classes start in a month," I said. "So, I need to start looking for a place to live."

"You can both stay here," Bobbi Jo said.

"Thanks, but I think we need our own place. You have no idea what it's like living with a teenager."

"Mom!" Sheridan protested.

"I just mean that you're in and out all the time. You have friends over. It's not what Bobbi Jo is used to." I smiled at Bobbi Jo. "Besides, you'll be busy getting ready for the baby."

"I guess," Bobbi Jo said. "But you could still stay here. At least take your time finding a place."

"I appreciate the offer. And it might take some time to find just the right place."

"Bobbi Jo, it's not like you won't see them again." Lily reached over and squeezed Bobbi Jo's hand.

"I know. It just going to feel weird to not have anyone in the house." Bobbi Jo smiled at me. "You know, you have a lot to look forward to now."

"And what would that be?" I asked.

"Oh, tons of things. Your first date, your first

boyfriend."

"Yeah, that's something to really look forward to," I said.

"Your first kiss. Remember how wonderful it felt to kiss some guy the first time? It's the best." Bobbi Jo forked a chunk of watermelon and grinned at me.

"I don't even want to think about dating and boyfriends." I leaned over the table. "But I've already had my first kiss."

"When?"

"Who?"

"Mom!"

"Oh, it's not a big deal. Max kind of kissed me on a dare today."

"Why isn't it a big deal?" Lily asked.

"Well, because Max is gay. It didn't mean anything." The three of them were silent, staring at me as if I'd grown a second head. "What?"

"Mom, Max is so totally *not* gay!"

"Yes, he is," I insisted. "He told me about his partner leaving him."

Sheridan shook her head. "Everyone says partner now. It's the politically correct word."

"She's right," Lily said. "I knew Max's partner and I can assure you she was not a man. Max loves the ladies, so if he kissed you, it wasn't on a dare."

Oh, my.

CHAPTER ELEVEN

I drove through the Portland traffic with a smile on my face. In spite of the sweltering heat. In spite of Bobbi Jo's sour attitude. I'd heard from my doctor and my DNA test for HIV was negative. I was more relieved than I'd thought I would be. Maybe I just hadn't allowed myself to consider the possibility that Craig might have infected me. I also hoped that he was being careful. Maybe I should mention it to him? Oh, geez, I was thinking about his feelings again. I had to cut the ties to him. He was a reasonable, responsible adult. He didn't need me to tell him to be safe.

"The next apartment is on the east side of the river," Bobbi Jo said. "I'm not sure I want you living that far away."

"It's only over the river." I'd ditched the candle-making session in order to look for an apartment. Sheridan had speculated that I was avoiding Max, now that I knew he wasn't gay. I'd speculated that I still had enough influence with her father to pull her car keys. I threaded my way through downtown Portland trying to find a way to the Hawthorne Bridge.

"Well, it's farther than I like. I still think you should stay with me. I have tons of room."

"We've been over that, Bobbi Jo. Sheridan and I need to have our own place."

"I know. But I don't have to like it." Bobbi Jo folded the newspaper and looked at me. "I just want you as close as possible."

"I promise we'll be close by. No more than twenty minutes away."

"Hey, you just missed the turnoff for the bridge."

"No. Did I? Damn, I always get turned around downtown. Too many one-way streets." I turned left and searched the street signs. That didn't help because I was in an unfamiliar part of town.

"We're lost."

I scowled at Bobbi Jo and pulled over to the curb. We were in the industrial section of town. I could tell by the large warehouses all around us. Bobbi Jo unfolded the map and tried to pinpoint our location. I rolled the window down, hoping there would be a slight breeze to alleviate the heat.

"Okay, we're almost there. You just need to take a right a few blocks up here and then another right, then a left and there's the bridge."

"Huh?" I knew Bobbi Jo was talking, but I was mesmerized by a sign I'd just spotted.

"Just drive. I'll tell you when to turn."

"Just a minute." I got out of the car and considered the building across the street. The one with the big *For Rent* sign.

"What the hell are you doing?" Bobbi Jo got out and stomped around to my side of the car. "What? You're going to rent a warehouse?"

"It could be cool."

"It could be drafty."

"Bobbi Jo, living in loft apartments is very cool. They do it in all the big cities."

"What's wrong with an apartment?"

"Everything I've looked at is just a collection of small off-white boxes glued together to form a bigger off-white box."

"What about that cute Victorian house we looked at?" she asked.

"Oh, I loved the house. But it's too small. The bedrooms would barely hold a single bed and a dresser."

"Look, darlin', I know this all seems like a step down for you. You're used to that huge craftsman house. Why don't you just stay with me?"

"That's just it, Bobbi Jo. I don't mind taking a step down. But what I really want is a step to the side. I want something different."

"This is definitely different."

"I just want to check it out. The sign says warehouse

space and lofts." I headed across the street before she could voice any more objections. Bobbi Jo hurried after me on her two-inch-heeled thongs.

"You know, you should stop wearing those. Flats would be a lot safer for you."

"I'm pregnant, Skye, not disabled."

I pressed the button that had *doorbell* on a handwritten sign over it. A few moments later a buzzer sounded and I pushed open the door. "See, it has a security system. Very important."

"Especially in this neighborhood." Bobbi Jo followed me into the entryway and made a face. Really, I couldn't blame her. The small space was decorated in drywall with seams camouflaged by a rough application of joint compound. Someone had swiped three garish shades of paint on one section. I could only hope they were out selecting a fourth color. There were four metal mailboxes loosely attached to one wall. The elevator doors opened and Bobbi Jo and I both turned. A short, chubby man hoisted up the wood-slatted inner gates and grinned at us.

"Stan Simpson. What can I do you for ladies?"

"I saw your *For Rent* sign in the window." I started to offer my hand, glanced at the grease on his, and reconsidered.

"Yep. I got a big loft apartment available and some warehouse space. Now the warehouse space can be divided up in two-thousand-square-feet increments, depending on what you'd need."

"I'm interested in the loft."

"Well, then, let's go up and take a look at her." He motioned us onto the elevator. We stepped in; he closed the wooden gate and pressed a button. Surprisingly, the elevator operated smoothly and quietly. We stopped on the fourth floor and stepped out into the hallway. This area had been painted with a technique I recognized as Venetian plaster in a terra-cotta color. I'd thought of doing a similar treatment in my dining room, but had never gotten around to it.

"There're four lofts on this floor. This particular one is around two thousand square feet." He jingled an enormous ring of keys, looking for the right one. "This one's a steal because it's not really been built out yet. The last tenant had a photo studio in here so he didn't much care what the place looked like. But it's got a full kitchen and a bath and a half." He finally got the right key and pushed open the door.

The first thing I noticed was the light that poured in through the huge windows. Windows that looked out over the Willamette River. The adjoining wall was equally graced with windows and had a view of downtown Portland.

"I'll let you gals wander around. I know you want to talk about it. Be back in a few." Stan jingled his keys and waved from the door.

"It's a mess." Bobbi Jo walked across to the windows. "Nice view of the river, though."

She was right about the mess. The former tenant hadn't done much in the way of cleaning up. The floors were littered with papers, magazines, old paint cans, and some debris that I couldn't readily identify. The floors were hardwood, although they were scarred and had been painted a dull gray at some point.

"Is this the kitchen?" Bobbi Jo stood at one end of the loft, staring at what passed for a kitchen. Basically, they had lined up a refrigerator, oven, and sink, each separated by about two feet of counter covered in a hideous yellow speckled laminate. At the end stood a metal cabinet with one door that hung open. Next to the kitchen area, a door led to a large, if uninspiring, bath. The sink hung loosely from the wall with a spotty mirror over it. But there was a lovely claw-footed tub. Another metal cabinet served as the linen closet.

"It has possibilities," I said.

"For what? Condemnation?"

"It could be fixed up. A little cleaning, a little paint."

"A *little* cleaning?"

"Hey, you forget. I've been a professional house cleaner for the past nineteen years."

"I know you said you wanted a step to the side, but

really, Skye. This is like stepping off a cliff. It needs
a lot of work."

"What else do I have to do?" I walked to the
other side of the space and opened one of the three
doors to a large empty room. The second door led to
a bath. Stan had referred to it as a half bath, but it
actually contained a shower stall, sink, and toilet. I
turned the water on in the shower and was rewarded
with a forceful spray. Still needed a little fixing up,
but it was definitely usable. I opened the third door.
Total darkness. I peered into the room, but couldn't
see a thing. Bobbi Jo reached around and flipped the
light switch. The long, narrow room glowed with dim
red light.

"It's a darkroom." I walked inside to look at the
sinks and trays.

"Yeah, because of the red lightbulb."

"No, Bobbi Jo, it's a darkroom for developing
film." I inhaled the faint odor of photo chemicals and
smiled. "I used to develop my own black and whites
in college."

Bobbi Jo declined to enter the dark room. I followed her back to the main loft. She looked around
at the enormous space. "What about rooms? Doesn't
Sheridan need a bedroom? Haven't you been saying
she needs her own space?"

"She can have the big room for her bedroom."

"And what about your bedroom?" Bobbi Jo asked.

"I can make walls."

"Now you're a carpenter?"

"No. But I can make walls with screens and stuff. Or I can hire someone to build walls."

"Walls." Bobbi Jo shook her head. "Skye, you need to think about this."

"No. I don't need to think about it. It's perfect. It just needs some paint, some fixtures. It'll be great."

"You don't even know if you can afford it," she argued.

"Let's find Stan and see how much it is." I'd already made up my mind that I was going to rent the loft. It would take a lot of work to fix up. But it was different in a way that really appealed to me. This was the first place that I could call my own. It was perfect.

Bobbi Jo followed me back to the elevator. "Sheridan is going to hate you for this."

My elation at finding the loft faded a bit when my cell phone chirped and I saw Craig's number. Why now? Why couldn't he wait until I was already in a bad mood?

"Hello?" Like I didn't already know it was him.

"Skye. How are you?"

"Fine. Really fine. What's up?"

"How's Bobbi Jo holding up?"

What the hell did he want? Not that he didn't care about Bobbi Jo, but he would never call to see how she was. "Well enough. I think mostly she's ignoring the murder investigation. But the other day, she mentioned that the detective hinted that Jimmy McLaughlin was a prime suspect."

"McLaughlin? That's ridiculous. He and Edward were friends forever."

"I know. But I guess they have to look at everyone." I really didn't want to discuss this with him. I didn't want to even talk to him. So, I didn't. After a moment, he seemed to realize that.

"I figured you probably wanted a chance to yell at me about Sheridan's car." He chuckled.

That pissed me off a little. And I wasn't even sure that was what he was really calling about. "I thought you didn't want her to have a car yet."

"True. But then I realized that our little girl is growing up. Besides, I thought it would be easier for all of us if she had her own transportation. This way she can visit either one of us whenever she wants to."

"Did you think I'd refuse to let her visit you?"

"No, Skye, I just thought it would be easier if she could drive herself."

Damn. He was being so freaking reasonable. "Sure, I guess you're right."

"I signed the divorce papers today."

"I thought you'd want to discuss it before you signed."

"No. I made some changes, though. Your attorney approved them."

"What kind of changes?"

"I increased the spousal support. And I agreed to pay off the Escape."

"You didn't need to do that. I was happy with the agreement. Besides, I don't need more support. I want to take care of myself."

"Well, sure. But that might take a while." I could hear Craig sigh. "Skye, I don't want you to have to suffer any more than you already have because of me."

What was this? A guilt trip? I wasn't buying it. I certainly wasn't going to let him believe that I was suffering. Then it occurred to me that I didn't really feel like I was suffering. Was my irritation with Craig just an auto-response now?

"Craig, I'm fine, really. Don't worry about me." There was a pause, then Craig cleared his throat.

"Are you going to the musical at her school next weekend?"

"Of course. Aren't you?"

"Sure. I just thought I should tell you that—"

Another pause. "I thought I should let you know that I'll be bringing a friend."

"A friend?" So, this was the real reason for the call.

"Jack."

"I see."

"I don't want to hurt you, or make you uncomfortable. I'm just trying to be me."

"I understand." And in a weird way, I did.

"It's just that I'm done with lies. I'm trying to be true to who I am. Whoever or whatever that is. I finally realized that I don't have the right to lie to people. Not if it's going to hurt them."

"I'd have to agree with that."

"I know that I wasted a lot of years of your life. I wish I could take that back. It wasn't what I intended. I thought I could be happily married to you forever. I just had no idea this would happen."

My heart broke a little at the sincerity in his voice. At one time I'd thought I'd wasted years of my life by being married to him. But I was entitled to think that. It hurt too much to hear him say it. To admit to causing the pain. I was suddenly aware of how painful this had to be for him. Aware of how much pain he must have lived with for so many years.

"I can't wait to meet Jack. I have to run, but I'll see you there."

I closed the phone and then I cried. For the pain

Craig must have lived with all of his life. For having been cheated out of the possibility of a happily ever after of my own. For the good parts of our relationship that I'd never have with him again.

Remembering Bobbi Jo's prediction that Sheridan would hate the loft, I waited nervously while she inspected it. Sheridan walked the perimeter of the large space, giving scant attention to the kitchen area. She stopped in front of the large windows and turned to me.

"Mom, I don't know what to say."

"You don't?" That sounded ominous.

"I had no idea you were this cool." Sheridan grinned.

"It needs some work. A lot of paint. Even more cleaning."

"It'll be fun." Sheridan looked up at the twenty-foot ceiling. She sang a few scales and grinned. "The acoustics are incredible."

"We're going to be late if we don't leave." I'd promised Lily and Jasmine that we'd join them to listen to the band rehearse. Not that it mattered much. There was little chance of getting another band at this late date. "We can talk about decorating tonight." I hustled Sheridan out of the loft and we drove to a small bar in southeast Portland.

"This must be it." I pulled over to the curb and parked behind Lily's car.

"Cool. I get to go to a bar."

"Only because they aren't open for business." A member of the band owned the bar and they used it for rehearsals.

"Still, I can say I've been to a bar." Sheridan pushed open the black door and wrinkled her nose. "Man, it stinks in here."

Lily, Jasmine, Bobbi Jo, and Sean were having coffee while the band members tuned their instruments. Max was at the end of a hallway, propping open the back door, which I hoped would help disperse the odor of stale smoke and alcohol. We took our seats at the round table, and Bobbi Jo poured a cup of coffee for me.

"You want some coffee, Sheridan?" she asked.

Sheridan was busy soaking up the atmosphere of her first bar, but managed to nod. Lily and Jasmine said hi, then bent their heads over the list of songs the band had given them. Sean shifted in his chair, getting a little closer to Bobbi Jo. He draped his arm casually over the back of her chair and it almost looked like his arm was around her. I couldn't believe she didn't notice. I was going to have to have a little chat with her about him.

"Hey, Skye. Let me introduce you to the band."

Max waved the band members over. "This is Bill, Tim, and Clark. That's Ken on the drums." Ken waved his drumsticks at us.

"Okay. I checked off the songs I'd like to hear." Jasmine handed the list to Bill. "Mostly, I just want upbeat music that everyone can dance to."

"That'd be our specialty, ma'am." He turned to me and nodded. "Nice to meet you, Skye. Hope you enjoy our music."

Bill was a tall, lean man with graying hair, twinkling blue eyes, and a deep, sexy voice with a Texan accent. Max put his hand on my shoulder in what I could have almost sworn was a possessive gesture. That reminded me that Max was not gay. Which made me nervous. In a weird, giddy, happy kind of way.

The band started to play, and Sheridan bounced in her seat, singing along with them. Jasmine clapped, evidently delighted with the band. That was a relief. They finished the first song, waited for the smattering of applause and moved into the second one.

"Oh, I love this song." Sheridan leaned toward me. "I'm singing it in the show at school."

"Well, go show us your stuff," Max said.

"What?" Sheridan asked.

"Go on. Sing with the band."

"No, really, I couldn't. Could I?" Sheridan looked at me with a hopeful, puppy-dog look.

"Go on," I said.

"Hey, guys, you mind a little vocal assistance?" Max called over the music.

Bill grinned at Sheridan. "Get on up here, girl."

Sheridan hesitated just a heartbeat, then shot off her chair and up onto the stage. As soon as she had the microphone in her hand, she turned into a hair-tossing, hip-thrusting pop star. She sang. She flirted outrageously with Bill when they shared the microphone. She strutted over and danced around Tim while he did his guitar solo. What had happened to my little girl? Where the hell was my baby?

"She's great!" Max said.

Bobbi Jo leaned across Sean to add her enthusiastic approval. "I can remember when she was four and she'd get up on the coffee table and dance and sing for us."

Sheridan's snug T-shirt rode up, revealing a few inches of tummy above her low-riding jeans. I felt a frown of disapproval settle on my forehead and suddenly felt old. Or maybe I was just a prude. Yeah, like that was better. The song finally ended, and Sheridan bounded off the stage to everyone's applause. Max whistled. Jasmine pumped her arm in the air. Bobbi Jo stood to give her a hug when she returned to the table.

"Scary as hell when they grow up, isn't it?" Lily leaned over and grinned at me.

"You could have warned me."

"No fun that way," she retorted. "Besides, having the realization hit you like a ton of bricks is just another rite of passage for a woman. I wouldn't think of denying you that experience."

There were several experiences that I'd have been just as happy to live without. Realizing that my baby girl was a woman in more ways than I really wanted to consider was just one of them. Still, I was incredibly proud of her.

"Really, Skye, it's not so bad," Lily said. "It's the beginning of a transitional phase."

"Transitional? To what?"

"For the past eighteen years, you've been Sheridan's mother. She's growing up and that identity will start to fade. You'll get to be Skye again. Not that you won't always be her mother, of course. It's just the identity thing."

"Really." Sometimes Lily was just a little too out-there for me to connect with.

"It was like a blossoming for me when Jasmine and Beau left the house and started making their own lives. I hadn't realized how much of myself I'd invested in them. Not that I minded. Not a bit."

"Of course not."

"But it was like being free again. I found out things about myself that I'd never known. Or maybe I'd just buried them for so long I'd forgotten about them. Trust me, you'll come to like it."

I wasn't so sure of that. I liked being known as Sheridan's mother. Having that part of my identity fade away was unsettling because I wasn't sure what it left.

"Skye!" Jasmine pulled me into the house. "We have a little problem," she whispered.

"We do?"

"It's Claire," she was still whispering. "My future mother-in-law."

"What is it?"

"She's not happy with the fact that a Wiccan priestess is going to perform the ceremony. She wants a minister."

"A minister?"

"A Methodist minister, if possible."

I refrained from informing Jasmine that this was the sort of thing that is normally discussed before the wedding is even announced. Certainly before it's planned and *most* certainly before the wedding is about to take place.

"I had no idea she would be this obstinate," Jasmine added. "And David doesn't want to upset her."

I further refrained from telling Jasmine that this did

not bode well for her marriage, and that if David had any balls, he'd inform his mother that it was his wedding and he'd get married by anyone he chose. Jasmine took my hand and pulled me into the living room.

"Skye, this is David's mother, Claire Taylor. Claire, this is Skye, my wedding planner."

Claire looked down her nose at me. "I hope you can do something about this."

I glanced at David. He looked miserable standing between his fiancé and his mother. Actually, he looked like he might cry. Great.

"It's nice to meet you, Mrs. Taylor." I held out my hand, but Claire just looked at it like I might have pagan cooties. "Jasmine, why don't you and David get us some iced tea while I show Mrs. Taylor the wedding plans?"

Jasmine opened her mouth to object, but I waved them out of the room. "Has Jasmine shown you pictures of the bridesmaids' gowns? The different shades of blue are lovely, but they have this bow on the back that I just don't think needs to be there." I set my file crate on the coffee table and pulled out the folder with pictures of the gowns. "If you agree with me, maybe we can persuade her to get rid of the bows." I fanned the pictures out on the table. Claire's curiosity got the better of her and she took a step to the table to glance at the pictures.

"Oh, dear." Claire shook her head. "Those bows will make the girls' butts look huge."

"That's what I thought. Jasmine seems to think they're cute." I shook my head. "Sometimes I think the bride chooses the bridesmaids' gowns just to make herself look better."

"Oh, Jasmine would never do that. She's very aware of the feelings of others."

"I know, and I don't think she's doing it deliberately. She's just young, and I think she could use the guidance of a mature woman in some of her decisions."

"Of course, she could. God knows, I've tried." Claire shook her head. "Is it written somewhere that girls don't get along with their mothers-in-law? I'd always hoped David would marry a girl who would be like a daughter to me. I never had a girl, just the three boys."

"I know what you mean. When I got married, I thought my mother-in-law hated me. It took me years to realize that she really liked me and was only trying to help." I was such a liar. Craig's mother had never liked me. Wonder how she felt about Jack?

"But you're friends now?"

"Oh, we get along great." Every other year when I had been forced to see her at Christmas, we'd been civil to each other. My smile was genuine because I realized that I'd never have to do that again.

"That's nice. I hope Jasmine and I can come to

that eventually."

"My mother was much smarter about it than I was. When my brother got serious with Diane, Mom made a point of becoming a friend to her. And when they were planning the wedding, it really paid off." I pulled more files from my crate.

"How?"

"Diane had this crazy idea to serve sushi at the wedding reception. Mom hated it, but instead of putting her foot down, she just told Diane that some people might not be comfortable with sushi. Some guests might be allergic to fish." I shrugged.

"And Diane agreed to change the menu?"

"Mom suggested that she just add some other, more traditional items to the menu. It worked out great. Diane got her sushi, and Mom got a traditional buffet for the guests."

"Your mother sounds like a very wise woman. I just don't know what to do about this Wiccan priestess thing."

"I understand. It's not at all the usual thing to do."

"But I really don't want to upset Jasmine. I'm not a religious bigot or anything. It's just that David was raised a Methodist and I believe he'll be more comfortable with a minister performing the ceremony."

"I wish I could come up with a compromise to you." I laughed. "It's too bad Jasmine can't be married by a priestess and David by a minister." Did I have to write it on the wall for this woman?

"Well, why can't they?" Claire asked.

"What?"

"Why couldn't the marriage ceremony include a minister and a priestess?"

"Claire! That is an inspired solution. I never would have thought of that."

Just then David and Jasmine returned with a tray of glasses and a pitcher of tea. I couldn't have timed their entrance any better if I'd planned it.

"Jasmine, David! Claire has just had the most brilliant idea."

"She has?" David asked. Jasmine said nothing but looked a little wary.

"How about having the wedding ceremony per-formed by a minister and a priestess? That way both of your religions are tied in to the ceremony."

David looked relieved, but I could see Jasmine was thinking that her perfect wedding was being compro-mised.

"Jasmine, don't you think this is perfect? I mean, you're always saying that marriage is a joining of two people, two lives, two ways of being. This is the very essence of what you want."

Fortunately Jasmine bought it. She hugged Claire and grinned. "It's a great idea. I'm so happy you—"

"Oh, Jasmine, could you get me some sweetener

for my tea?" I wasn't about to take a chance on her blowing my careful manipulation.

"Oh, sorry. I'll get it."

As soon as she left with David right behind her, I leaned over and patted Claire's arm. "That was brilliant. I'll talk to Jasmine about getting rid of the bows on the dresses." Which would be easy since Jasmine had already ordered the dresses without the bows. "You don't mind if I mention that you don't care for them, do you?"

"Of course not, Skye. Do whatever you have to."

Another disaster avoided, thanks to my manipulative bitch powers. Now all I had to do was find a minister who didn't mind sharing a wedding ceremony with a Wiccan priestess and was available in two weeks. My cell phone chirped and I glanced at the display. Marjorie Tillis. The Queen of the Country Club. She'd made me feel like an interloper ever since Craig and I had first joined. She'd called my cell phone several times in the past few weeks, and I'd been avoiding answering her calls or calling her back.

That made me feel like a chickenshit. I excused myself and said hello as I walked outside to the porch.

"Skye, I'm so glad I finally got you." Marjorie's voice had that fake enthusiasm that made me want to grind my teeth.

"I tried your home number but kept getting voice

mail."

I'd never really been comfortable with Marjorie or the other women at the country club. Too many of them seemed to take an unwarranted amount of pride in whom they had married. Like their value as a human being was based on how well they'd played the mating game. But Craig had wanted to join years ago, when we could barely afford it. He was determined to network with other men who were clawing their way up the corporate ladder and hopefully become friends with the ones who'd already made it to the top rung. I'd agreed and even been deemed marginally acceptable and included in bridge games and charity events over the years. But I knew that it was my handsome, laughing, slightly flirtatious husband who'd really been found acceptable by them. I'd only been a necessary accessory. Well, there was no point in playing Marjorie's game now.

"Actually, Craig and I aren't living together any longer."

"Oh, Skye, I had no idea. Although we've wondered why we haven't seen you two around lately. Is it temporary?"

"The divorce papers have already been filed."

"I see. Well, I hope you're all right."

"Oh, I'm fine. What did you call about?"

"I was going to ask you to serve on the winter

dance committee."

I was betting that she was having a change of heart and watching her squirm out of it would give me some entertainment.

"Really? I'd love to do that. It sounds like fun."

"Well, yes, I'm sure it will be. However, when I couldn't reach you, I had to fill the spot with someone else. Can't leave these things until the last moment, you know."

"Of course. I understand. But if you'd already filled the spot, why did you call?" I almost laughed with the giddy freedom of confronting her. I'd never had the nerve to question her when I was with Craig. Too much pressure to fit in and be the perfect wife. Now, I didn't have to be perfect for anyone but myself.

"Well, I, ah, I just wanted to make sure you were all right . . . since I hadn't been able to get in touch, you know."

I snorted and covered the phone with my hand to cover it. "Sure. Well, I'm fine."

"I'm so sorry to hear about you and Craig. Are you sure you can't reconcile?"

"I'm certain."

"I just can't believe you won't be Craig's wife anymore," she murmured.

"No, I'll be Skye, now. Skye Donovan." I surprised myself by using my maiden name. But it felt right. I

If it's not one thing, it's a Murder

wasn't Skye Williams anymore.

Bobbi Jo hung up the phone and sat on the edge of the sofa. "That was Jimmy. He's finally explained his financial situation to the police."

"You mean about the eight million he needs for the buyout?" I asked.

"He gave them all the paperwork and documents showing them he could get the money he needed easily enough, so I guess he's not a prime suspect anymore. I'm relieved, but I just wonder how long it's going to take them to find the real murderer."

"They'll find the person. It's just going to take some time."

"I hope it's soon. I feel like I can't let go of it until they do." She turned to look at me. "Shouldn't you be getting dressed?"

"I have nothing to wear."

"Nothing?" Bobbi Jo lifted an eyebrow.

"Nothing I want to be seen in."

"What about that beige dress?"

"I hate it. It pulls around the arms." I flopped down on the sofa in my robe and propped my feet on the coffee table. Bobbi Jo looked up from her magazine.

"Then wear the tan pantsuit."

"The pants are too baggy."

"What about the brown skirt and sweater set?"

"No shoes that match."

"Sucks to be you." Bobbi Jo laughed. "Go get something from my closet."

"All your clothes would be too long for me."

"What about that outfit you wore to Max's party?"

"He's my escort tonight so it would look stupid to wear the same thing."

"Oh, I have just the thing." Bobbi Jo put down the magazine and got up. I followed her to her bedroom and stood outside the walk-in closet while she rummaged through her clothes.

"Here!" Bobbi Jo emerged from the closet holding a hanger draped with a flaming red silky thing. I felt an unaccountable thrill. I was pretty sure I hadn't owned anything red since I was five years old.

"You know what this is all about, don't you?" Bobbi Jo asked.

"What?" I was entranced by the feel of the flaming red garment. I didn't even know what it really looked like yet.

"This whole clothes thing. You're bored with all your drab clothes. Just like you're bored with your drab life. Time for a change." Bobbi Jo took the garment off the hanger and threw it on the bed where it miraculously arranged itself into slinky pants and a flowing top.

"It'll be too long," I wailed. I was heartbroken. The outfit was gorgeous. It was glamorous. It was exciting. It was so not me.

"It'll be fine. I've never worn it because the damn pants are too short."

"Really?" Hope flared in my heart. I tentatively picked up the top and stroked the silky fabric.

"Put it on."

I ripped off my robe and pulled the top over my head, then pulled the pants on. They were too long.

"No problem." Bobbi dove back into the closet and emerged with a pair of strappy red heels. "Try these on."

For a tall woman, Bobbi Jo has ridiculously tiny feet. I sat on the edge of the bed and slipped the heels on. I'd gone to the salon with Bobbi Jo a few days earlier and let her talk me into gold polish for my toenails. It perfectly matched the glittery stuff sprinkled over the outfit. I lifted my arms and the batwing sleeves spread out in a graceful arc.

"Can I do this?"

"You *have* to do this." Bobbi Jo stood back and looked at me. "It's like a rite of passage."

Another rite of passage? Was there no end to them? Still, the outfit was striking. I didn't even feel like myself. I wasn't sure what or who I felt like. I just knew it was different. And it was good.

"This is your first date, Skye. You should wear something special."

"Date? This isn't a date. It's Sheridan's school play."

"But you're going with Max, right?"

"Yes, but it's not a date. Sheridan invited him when we were listening to the band last week."

"It's a date."

"It's not a date. I can't date. I'm not ready to date."

"Get ready, darlin', 'cause it's a date." Bobbi Jo cocked her head to the distant sound of a car pulling into the driveway. "There's your date now. Go put on some makeup; I'll entertain him."

"I already put on my makeup."

"Well, do it again. And use some color this time." Bobbi Jo left me standing in her bedroom. I walked over to the mirror on her closet door and looked at my face. It looked all right. Kind of. A little pale. Maybe a brighter lipstick would help. Not that I owned a brighter lipstick. I eased into Bobbi Jo's bathroom and opened the top drawer in the vanity.

She had everything. I opened a few tubes of lipstick before I found a red that I thought I could wear. Then my cheeks looked too pale. I applied some blusher but it looked too harsh, so I wiped some of it off with a tissue. Maybe the eyes. I found a smoky eye shadow and stroked some on my eyelids. Perfect! Well, better, anyway. I straightened my shoulders and marched into the living room.

"Wow, you look great." Max stood up when I came in. "And tall." We both laughed at our inside joke.

"Are you sure you don't feel like coming with us?" I asked Bobbi Jo.

"I'm just too tired." Bobbi Jo shook her head. "The doctor said it would go away in another month. Give Sheridan a hug for me and tell her I'll be at her next show."

"Okay. Go to bed early and get some rest." I gave her a hug on the way to the door.

I relaxed a little after the first half hour of the drive. Max was charming and entertaining and almost made me forget that Craig would be there with his new *friend*.

CHAPTER TWELVE

Skye, you look marvelous." Craig took my hands
and leaned in to kiss my cheek.

I tottered a bit on the four-inch stilettos and
took Max's hand to pull him forward. Also to balance
myself. "Craig, I'd like you to meet Maxwell Harrison."

"Max Harrison? I love your books. I've read the
Amber Crystal series three times."

"Thanks. I really enjoyed writing that series."

"Are you going to write more with those charac-
ters? It was a little uncertain what was happening with
Annis and Thara at the end."

"I'm working on a new series, but I always like to
leave it open, just in case."

"Great. I look forward to the new books." Craig
grinned and I felt suddenly at a loss. Out of place. Of
no use whatsoever. How the hell had that happened?

"Oh, this is Jack Kester." Craig gestured at the
man next to him.

"Hi, nice to meet you." Jack directed the comment

toward both of us.

So this was the new friend. The man who had replaced me. I'd expected to feel a certain animosity. I'd prepared for that and was surprised that mostly I just felt curious. Which was weird. Jack appeared to be quite a bit younger than Craig. Certainly no more than late twenties, possibly early thirties. A good twelve to fifteen years younger than Craig. And me.

I murmured a greeting, shook his outstretched hand, and breathed a sigh of relief when the lights flashed signaling us to take our seats. As much as I was all right with the divorce and everything, meeting the other man was strange.

Sheridan was outstanding. She sang with gusto. She danced with grace. Her performance took my mind off the situation. Until the intermission.

"I'm going to the ladies' room," I whispered to Max as I rose from my seat.

"I'll go with you," Jack said.

I turned and stared at him. He was going to the ladies' room with me? What were we, girlfriends? I couldn't think of an appropriate way to refuse, so I stepped past Max and made my way to the aisle. When I glanced back, Craig and Max were chatting and Jack was right behind me. I wasn't sure whether I was more concerned about talking to Jack or leaving Max and Craig alone together.

He placed his hand under my elbow and guided me up the aisle until we were stopped behind a clog of people who evidently had the same idea.

"I'm really happy I had this chance to meet you, Skye."

"Really? Why is that?"

"You mean a lot to Craig. That's important to me."

"Is it?" I was on the verge of sounding like a bitch and reeled myself in a bit. "Craig means a lot to me, too."

"I understand. I mean more than just that you used to be married. I know this can't be easy for either of you. But, well, I love Craig. I want him to be happy. And I know that this phase is hard for him. It was hard for me when I first came out, too."

"Yes. It's a difficult time for everyone."

"Sheridan seems to be dealing with it rather well," Jack said.

"Yes, she is. I'm glad about that. Both for her sake and for Craig's." I nudged the couple in front of us, hoping to push through the bottleneck and escape to the ladies' room. Hoping that Jack wouldn't actually follow me in there. The crowd parted enough for me to squeeze through. Jack stayed right on my heels and pulled me into an alcove before I reached the ladies' room.

"Skye, Craig feels badly about what he's done. I mean, he feels badly that you have been hurt by all this. But he's coming to terms with who and what he really is now."

The situation was starting to piss me off. I wanted to support Craig in this, but I was still having some emotional response to the whole thing. "Craig feels badly? How sad for him. Tell me, Jack, is that supposed to make what he did okay?"

"Skye, it's not like he has a choice. He can't help the fact that he's gay."

"I understand that sexuality isn't a choice. But behavior is. The fact that he's gay doesn't excuse what he did. He betrayed me. He made our marriage a sham."

"I'm sorry you see it that way." Jack was looking a bit uncomfortable. Like maybe he was the one who wanted to escape now.

"I understand that Craig is going through a difficult time coming to terms with his sexuality. I just don't think that excuses his past behavior." I turned to leave, then looked back at Jack. "What makes you think he won't betray you? He cheated on me after almost twenty years of marriage. I'd imagine it would be even easier to cheat on someone he's only been with a short time." Jack paled and I felt a twinge of regret at my harsh words.

"Right now, he might seem to be selfish, but it's just a part of what he's dealing with. He needs to be focused on himself right now. It needs to be all about him. For now."

I wanted to hate Jack. But I had to admit that he was probably right. Jack was looking at it from Craig's point of view. I'd been looking at it from mine. Neither was right or wrong.

That kind of pissed me off, because I really wanted everyone to see it from my perspective. I wanted to be right. I wanted to be the injured party. I wanted to be the victim, damn it.

I almost choked on the thought. The victim? Is that what I really wanted to be? What I wanted other people to see when they looked at me? Hell, no! That's not what I wanted at all. So, why was I being such a bitch?

I had nothing more to say to Jack. He'd been Craig's lover for a few weeks; I'd been Craig's wife for two decades. What right did he have to tell me how to deal with Craig? I made my way to the ladies' room where I stood in line for fifteen minutes and thought about it. They weren't pretty thoughts.

Craig had arranged to take Sheridan out for a late dinner after the show. I had no desire to spend any more time with him and Jack than necessary and declined their invitation to join them. I waited until Sheridan had changed out of her costume, told her how outstanding she'd been, and got a promise from her to call me the next day. Max and I were headed home by ten thirty.

"Was that hard on you?"

"What? Meeting Craig's boyfriend?" I shrugged. "Not as hard as I'd have thought. I guess that's a good sign."

Max laughed and shook his head. "I think you're amazing. I certainly wouldn't be as understanding as you are."

"You never know until you're in that position. I care a great deal for Craig. It's not his fault he likes men more than women." It was easier to be generous and understanding about Craig when I was sitting next to a handsome and charming man who showed more than a little interest in me. "I think it's the betrayal that hurts the most. I've always thought that if you're married and you want to be with someone else enough to risk your relationship, then why not just be up front about it? Why not just go to the other person and say, I'm going to do this?"

"I suppose it's because some people think they can have it all."

My cell phone chirped and I dug it out of my evening bag and looked at the caller ID. Bobbi Jo's cell phone. That struck me as odd since she would normally use her home phone unless she was out. But she'd said she was turning in early tonight.

"Hey, Bobbi Jo."

"Skye. I'm in jail!"

"What do you mean you're in jail?"

"Well, I'm not actually *in* jail. I'm downtown

at the central precinct. Can you come pick me up?" Bobbi Jo sounded more angry than upset.

"What are you doing there?"

"It's a long story, but Brian was almost killed, and Detective Madison decided that I was the most likely suspect so he brought me down here to talk to me."

"Are you all right, Bobbi Jo? Did you call your lawyer?"

"No. I figured a corporate lawyer wasn't going to do me much good and besides, I don't have anything to hide. I didn't kill Edward or try to kill Brian. So, I just answered their stupid questions."

"We're still at least an hour away."

"Oh, don't worry about it then. I'll call a cab. I should have thought of that first."

"What about Brian? Is he still in the guest-house?"

"Not tonight. They're keeping him in the hospital for observation. Look, I'll explain the whole thing when you get home. I should be there by the time you and Max arrive."

She hung up and I stared at my cell phone for a moment.

"What was that all about?" Max asked.

"I'm not really sure, but Bobbi Jo was at the central precinct being questioned tonight."

"About Edward's death?"

I shook my head. "About Brian. Something about his near-death. She said she'd tell us all about it when we get there."

When we arrived, Bobbi Jo was sitting on the patio with a cup of herbal tea. She seemed calm enough and I was almost reluctant to ask for the details.

"Oh, hey, y'all." Bobbi Jo waved when we came out. "Max, there's some beer in the fridge if you want some."

"Sounds good." He headed back inside for a beer and I sat down across from Bobbi Jo.

"What the hell happened?" I asked.

"Gawd only knows, Skye. Detective Madison came over and told me that Brian had been in an accident on his way to the coast. He's okay but pretty banged up. And when they inspected the car, they found that the brake lines had been cut."

"Cut? You mean someone was trying to kill Brian?"

"That's how it looks. And evidently Detective Madison thinks I did it." Bobbi Jo sipped her juice, then set the glass on the table with a shaky hand. "He thinks I killed Edward, too."

Max came back with his beer and sat in the chair next to me. "Who thinks you killed Edward?"

"Detective Madison." I remembered Scott telling me that he was fairly certain Bobbi Jo hadn't killed her husband. Had he been lying to me or was he changing his mind now? Either way, it really pissed me off.

"Oh, I suppose it makes sense to him." Bobbi Jo waved her hand. "He thinks I killed Edward to get his money, and then tried to kill Brian because he's contesting Edward's will."

"That seems like a giant leap to a conclusion," Max said.

"Well, I guess it does, in a way. But when you add in the fact that I actually *know* how to cut a brake line because I used to work in my daddy's garage, it becomes a little more believable."

"That's ridiculous," I said. "And Scott is just wasting his time suspecting you. Time he could be spending finding the real killer."

"Don't be so hard on him, Skye. He's just doing his job." She smiled and shook her head. "I never should have called you. I was just so mad at being hauled down to the precinct to be questioned. So, tell me. How was Sheridan's play? And what was Craig's boyfriend like?"

Okay, I'd dish with her for now, but I wasn't letting Scott off that easily.

I hung up the phone and burst into tears. It was either that or explode from the building anxiety.

When Sheridan fell in love, I was going to hand her a check for as much money as I could get my hands on and tell her to elope. There was a knock at Lily's back door and I threaded my way through the multitude of white flowers to open it.

"What's wrong?" Max stepped inside, worry creasing his brow.

"The flowers arrived half an hour ago."

"That's a problem?" Max pulled a handkerchief from his back pocket and dabbed at my cheeks.

"They're all white. Every single one of them. Not a blue blossom in the bunch."

Max walked past me to look into the dining room where the flowers had been placed. "Did you call the florist? They must have delivered the wrong flowers."

"I just got off the phone with them. According to their records, all the flowers are supposed to be white. The only thing they could offer was to redo the bouquets for the bride and the bridesmaids."

"Well, that's something."

"It's not enough. Jasmine will be crushed. She wanted every single thing about this wedding to be blue."

"Maybe we can fix them."

"How? With spray paint?"

"With a little grade-school science project." Max grinned at me. "Is there any blue food coloring around?"

261

"I have no idea. But how will that help?"

"We just put the flowers in water with blue food coloring. They'll soak up the color overnight and by tomorrow we'll have blue flowers."

"You are a genius." Relief poured through every cell in my body.

"Let's take the flowers to my place. That way, when Jasmine gets home from the rehearsal dinner, she won't see them."

"Great idea."

"Even better, I'll take them over while you go buy some blue food coloring." Max picked up a container of white gladioli. "Get a lot of it."

An hour later, we had all the flowers in Max's living room and his kitchen counter was littered with a dozen empty bottles of blue food coloring.

I poured the last bottle of food coloring into a vase. "I really hope this works."

"It has to." Max smiled at me. "But now, I need your help."

"With what?"

"Well, the clematis that I grew for the arbor isn't blooming."

"Jasmine was really counting on that arbor being in full bloom."

"And it will be with a little help from us." Max pulled a large plastic bag from the closet and opened it.

I peered into the bag. "Blue flowers."

"Blue silk flowers, to be exact."

I picked one out of the bag. "So, this is what a clematis bloom looks like."

"It is now." Max waggled his eyebrows at me. "I doubt Jasmine knows the difference. As long as she sees blue flowers, she'll be happy."

"And if the bride is happy, we're all happy."

"I think we need some wine to do this correctly."

"Sounds good to me." I followed him into the kitchen. "How are we going to attach the flowers?"

Max handed me a glass of wine and poured one for himself. "Floral wire. It'll be a piece of cake." He picked up the bag and led me to the patio. "If that doesn't work, I've got a staple gun, a glue gun, and duct tape."

Even without the flowers, the arbor was beautiful. The vine of bright green leaves twined up each side of the arbor and across the arched top. I set my wineglass down and picked up a silk flower and a strip of floral wire. The flower attached with a twist of the wire, and I breathed a sigh of relief. At least this would be easy.

Three hours later, I never wanted to see another silk flower again. My arms ached, my fingers throbbed, and I saw blue blossoms every time I blinked. But the damn thing was done. Max attached the last of the blooms to the top and stepped down from the ladder.

"Now for the crowning touch." Max pulled a bolt

of pale blue tulle from another bag. "Jasmine doesn't know about this part." He grinned and started unrolling yards of the tulle. "Hand me that staple gun on the table."

Max worked on the underside of the arbor, bunching and stapling the tulle to cover the lathing strips. The tulle had a silver thread in it that sparkled in the patio light. Jasmine would look like a fairy princess under the arbor. Max placed the last staple and stood back.

"What do you think?"

"It's beautiful. The tulle is perfect, and no one will notice that the flowers aren't real."

"They are real," Max insisted. "Real imitation silk."

"They're blue. That's the important part. I wonder how the real flowers are doing?"

"Let's go see."

I thought I could detect a little blue in most of the flowers. But it made me nervous. "What if they don't all turn blue by morning?"

Max sat down on the sofa and pulled me down next to him. "They will." He squeezed my hand. "Of course, we could sit here all night and make sure it happens."

I laughed. "You're right, they'll either be blue or not. I'm sure Jasmine will get over it if she has white flowers at her wedding."

"And there's always spray paint."

"I should get going. Tomorrow will be a long day, and it's going to start early."

"Not yet." Max put an arm across the back of the sofa and let his hand rest on my shoulder. "You've had wine. I think you should wait a little while before you drive."

"Probably. Although I don't really feel the wine."

"Just an hour. Just to be safe."

"Okay. Maybe the flowers will turn blue by then."

"I can think of better things to do for an hour than watch the flowers." Max's voice had dropped into a soft purr. I turned to him and realized his lips were just inches from mine.

"You can?" My voice was a breathy whisper and I wasn't sure if I was scared or exhilarated.

"Sure. Lots of things."

His lips were almost touching mine yet somehow I couldn't bring myself to pull away. Probably because I didn't want to pull away. I liked the feel of his breath on my lips.

"Like what?" I asked.

"Mmmm. Let's see." He brushed his lips across mine so gently I could barely feel it. "We could just talk for a while."

"Talking's good. Anything else?"

265

"Well, there's this." His lips finally made contact with mine.

Dear God, the man could kiss. He nibbled at my bottom lip, then ran the tip of his tongue across it. He pulled back a fraction of an inch and I leaned in, reluctant to let him go. He grinned and dipped his head to kiss just under my ear. I'm pretty sure I whimpered at that point.

I couldn't help myself, and I didn't want to. His hands moved around to caress my back. That felt good. Almost as good as when he slipped me his tongue. Before I could get used to that, he pulled back again and sprinkled little kisses over my face. He was starting to breathe hard and I realized I was, too.

"Kissing you is exhilarating."

Exhilarating? Me? I'd never been told that. I liked the sound of it, though.

Max moved his lips over mine again, effectively removing all coherent thoughts. I was lost in the sensation. My hand moved up to curl around his neck. He seemed to like that. He deepened the kiss and one of his hands drifted down to my waist, pulling my body up against his hard chest. Damn. Had I ever been kissed like this before? Certainly not by Craig. And I had very little experience with men other than him. I'd started dating Craig when I was a senior in high school and we were married three years later.

Thinking of Craig was like having a bucket of cold water thrown on me. Suddenly desire turned to hesitation. I pulled back and felt my entire body tense. "I should really be going."

"Now?"

I squirmed away from Max. "I have to get up early."

"Sure." Max stood up and held out a hand. It shook a little.

I took his hand and stood up. "This was nice."

"It was very nice." He pulled me close and kissed me lightly.

"I'm just not sure I'm ready, you know?"

"That's okay. I'm a patient man."

Max walked me to my car and kissed me good night. I drove to Bobbi Jo's wondering if it really was okay with him that we'd stopped when we did. He'd said it was okay, but did men ever think it was okay to stop in the middle of something like that? I had no doubt we'd have ended up in bed if we'd continued for another five minutes. I still wasn't sure how I felt about that. I wasn't even sure I wanted to think about it.

I pulled into Bobbi Jo's driveway, and the porch light automatically turned on. The house was dark, and I guessed she'd already gone to bed. She was still experiencing the fatigue so common in the first trimester and usually turned in by nine. Which meant she wouldn't be awake to hear me call Scott Madison and ask him what the hell he was thinking by dragging my best friend in for questioning.

How could he even *think* Bobbi Jo would kill anyone? Much less for money. He hadn't bothered to learn anything about her. He was being a typical cop. Just because Bobbi Jo could have done it, he was more than willing to assume she was guilty. I wasn't about to let that happen.

By the time I'd found his card and picked up the phone, I'd worked up a righteous anger. I punched in his cell number, ignoring the fact that it was almost eleven o'clock.

"Madison."

"Detective Madison, this is Skye Donovan."

"I thought your name was Williams."

"I'm going back to my maiden name." I was immediately annoyed that somehow he had started the conversation so that I was answering his questions rather than him answering mine. "I understand you took Bobbi Jo to the precinct for questioning?"

"Yeah, but it was just routine. You know cops. We do it all the time."

"Save the flippant attitude for someone who might appreciate it."

"Sorry."

"You told me that you didn't think Bobbi Jo was

really a suspect, so why the questioning?"

"Well, that was then. This is something different. Listen, Skye, you have to admit she had the motive, means, and opportunity to commit both murders. I can't really ignore something like that."

"Oh, this is ridiculous. Bobbi Jo didn't kill anyone or even try to kill anyone."

"Did you know that Brian is contesting Edward's will? He thinks he should be getting all the millions that Bobbi Jo is getting?"

"Yes, as a matter of fact, Bobbi Jo told me that. Did you know that Bobbi Jo was the one who talked Edward out of disowning Brian altogether?"

Scott paused. "Did you actually hear that conversation?"

"Of course not. I don't normally listen in on my friends' personal conversations."

"So, you only know that because Bobbi Jo told you about it?"

Damn. He had me there. Which only pissed me off even more.

"Skye, all I can tell you is that I still don't believe Bobbi Jo had anything to do with her husband's death. I also don't think she made an attempt on Brian's life."

"Then why did you bring her in for questioning?"

"Because that's what I do. It's my job. I question

everyone. I question everything. I report what I find and the DA takes it from there."

"The DA? You mean they might arrest Bobbi Jo?"

"I really don't think they will. It's just one of those cases where someone looks like she is the perfect suspect but I have to tell you, no one working on this case likes Bobbi Jo for this."

"How can anyone not like Bobbi Jo? And I really don't think that your personal opinion of someone should factor into this."

"No. That's not what I meant. It's just copspeak."

"Copspeak?" I asked. What the hell was that?

"If a cop thinks someone actually committed a crime, we'll say we *like* them."

"That's weird."

"Only if you're not a cop."

"So, if you really, really believe they did something, do you love them?"

"It doesn't really work that way."

"I see. So, you don't think anyone is seriously considering Bobbi Jo a suspect?"

"No," Scott said. "I really don't. Now, are we still friends?"

CHAPTER THIRTEEN

I pulled on the gray silk pantsuit I'd bought for the wedding and buttoned the jacket over a lavender chemise that matched my new suede flats. The three-way mirror reflected a polished, organized, professional event planner who could handle anything. God, I never wanted to do this again.

"Hey, Skye. Are you about ready?" Bobbi Jo called from the front room.

"As ready as I can be." I picked up the bag that held a clipboard and my cameras, and went to join Bobbi Jo.

She looked stunning, as usual. Disappointed that she really wasn't showing enough to wear any of her new maternity clothes, she'd chosen a flowing dress in yellow crinkled silk with flowers splashed about the hem, tendrils of leaves and vines creeping up to the low neckline. It was topped with a floppy brimmed hat and complemented by low-heeled sandals in a mossy green.

"You know, you really don't have to go so early," I

said as we climbed into my SUV. "You could wait and come later with all the other guests."

"Oh, I know, darlin'." Bobbi Jo waved her hand. "I just thought maybe I could be of some help. Besides, I need to keep busy."

I knew what she meant. Even though Scott had assured me he didn't really believe Bobbi Jo had murdered Edward or cut Brian's brake line, Bobbi Jo was still a suspect. I could only imagine what that felt like. To have anyone think you might have murdered the man you loved more than anything in the world. And I had a feeling that Bobbi Jo needed to know who really did kill Edward. Just to give her some closure.

I reached out and squeezed her hand. "I appreciate it. I really do. I hope this all goes off without a hitch." And I hoped those damn flowers were blue by now.

We arrived at Lily's house a few minutes after nine. The wedding was scheduled for noon. I already felt like I was running behind. I had to check on the flowers, make sure the bridesmaids were dressed, direct the caterers when they arrived, tell the band where to set up, hope the florist had managed to remake the bouquets with blue flowers, see that the tables were set up correctly, and keep the groomsmen from getting drunk before the ceremony. After the ceremony, I didn't really care what anyone did. Personally, I was hoping to get a tiny bit drunk, go home, and take a long nap.

"You know what you can do, Bobbi Jo?"

"What?"

"You can make sure that David's mother is taken care of. The last thing I need is for her to get upset and make a scene or anything. Her name is Claire Taylor. You'll recognize her by the icy expression."

"No problem, darlin'. I'd recognize her kind anywhere."

"Thank the Goddess you're here!" Lily threw the front door open.

"Why? Is there a problem?"

"No. Not at all. Not really. Well, not yet."

"Not yet?"

"I'm just so emotional. I didn't expect to be, but my baby is getting married." Lily threw her arms around me and blubbered. "I didn't feel this way when Beau got married. And I didn't even like the woman he was marrying."

"Now, Lily, this is no time to get emotional. You can cry later. You don't want puffy eyes, do you?" I wiped the tears off her cheeks.

Just then two little boys screamed through the room. Really. Screamed. At the top of their lungs. They appeared to be about five. They also appeared to be hell-bent on trouble.

"Brandon, Justin, slow down. You'll knock something

over." Lily smiled at them. "Come here, boys, I want you to meet someone."

The boys glared at me and I could have sworn I saw a malicious glint in their eyes as they walked over. I had no doubt I'd probably recognize them on a most-wanted poster in the future.

"This is Skye. She's helping with the wedding," Lily said to the boys. They didn't appear to be impressed.

"Brandon and Justin are Beau's twins. They're going to be the ring bearers."

I felt a tug on the hem of my jacket.

"I'm gonna be sick."

I looked down at a tiny girl who had her hand plastered across her mouth. I scooped her up, running for the bathroom, hoping it wasn't occupied.

I didn't make it. The little girl spewed her breakfast over the hallway floor. Looked like Cheerios to me.

"Is she all right?" Lily asked from behind me.

"I think so, but your floor's not." I stepped across the mess on tiptoe. Now the girl was crying. "It's okay, sweetie. You're going to be fine." I patted her back and hugged her tight.

She hiccupped and wiped at her eyes. "I made a mess."

"It's all right. Someone will clean it up. Does your tummy hurt?"

She shook her head. "Not anymore. I'm the flower

girl."

Perfect. A puking flower girl and demon spawn for ring bearers.

"Are you nervous?"

The little girl nodded. "Mommy says I always get sick when I get excited."

"Where's your mommy now?" I hoped she was someplace close. Like in the next room.

"I don't know. She's going to be here later."

"Giselle's mom will be here soon. She dropped her off early so I could get her dressed." Lily threw a handful of paper towels into a plastic bag and tied a knot in it.

"I don't think I'd dress her until the last minute. Just in case."

"Good point," Lily agreed. "Giselle, you go play, honey, and I'll help you put your dress on in a little bit."

"Okay."

I lifted Giselle down from the counter and she ran off, evidently in excellent health now that she'd relieved herself of her breakfast. "I also wouldn't give her anything to eat."

"Holy Goddess, are we going to live through this?"

"Absolutely," I assured her. "It's only a few more hours. Then it's all over."

"Can't be too soon for me. I have a life to get on

with."

"Has the florist delivered the bouquets?"

"Oh, yes, they arrived just before you got here. I've got them in the extra refrigerator in the garage. They're lovely, Skye. And Max will be putting out the other flowers soon."

The other flowers. I offered up a little prayer that Max's chemistry experiment had worked. But Max would have called if there had been a problem. Or he would have gone out for spray paint.

"What about the caterers?" My question was punctuated by the doorbell.

"That must be them now. Can you take care of it while I get rid of this?" Lily trotted off to the kitchen without waiting for a response. I greeted the caterers, directed them to the reception tent set up in the back-yard, and headed for Jasmine's bedroom.

She was surrounded by her three bridesmaids, all in some stage of undress, or about to be dressed. They fluttered around her as she sobbed into a towel.

"Skye!" Jasmine lowered the towel. "I'm going to be married today." Then she burst into tears again.

"I know. You're also going to have a puffy face and red eyes if you keep this up."

"I know!" Jasmine wailed.

I ran to the kitchen, found a blue-ice pack in the freezer, and wrapped it in a hand towel.

"Here, put this on your face."

Jasmine leaned back against the headboard and held the ice pack to her face while I shooed the brides-maids out.

"Take your gowns to Lily's room and get dressed in there. I think Jasmine needs a little solitude," I instructed. The girls gathered up their blue chiffon gowns and chattered as they left the room.

"Feeling better?" I asked Jasmine when they were gone.

Jasmine sobbed a couple of times and lowered the ice pack. "I just didn't expect to be so emotional. I didn't sleep at all last night."

"I know. It's okay. You'll be fine. But you don't want to have a tearstained face for the wedding. Just lie down for a few minutes. Get some rest and I'll check on you in a bit."

I left the room, closing the door softly behind me. With any luck, she would pass out and sleep until she needed to get dressed. The bridesmaids were gig-gling and dressing in Lily's room, the demon spawn were running in the front yard, and the flower girl was asleep on the sofa. I checked my watch. Two hours until the wedding.

"Hey." Max walked in from the sunroom. "The flowers are all in place. The tables are set up for the reception. I put down the blue carpet for Jasmine to walk down, but you probably need to take a look at the altar area."

"Hi, Max," Lily called without turning around. She looked too tired to even move from her chair.

"I'll go check the altar. You rest for a minute, then kick the bridesmaids out of your room so you can get dressed." I grabbed my bag and followed Max outside.

"They're all blue," he said.

"Really?"

"Really. Some are more blue than others, but I didn't have to spray paint any of them." He grinned at me and I giggled. We reached the wedding area and I stopped at the arbor, covered in fake clematis blossoms.

From the arbor, a powder blue carpet ran twenty feet to the altar. The altar was flanked by tall stands of gladioli, in a glorious shade of blue. I grinned at Max. "You did it. You turned the flowers blue."

"Simple science."

"Right now, I consider it magic. I want to look at the reception tent." We walked over to the large tent where the caterers were setting up the buffet. Everything looked perfect. I pulled one of my cameras out of my bag and snapped some pictures of the tables and the altar. Jasmine would probably like to know what it looked like before the guests arrived. The photographer's van pulled into the driveway and I ran back to the house to direct him to the backyard.

One of the hellion boys tore through the living room, emitting a high-pitched scream. Did these children do anything but scream? And where the hell was their father? The other demon spawn came down the hallway screaming and holding one of Jasmine's blue satin shoes in his grubby little hand. I nipped the shoe from his hand and barely resisted the urge to swat his bottom. That was fortunate because the father of the little brats walked in.

"Hey, Skye, have you seen Brandon and Justin?"

"That way." I pointed toward the sunroom. "They need to get their suits on. And watch they don't get dirty before the ceremony," I called after him.

I took the shoe to Jasmine's room. She was surrounded by her bridesmaids in their fluffy chiffon gowns. Other than her missing shoe, Jasmine looked like a fairy princess. The ice-blue wedding gown fit her perfectly, and her eyes sparkled under the wreath of blue flowers on her head. Even the puffiness from her crying jag had disappeared.

"Looking for this?" I waved the shoe at her.

"Oh, Skye. Where did you find it?"

"One of the twins had it."

"Those boys are such pranksters." Jasmine slipped the shoe on. "But they're sweethearts. It's so cool how Beau lets them express themselves."

I would have muzzled them. "Everything's all set,

so just stay here and I'll send your father for you when it's time." I ran out to the yard again for a final review.

The caterers were set up in the reception tent. The guests had gathered in the area where the wedding would take place. The harpist who would play during Jasmine's walk down the blue carpet was positioned to one side. Even the minister and priestess were at the altar, chatting amiably. Claire kept glancing nervously at the priestess, but Bobbi Jo was keeping her distracted with nonstop chatter. I trotted over to the guesthouse and knocked on the door.

"Is it time?" Grant asked.

"It's time. You go get Jasmine, and Kyle can make sure David gets to the altar."

"I can't believe my baby girl is getting married."

I patted him on the back and guided him toward the house. Once David was in place and Jasmine and Grant were poised for her entrance, I set down my clipboard and hung both cameras around my neck. Finally my job was over and I could enjoy taking some photos for the scrapbook I planned to make for her.

I got a few shots of Grant and Jasmine as they whispered quietly to one another, then the harpist began playing. I hung back and continued taking photos during the ceremony and as the guests moved into the reception tent.

"You did it," Max said.

"And I'm fairly certain I don't ever want to do it again."

"But you're so good at it." Max grinned.

I grinned back. I liked Max. A lot. He was fun, easy to talk to, and he'd saved my butt with the blue flowers. I just wasn't sure how much I liked him or how much I was ready for.

"I need to change my film."

"Just a minute." Max looked down at his feet. "I wanted to talk to you about last night."

"Oh."

"I thought maybe I was rushing you a bit. Was I?"

"I don't know. I think maybe I was the one rushing. I just don't know what I'm ready for. Does that make any sense to you?"

"I understand. It takes a while. Especially after having been with someone for so long."

"I guess it does."

"I just wanted to let you know that I understand. I don't want to do anything that makes you uncomfortable."

"Oh, you didn't. Well, I mean, I enjoyed . . ."

"Me, too. Skye, we can take this as slowly as you like."

"We can?"

"Of course. If you just want to keep it at friendship for now, I'm fine with that."

"Does that mean you'll help me paint my loft?" I was teasing but his answer pleased me.

"Absolutely. What are friends for?" Max leaned over and kissed my cheek. "But I won't pretend that I wouldn't like the possibility of more, eventually. I think you're worth waiting for."

That sent a little shiver through me.

I fumbled the key to Bobbi Jo's front door into the lock and pushed the door open, almost dropping the bottle of wine I'd bought on the way home. Bobbi Jo took the bottle and set it on the table as she sprinted for the ringing phone.

"Oh, hi, Max."

I shook my head at Bobbi Jo. I'd been avoiding his phone calls and I knew I should talk to him but not now.

Bobbi Jo frowned at me. "No, she's not here. She's been out on interviews all day." She made frantic arm and hand gestures to me, which I ignored. "Sure. I'll tell her." She hung up the phone and stared at me for a moment. I kicked off my shoes and collapsed on the sofa.

"Max said to tell you he's calling your cell phone and if you don't answer he's leaving a message and you should listen to it because it's important."

My cell phone chirped and I ignored it in favor of ripping off my thigh-high stockings and stuffing them in the pocket of my jacket.

"Skye, why won't you talk to Max?"

"I will. Just not now."

"This is a very big bottle of wine." Bobbi Jo eyed the bottle a little wistfully.

"I know. I should have gotten two because Lily is coming over tonight. I swear I could drink one all by myself."

"No luck with the interviews?"

"Depends on what you call luck. I've been offered a variety of positions, most of them suitable to a high school student who is unlikely to advance her education. I actually had to take a test to see if I could file alphabetically."

Bobbi Jo disappeared into the kitchen with the wine and returned with a full glass for me.

"Thanks."

"What are you going to do?"

"I don't know. I've pretty much gotten to the point of realizing that I have no marketable skills. Maybe I should go back to school."

"You mean grad school?"

"God, no. I didn't really like college all that much the first time. I can't see going back full-time to get a master's degree in something that I have no interest in anyway. I'm thinking of just taking a few courses. Computers, office skills, accounting. That sort of thing."

Bobbi Jo shuddered. "Will that make you happy?"

"No, but it might make me employed." I sipped the wine and grinned at her. "So how are you doing? How's the bambino?"

"I'm fine. And I have my first ultrasound this week. Will you go with me?"

"I'd love to. Why? Are you nervous?"

"Darlin', I'm nervous about everything to do with this baby. I just want you to hold my hand. And I guess I want someone to share it with."

I put my glass down and hugged Bobbi Jo. "It's got to be hard not having Edward here."

"Well, sure. But nothing will change that. I'm just so happy that he left me the baby." A tear ran down her cheek. "Damn, I cry all the time now."

"It's normal. Just pregnancy hormones. They say it goes away after the first trimester, but I cried all the way through my pregnancy."

"Nice to know I'm normal, then."

"I'm going to change into shorts. Did you have anything planned for dinner?"

"Me? You've got to be kidding. The only dinner plans I make are reservations."

She followed me down the hall to my bedroom. I ripped my interview clothes off and pulled on a pair of shorts and a tank top. "That's going to change, you know. Children expect to be fed on a regular basis."

"That's what the housekeeper is for, darlin'."

"You don't have a housekeeper," I pointed out.

"I will before the baby comes."

"How does pizza sound for dinner?"

"Yeah, I've been wanting pizza. Can we have anchovies and pineapple?"

"Only if we get separate pizzas."

The doorbell rang and Bobbi Jo waved me toward the door. "I'll call for the pizza, you let Lily in."

I poured wine for Lily and myself, and juice for Bobbi Jo. Lily and I took our wine out to the patio while Bobbi Jo ordered the pizza.

"How's she been?" Lily asked.

"Well enough. Physically, she's fine, but I think she's really stressing out over the murder investigation."

"Nothing new?"

"Not a damn thing. It seems like they focus on one person and then that gets cleared up and they turn to another person. She doesn't seem to be all that concerned that they consider her a suspect."

"I guess they have to."

"Scott told me that he really doesn't think Bobbi Jo killed Edward, but they have to consider her a suspect because she had the means and opportunity."

"What about motive? Why would she kill the man she loved?"

"Scott said the cancer Edward had would become incredibly painful before it killed him. The police are considering that Bobbi Jo might have put him out of his misery. And then there was that attempt on Brian's life."

"Well, obviously Brian doesn't think Bobbi Jo cut his brake line since he's still staying here."

"What bothers me is, who would want Edward and Brian both dead? And is Bobbi Jo next?"

"Dear Goddess," Lily said. "I hadn't thought of that."

We both fell silent when we heard Bobbi Jo come outside.

"It should be here in half an hour. So, what's going on in your life, Lily?"

"I've decided to leave Grant and Kyle," Lily said.

"What? Because of Derek?" I poured myself another glass of wine. It was going to be a long evening.

"Darlin', do you really love Derek enough to give up Grant and Kyle?" Bobbi Jo asked.

"It's not that. I'm not going to see Derek, either."

"Have you become a lesbian, Lily?" Bobbi Jo asked.

Lily laughed. "No, nothing like that."

"Well, that's a relief." Bobbi Jo fanned herself.

"I've got enough to deal with right now."

"So, what's this all about, Lily?" I asked.

"I've been thinking about it for a couple of months and it finally dawned on me that I do this every ten years."

"What?" Bobbi Jo asked.

"Get into another relationship," Lily explained. "I'd been married to Grant for about ten years the first time it happened. I became attracted to another man and we broke up for a while. I dated the other man, but eventually, I missed Grant so much and he missed me. I broke it off with the other man and Grant and I got back together."

"You never told us that," I said.

"Well, it's ancient history. But then ten years later, I met Kyle. I think Grant was afraid the same thing would happen and he suggested our present arrangement as a way to work around it."

"He must really love you to have done that."

"Edward would never have done anything like that," Bobbi Jo said.

"In the beginning it was a little awkward, but then as Grant and Kyle got to know each other, we all settled into it rather well."

"And now it's ten years later and you're wanting something with Derek." I reached for the wine bottle and refilled Lily's glass.

"Exactly. It seems like every ten years I need a new man, or something different. I don't know what exactly."

"So how is leaving Grant and Kyle going to get you an answer to that?" Bobbi Jo asked.

"I thought about it for a long time and I've decided that I go through this because I feel like something's missing. I think it's got to be something within me."

"Maybe you're just looking for some excitement," Bobbi Jo suggested. "Maybe you should just have an affair."

"That's never been my way, Bobbi Jo. Besides, when would I have time? I've already got two men to take care of sexually. I don't even know why I was thinking about adding another one to the mix."

"You're sure about this?" I asked.

"I'm sure." Lily nodded her head. "I need to find out what's missing. I can't go through the rest of my life looking for someone else to fix this."

"Have you told Grant and Kyle?" I asked.

"I told them today. I'm not sure they really believe me yet."

"What are you going to do?" Bobbi Jo asked.

"What do you mean?"

"Where will you live?" I asked.

"I'll get a little apartment somewhere. Something temporary, and then I'll just see where everything leads me."

"This is really amazing. All of our lives are changing because we're without husbands. One's dead, one's gone over to the dark side, and the other two have just been hung out to dry."

"Bobbi Jo! That's terrible. Craig hasn't gone over to the dark side. He can't help being gay," Lily said.

"Oh, I know, darlin'. I just don't have any control over my mouth these days. Must be the pregnancy."

I narrowed my eyes at her. "You can't blame everything on the pregnancy."

"I don't see why not."

"Our lives certainly are changing," Lily agreed. "But it's up to us to take charge of the change."

"It is?" Bobbi Jo asked.

"Of course. If you don't take charge of your life, someone else will and you won't like it. You'll have to take charge of your life and your baby's life. You'll have to learn to be a single parent, and I know you'll be good at it. Skye has to build a new life for herself and I'll have to find what I'm missing. It's up to us to orchestrate the changes, no matter what the catalyst was."

The three of us were silent for a moment, considering Lily's words of wisdom.

"Oh, I have an idea," Bobbi Jo said.

"I'm almost afraid to ask," Lily said.

"Why don't you move in here and be my doula?"

"What's a doula?" I asked.

"It's a woman who helps you through the pregnancy and childbirth," Lily explained. "It can be anything from just being the birth coach to going to the doctor and midwife appointments, making sure the mother has vitamins and wholesome food."

"I thought that's what the husband was supposed to do." I bit my lip. "Sorry, Bobbi Jo."

"Don't worry about it. But even women with husbands are using doulas now."

"And to think, I made do with just Craig."

"Oh, I think a doula is a wonderful idea. I don't think men are any good at the whole pregnancy thing," Lily said.

"But don't the fathers want to be in the delivery room?" I asked. "Craig was there and he loved it."

"I think some do," Bobbi Jo said. "But some don't want to and some are just useless. They get hysterical during labor and pass out at the delivery."

"After a few million of us dragged our husbands kicking and screaming into the labor and delivery rooms, we finally realized that they aren't particularly well suited to the task. So now, we hire doulas," Lily said.

"So, what do you say, Lily? Will you be my doula?"

"Are you sure about this, Bobbi Jo?"

"Absolutely. And you can live here. I'd like to

have someone around during the pregnancy."

"But I'm at the shop most of the time."

"That's okay. You don't need to be here every second. I'd really feel good if you'd do it."

"Fine. I'll do it. But only until the baby comes. Then I'm moving out."

"Whatever you say. I'm having my first ultrasound this week. Can you come?" Bobbi Jo turned to me. "You can still come, too."

"What kind of doula would I be if I didn't go to the ultrasound?" Lily laughed. "This could be fun."

"Oh, there's the pizza," I said at the sound of the doorbell. "I'll get it."

Bobbi Jo and Lily talked about baby stuff while I set out the pizza and refreshed our drinks.

"So, what message did Max leave on your cell phone that was so important?" Bobbi Jo asked.

I'd just bitten into a luscious slice of pepperoni and cheese, so I waved my hand to indicate I hadn't listened to the message yet.

"Why not? Go get your cell phone right now."

"Max is calling Skye?" Lily asked.

I swallowed the lump of pizza. "It can wait. I'm eating." I looked at Lily. "Max has only called a couple of times. I've been too busy to call him back."

"Too busy, or too scared?" Lily asked.

"I'm not scared. Why would I be scared?" I

objected. "I'm busy. I've been interviewing for jobs and I still have to paint the loft before I move in."

"Oh, I can't wait to see the loft," Lily said. "When are you moving?"

"All I need to do is finish a few repairs and paint. I've ordered the furniture and appliances already."

"Listen to the message, Skye," Bobbi Jo ordered.

"Fine." I put the pizza down and retrieved my cell phone from the living room. I punched in the voice-mail number as I walked back to the patio and listened to Max's voice mail.

"So, what is it?" Bobbi Jo asked.

"Evidently, I'll be painting the loft on Wednesday. Max said he and some friends are showing up at ten and I'd better have the paint ready."

"How sweet of him," Lily said.

"Yeah, sweet." I put the cell phone down and picked up my wineglass.

"You have a problem with that?" Bobbi Jo asked.

"No. I've already bought the paint. I just don't know why he's doing this."

"Well, I'd suppose it's because he likes you. He wants to help," Lily said.

Bobbi Jo smirked. "He wants you, Skye."

"I'm not sure I'm ready to be wanted."

"Now, darlin', I know this whole situation with Craig had to be a shock. But you can't let it stop you from finding someone you can be happy with," Bobbi Jo said.

"That's not it, Bobbi Jo. Certainly I wasn't prepared to find out that Craig is gay, although looking back on our marriage I can pinpoint some things that should have been clues."

"Like what?" Lily asked.

"Once we were discussing sexual fantasies. I'd read an article about it and asked Craig what and who he fantasized about. He said that he never thought about having sex with other people. Not women. People. I remember at the time thinking that it sounded funny but I just chalked it up to him not wanting to admit to having a sexual fantasy."

"It's not your fault that you didn't see it, Skye," Lily said. "I'd imagine Craig didn't want to admit it to himself for a long time."

"That's probably true," I agreed. "And I'm not beating myself up for not knowing. Not anymore."

"So, why aren't you eager to date Max?" Lily asked. "Are you still in love with Craig?"

"No. I mean, I'll always love Craig. But I'm not in love with him now."

"It's been long enough since you left Craig. I think it'd be good for you to start dating." Lily patted my hand.

"I don't want to date." I stared at the cheese coagulating on my pizza. "I haven't dated since I was in college. And not much before that."

"Well, it hasn't changed all that much," Bobbi Jo said. "Although I hear that some men actually expect you to pay for dates. At least some of the time." Bobbi Jo took a delicate bite of pizza. "I've never done it, though."

"Why am I not surprised?" Lily asked. "Of course when I was young, we didn't really date. We only had money for pot, so we just kind of met and went to bed."

"You're kidding?" Bobbi Jo looked appalled.

"So, what was your criteria for going to bed with a guy?" I asked her.

"There was a lot. When I was dating, it was all about getting married. So, we looked for a stable income, a man who would make a good father." Bobbi Jo squinted in thought, then grinned. "But usually we determined that by who was best in bed."

Bed? I wasn't even ready to have dinner with a man. I wanted some time to find out who and what I was now. I wanted a career. I wanted to have my own place. I wanted to be myself without having to worry about what someone else thought of me.

CHAPTER FOURTEEN

"H ey, nice place." Max stood in the doorway of my loft with a gang of men and a few women behind him.

"Hi. I can't believe you're doing this." I closed the door of my new side-by-side refrigerator and gestured them to all come in.

"What? It's just a little painting." Max looked around the huge room. "Okay, a lot of painting."

"It's big, isn't it?"

"Oh, yeah, it's big." He waved everyone in. "I brought some rollers and brushes and paint trays."

"I got some too. And paint. And I borrowed two ladders from the super."

"We'll definitely need them." He glanced up at the ceiling. "What color did you get?"

"A pinky beige. I figured that was a safe bet. If I decide to use a different color later, it'll be easy to paint over." There must have been a dozen people with him. Max made introductions as they filed in, and I promptly forgot most of their names. "There's beer, soda, and water in the fridge. And snacks on the counter."

Max turned toward the counter. "What's this?" He pointed to a stack of photos.

"The photos I took at Jasmine's wedding. I thought I'd take them over to Lily later."

"How's she doing?" he asked.

"She's good. How are Grant and Kyle?"

Max shrugged. "I guess they're fine. They took off on a fishing trip this morning."

"It was kind of surprising," I said.

"Yeah. I thought those three would be together forever. Well, let's get started. Where's the paint?"

Max's friends worked until eight that night. When they left, my entire loft had a fresh coat of paint. I fed them Kentucky Fried Chicken for lunch and pizza for dinner and thanked them profusely at every opportunity.

"I love this. I'm ready to move in now." I walked through the loft admiring the fresh paint. "I can't thank you enough."

"Then have dinner with me," Max suggested.

"We just ate pizza."

"No, I mean some other time."

"I think I need to be really up front with you. Max, I'm not sure I'm ready to date."

Max smiled and nodded. "I know. You've mentioned that before. I told you, it's not a problem for me."

"Right, I forgot."

He held up a hand. "That's not what I meant. I like you, Skye. I enjoy spending time with you. And I'm a patient man. I can wait until you're ready. But we can still hang out until then, can't we?"

I hoped he really meant that. Max was easy to be around. He was fun. He was a friend. I needed that. "In that case, come over here for dinner next Saturday night."

"Really?"

"Sure. I'll be moved in by then."

"You need help moving?"

"No. Even if I did, you've done more than enough. But the furniture is being delivered. All I have to move are a few things from Bobbi Jo's and some stuff from Craig's house." That was the first time I'd thought of it as Craig's house and somehow it didn't even feel weird.

"Okay, then. I'll see you Saturday night. About seven?" Max kissed me on the cheek and opened the door.

"Sounds good." I waved as he got on the elevator and closed the door wondering why I was disappointed at the kiss. I refused to think about it and turned back to the loft.

I had my own place. My very own place. The thought was astounding to me. I'd never lived on my own. I'd lived with my parents, then in the dorm at college until Craig and I got married. Of course, Sheridan would be with me most of the time, but I wouldn't be living with a man who took care of me. I'd be on my own. That thought was a little scary and a little exciting. I decided to go with exciting. I'd decorate it the way I liked, I'd have food that I wanted, when I wanted it. No more meals on a schedule for me. I'd pay my own bills.

My bubble of excitement burst. I'd be paying them with Craig's money. He'd been very generous in the divorce settlement. He'd bought my half of the house and given me more than enough alimony. Not that I wasn't grateful, but I really wanted to be on my own. I wanted to make my own money. Pay my own way. I'd given up my independence before I'd ever really had it. Now I had an immense hunger for it. I even wanted the hardships that came with it.

But a temp job as a receptionist at little more than minimum wage wouldn't cut it. I needed more. I needed to go back to school and learn something more useful than art history and design theory. I locked up the loft and drove to Bobbi Jo's. I was almost too tired to think and could only hope that I'd wake up bursting with job ideas and the energy to follow through on them.

The next morning I slipped out of the house after Lily left for her shop and before Bobbi Jo got up. At

Portland Community College, I picked up several brochures and a registration packet and drove to a small coffeehouse to peruse them. After two lattes and a minimum of soul searching, I drove back to the college and enrolled in three courses. A business computer course that taught the popular word processing and spreadsheet programs, a course that promised to give me the skills I needed to reenter the workforce, and a photography course. The first two would hopefully prepare me for a real job and the photography course would give me something to do that I really enjoyed.

I paid the registration fee and drove to Craig's house. He'd offered to help me move, but I'd finally convinced him that all I needed to do was box up some things and have the movers pick them up. Sheridan was already there, packing some of her own things.

"Hey, Mom. I'm almost finished here." Sheridan stood in the middle of her room. There were still a few posters of some pop rock groups on the walls. Her bed and furniture was white French provincial. The ruffled yellow curtains matched the bedspread, and there were stuffed animals on a high shelf along one wall.

"I can't believe we never redecorated your room. It hasn't really changed since you were thirteen."

"That's okay. It's good to have a room the same for a while. Gives you a sense of security, you know."

"Do you want to move the furniture to the loft?"

I asked. I hadn't even considered that she might want the security of her own furnishings.

"Are you kidding? No way. I want the new stuff we ordered." She looked at the small nightstand. "Besides, condoms would look so out of place on this nightstand. I need something more sophisticated."

"I am not ready for this."

Sheridan laughed. "Just kidding, Mom." She turned back to the box she was packing. "I never use condoms. They're a hassle."

"Sheridan!"

"It's a joke, Mom. Relax." She sat on the bed. "I'm sorry you and Dad broke up, but this is kind of exciting, you know?"

"I know. And don't be sorry. It was just something that had to happen."

"Are you really okay?"

"Perfectly fine," I assured her.

"You don't hate Dad, do you?"

"Oh, honey, no. It's not your dad's fault he's gay. It's not even a choice. Although there are times I wish he'd been honest with himself before we got married."

"No kidding."

"Still, I think he's going through something much harder than I am."

"You're really cool, Mom."

"You aren't just saying that because you want

something, are you?"

"That only works on Dad."

I laughed and swatted her hand. "Finish up in here and then come to the kitchen and help me."

"Okay." Sheridan turned back to packing and I walked to the kitchen.

There really wasn't much I wanted. I opened a lower cabinet and removed my cast-iron skillet and Dutch oven. Craig had set the silver serving platters on the counter. He knew how attached I was to them. He knew a lot about me. I knew a lot about him. But I thought maybe we'd never known the *right* things about each other.

"Hey, you need any help?"

I turned at the sound of Craig's voice. "You're okay with me taking the platters?"

"Sure. I figured you'd want them."

"Thanks. I appreciate it."

"I packed up the rest of your clothes and put them in the garage. And there were some boxes of stuff I thought you'd want."

"Like what?"

"Really old boxes. Your stuff from college. A couple of boxes of photos that you took."

"I'd forgotten they were even there."

I followed Craig through the kitchen to the garage. One of the boxes was opened and I pulled back the cardboard flap to look inside.

"Oh, look." I pulled out a photograph. "This is from that white-water rafting trip we took before I got pregnant with Sheridan."

Craig took the photo from me and looked at it. "Damn, you were a feisty thing back then."

"I'm still a little feisty," I argued.

"Oh, I don't doubt it at all. That was a fun trip. Remember when Mike got up to take a leak in the middle of the night?"

"And he thought a bear was chasing him."

"God, he was a funny sight. Running through the camp with his shorts around his ankles. And it turned out to be a raccoon."

"A baby raccoon at that!" We both laughed at the memory and it felt good. We'd always been friends, and I liked that we weren't going to lose that part of our relationship.

"He was so embarrassed when he stopped and everyone was staring at him standing there with his dick hanging out."

"Well, that's understandable."

"You know, Mike is gay. He e-mailed me a couple of years ago. He's living in San Francisco with a partner."

"Did you know back then?"

"About Mike? No." Craig shook his head. "But he did. He told me he only dated stupid girls because they were easier to fool. After college, he married one of them. But it didn't last even a year."

I put the photo back in the box and closed the flap. Craig ripped off a strip of tape and handed it to me.

"Did you know you were gay back then?" I asked.

"I'm not gay."

"What?" I was surprised that he'd deny it.

"I consider myself bisexual," Craig explained.

"You do?"

"I'm equally attracted to men and women."

"So, our marriage wasn't a sham for you?"

"Absolutely not. Skye, I loved you very much. I still do." Craig sat down on a box and looked up at me. "When we married, I thought we'd be together forever."

"What happened?"

He laced his fingers together and lowered his gaze to the floor. I recognized the movement. It's what he always did when he talked about something he was uncomfortable with.

"I'm not sure myself. Maybe I should have experimented more when I was younger. I knew I was attracted to men, but I just pushed it aside. Maybe if I'd dealt with it then, this wouldn't have happened."

"You never had sex with a man when you were younger?"

"Oh, I had a few encounters from the time I was

303

a teen. But I really wanted a family. I wanted a normal life."

"So you married me."

"No." He looked up at me again. "I married you because I loved you. I thought that part of my life was just a phase. I thought it was gone forever. I can't explain it. It just happened. Suddenly I was more attracted to men than to women. Sexually."

"I see."

"I tried to deny it. But the more I tried, the stronger the urge became."

"That's when you started going online to meet men?"

"I thought if I just played around with it, the urge would go away. I thought I could do that and still keep you and our life."

"I think it happened for a reason. I think it's something you need to experience or deal with or whatever."

"I'm sorry I hurt you, Skye." He stood up and put his arms around me and rested his chin on my hair. "I'm so sorry."

I put my arms around his back, and we settled into a familiar stance. Just two people who had been friends forever. So close in some ways that words were unnecessary. While a part of me was sorry that our marriage had ended, I didn't have any regrets about leaving that life and starting a new one. Standing there, holding each other was like a memorial service for our marriage.

Talking with Craig made me think about a lot of things. I knew this was difficult for him, but I hadn't considered just how much he was really going through. Somehow, that brief conversation with him had made me realize that if he could face his future with strength, then I could do the same. He had to deal with his sexuality and how the people he knew would react to it. All I had to do was get a job and learn to date. That opened up the possibility that maybe Max and I could be more than just friends. Lily was right. I had to take charge and orchestrate my own life changes.

"Hey, Mom, you're taking the business skills course?" Sheridan held up my class schedule.

"Yes, why?"

"Oh, I'm taking it, too. Tuesdays at ten."

"My class is Thursday, so you're safe." I'd had a little trepidation about how Sheridan would feel about me attending the same college, but she'd been fine with it.

"Too bad. It would have been fun taking a class together." Sheridan slung her backpack over a shoulder.

"I'm outta here. You and Max have fun tonight." She leaned over and kissed my cheek.

"You sure you don't want to stick around for dinner?"

"Mom, you don't want me here for your date."

"It's not a date. It's just a couple of friends having dinner."

"You might get lucky," she suggested. "Besides, Donna and I are going to see a late movie tonight, so I might as well stay at her place. And I'm going shopping tomorrow afternoon. But I'll be home before that."

"Did your father give you money?"

"Of course. I convinced him I couldn't possibly go back to college with old clothes." She opened the door and looked back. "I think he's beginning to get over the guilt thing though. He didn't give me nearly what I asked for. I think that's a good sign."

"Have fun and be safe."

Sheridan dug a hand into the side pocket of her backpack and pressed something into my palm. "You be safe, too." She darted out the door, leaving me standing there, staring at a condom packet in my hand.

I'd kind of been hoping that Sheridan would hang around for dinner. I still wasn't sure about how far I wanted to go with Max. Surely not far enough to need a condom. Or did I? I took the condom packet into the bathroom and tucked it in a drawer. I wanted something more than friendship with Max but I couldn't put my finger on exactly what that would be. Was there a middle ground between friendship and sex with a man?

I took a shower and found myself shaving my legs and underarms, although I'd just shaved the day before. Did I subconsciously want something to happen? Just the idea of making love both terrified and titillated me. It had been a long time since Craig and I had been intimate. And even before that our love life had never been passionate. What would it feel like to make love to a truly passionate man?

We were having a last blast of summer heat so I pulled a loose cotton dress on over my lacy bikini panties and matching bra. Who was I kidding? No one wears panties like that unless she wants them to be seen. I twirled around in front of the full-length mirror. The dress floated and swirled around my calves. One of those dresses that make you feel pretty and feminine. Every woman should have at least one.

By the time Max rang the doorbell, I had the chicken Florentine simmering and water boiling for the fresh pasta. I buzzed him in through the front door and took a quick glance around the loft. I still got a thrill from having my own place. I'd given Sheridan the room next to the darkroom and had a second bedroom built next to the bathroom. Even with that addition the loft was still airy and spacious.

Max knocked at the door and I opened it.

He was holding a bunch of flowers and a bottle of wine and he looked better than ever. I felt a hum of energy run through my body when he leaned over and brushed his lips across mine.

"The flowers are beautiful." The arrangement included birds-of-paradise, orange and yellow daylilies, and purple hydrangeas. I took the flowers from him and carried them into the kitchen. I hadn't thought to buy a flower vase so I put the flowers in a glass pitcher and filled it with water.

"Thanks. They're from my yard. And I brought some sauvignon blanc for dinner."

"One of my favorites. You want to open it now?" I handed him a corkscrew. "Dinner will be ready in about five minutes."

"You look nice," Max said. "Smell good, too."

"Thank you." I dumped the fresh pasta into the boiling water and stirred it. Max poured two glasses of wine and took them to the small table I had set. I drained the pasta, poured the chicken Florentine over it, and carried the platter to the table.

"Would you get the bread from the counter?" I asked.

"Sure." Max came back with the bread and an envelope of photos. "Are these the photos you took at Jasmine's wedding?"

I nodded. "I keep forgetting to take them to Lily."

"Can I look?"

"Sure." I opened the envelope and pulled out the black and whites I'd done. "I took some color shots, too, but I like the black and whites better."

Max leafed through the photos and whistled. "These are great, Skye. I had no idea you were such a good photographer."

"It's been a hobby for years."

"This one is amazing." He held up a shot of Grant and Jasmine. Grant pressed his lips to Jasmine's forehead and a single tear trickled down his cheek. "It captures how he must have been feeling."

"Thanks."

"You know, I have a friend who's a photographer. He just told me he's looking for an assistant."

"Really?" My breath caught.

"Would you be interested?"

"Oh, yes!"

Max grinned. "He'll work you to death, though. Ben is known for going through assistants."

"That's okay. Does he have his own studio? What kind of photography does he do?"

"Yeah. Steinhart Photography. He does lot of advertising, publicity, some events. Then there's the artsy stuff." Max put the photos back in the envelope and set them on the counter. "I'll call him tomorrow and set up an interview for you."

"*Benjamin Steinhart?*"

"Yeah. You know him?"

"I know *of* him. He's considered one of the best photographers in the Northwest."

"Ah. That explains his ego, then."

"I didn't know he did commercial photography. I only know about his art photography."

"He enjoys an extravagant lifestyle," Max said. "The commercial photography pays better than the art."

I didn't hold out much hope. My only experience was as an amateur photographer. Steinhart was probably looking for someone who'd done the job before. Still, it was nice to think about.

When we finished dinner, Max insisted on doing the dishes.

"You don't have to," I objected.

"You don't seem like the kind of woman who likes to wake up to a sink full of dirty dishes." Max ran water in the sink and added a squirt of detergent. "You can dry, if it'll make you feel better."

We did the dishes in silence and somehow it felt all right. I was a little surprised how at ease I felt with Max. Another sign that I was ready? Max drained the sink, rinsed it, and put the sponge in the dish I'd bought for it.

"Are you always so neat in the kitchen?"

"Not really, but it looks like you are. Just trying to be a good guest."

"You want some coffee?"

"No way, there's still wine left." Max picked up the bottle and filled our glasses.

"That's because you got the big bottle."

"Didn't want to run out." Max led the way to the living area. "Nice furniture."

"Thanks. I had a good time choosing it. Most of it's from Pottery Barn and Pier One." Craig had always hated those places so I'd never bought anything there. But this was for me.

"I like it." Max sat on the sectional and placed our glasses on the coffee table. "You have a great sense of style."

"Thanks." I settled beside him.

"I envy someone who can pick out the right furniture and colors and accessories. I can barely match my clothes and you always look terrific."

"I do?" I felt heat bloom in my cheeks. I wasn't used to men complimenting me, but I liked it.

"Yes, you do. You have a knack for selecting clothing that brings out your best features."

His arm moved around my back to rest a hand on my shoulder. "Does this make you uncomfortable?"

"No, it doesn't." I had to smile at the surprise on

his face.

"That's nice to hear." Max pulled me closer and kissed my temple.

Just a little kiss, but it sent shivers down my neck. He turned my head and brushed his lips across mine. My breath stopped, wanting more. He pulled back and looked into my eyes and I didn't think he would ever look away. That made me a little nervous and I dropped my gaze to his lips. He had really nice lips. My hand moved up to trace a finger over them. I remembered how they had felt that night at his place and leaned in just a bit.

Max seemed to think that was a good idea and covered my mouth with his. His lips moved softly over mine, his tongue tracing their outline. I felt his hand slip from my shoulder down my arm and underneath my breast. I leaned into his hand even as I thought it probably wasn't a good idea. When his hand cupped my breast, I decided it was a very good idea. I felt a little light-headed and wondered if I'd forgotten to breathe. He pulled me to my feet and I almost whimpered as we lost body contact for a moment. I wanted his shirt off. I wanted to touch his flesh. Now. I pulled his shirt out of his pants and he leaned back to give me better access.

His hands left my breasts and I would have objected, but they moved to my waist, then drifted lower to cup my bottom, pulling me up against him. Oh, yeah. That's what I wanted. My breath was coming in short, harsh gasps as I fumbled with the buttons and finally got his shirt open.

"We need to stop."

"What? Why?" I didn't want to stop. I wanted the logical conclusion to this. And I wanted it right *now*.

"I don't have any protection."

"You need protection?" From what? What was I going to do to him that he needed protection from?

"A condom. I don't have any with me."

"I have one." I took his hand and pulled him across the loft to my bathroom. I opened a drawer. No condom. What the hell had I done with it? I opened the next drawer and breathed a sigh of relief when I saw the packet.

"Thank God." Max pulled me into the bedroom. We stopped at the foot of the bed and he pulled me up against his almost naked chest. I was a little distracted from his kiss when I felt him unzipping my dress. In my haze of passion, I'd forgotten this would involve him seeing my naked body.

No man had ever seen me naked but Craig. Even the only other man I'd been to bed with hadn't really seen me naked because we'd done it with the lights off. My body is in reasonably good condition, but at forty-two nothing was as firm as it had been. Lust whipped through me when Max started nibbling on my neck. It would be all right. After all, I had the pretty bra and panties on.

I felt the dress drop off my shoulders and fall to my feet. The snap on his pants came apart under my fingers. I pulled the zipper down and pushed his pants off his hips. Max shrugged his shirt off, then pushed off his loafers and stepped out of his pants. We stood there in our underwear and looked at each other. He was hard and ready, pushing against his blue silk briefs.

"You're beautiful," he said.

"So are you."

"Where's the condom?"

What the hell had I done with the condom? I looked around frantically and finally found it on the floor next to his pants. I picked it up with shaking hands and held it out to him.

CHAPTER FIFTEEN

I poured myself a cup of coffee and sat on a stool at the counter. Max had left at some point during the night without waking me. I felt a little weird about that. Why had he left? Did it mean something? Did he not want to sleep with me? I mean, really sleep as opposed to what we'd done before I'd fallen asleep. Maybe I snored. Craig had never mentioned it, but there were a lot of things Craig had never mentioned.

I was staring at the phone when it rang and I jumped, sloshing coffee onto the counter and my robe. Was it Max? Should I answer it? Did I want to talk to him? The front door opened on the third ring. Two more rings and it would go to voice mail.

"Mom, answer the phone. It might be for me." Sheridan dumped her backpack on the floor and ran for the phone.

"It's for you." She held her hand over the mouthpiece. "Some guy named Benjamin Steinhart. How many men are you dating?" She handed the phone to me.

"This is Skye Donovan."

"Benjamin Steinhart. Max tells me you'd make a good photographer's assistant. I don't really believe him, but I'm willing to give you an interview."

He rattled off an address and I wrote it down, too stunned to say anything.

"Be here at three on Monday. We'll talk."

I hung up the phone when I realized I was hearing a dial tone.

"Who was that?"

"A photographer," I said. "A friend of Max's. He's looking for an assistant."

"You? Mom, that would be great. You've always loved photography."

"I know. I probably won't get the job. I mean, I'm sure he's looking for someone with experience. Still, it's a chance."

"Don't be negative. All an assistant does is whatever the boss tells them to. And you know lots about photography." She gave me a one-armed hug. "He'd be lucky to have you."

"Thanks. How was your evening?"

"Okay. How was yours? Did you get lucky?"

I knew Sheridan was joking, but it was cutting too close to the truth to be comfortable.

"What movie did you see?"

"*Casablanca*. Those old movies are so great."

"That one's a classic," I agreed.

"I cried at the end when she had to choose between Rick and her husband."

"We've all cried at that part."

"How could you make a choice like that? The man you love or the man who's going to do a lot of good for the world? I think I'd be too selfish to make the right choice."

"Most of us would be. That's what makes the story so poignant."

"I guess."

The phone rang and since I was still holding it I got to answer it before Sheridan grabbed for it.

"Hi, Skye, it's Max. How are you?"

"I'm fine." I glanced nervously at Sheridan. Why did I feel so guilty?

"I'm taking a shower before I go shopping," Sheridan called as she headed for her room. I waved and turned my attention back to the phone.

"When did you leave?"

"Oh, about six, I think." Max paused but I didn't know what to say. "I didn't know if you might feel strange waking up with me there, so I thought I'd leave."

"Oh, I see."

"I called Ben. He said he'd give you a call."

"He already did. I have an interview with him

tomorrow. He didn't seem very positive."

"That's Ben. He can be a gruff son of a bitch. I probably shouldn't have told you about him."

"No. I'm thrilled. Even if I don't get the job. Although I'd love to work for a photographer." I couldn't imagine a better job than working for a professional photographer.

"Then, I hope it works out. I have to run. I'm seeing some friends this afternoon. Let me know how the interview goes, okay?"

"Sure." That was it? Let him know about the interview?

"Skye?"

"Yes?"

"I had a really good time last night."

"Me, too."

"I'll call you later."

"Okay." I hung up the phone and stared at it for a moment. I wasn't sure what any of our conversation meant. Was he going to call me? Before my interview on Monday? Should I call him after the interview with Benjamin Steinhart?

"I knew it! You got laid!"

I turned to look at Sheridan, still standing in the doorway to her room. "Excuse me?"

"You got lucky with Max, didn't you?"

"Sheridan, I'm not about to discuss my sex life

with you."

"This is so cool, Mom. Was it good? I'd think Max would be good."

"Aren't you going shopping or something?"

"If you can bring men home, does that mean I can bring my dates back here, too?"

"Sheridan!" I glared at her.

"Okay, okay. We can talk about it later. I gotta take a shower, then I'm meeting Donna at Washington Square."

I was prevented from continuing the conversation by the phone ringing again. "Hello?"

"Skye, Scott here. I wanted to update you on that lead."

"You mean Matt Nichols?"

"I checked him out and you were right; Mr. Melrose took over his company. Nichols had gotten into a lot of financial problems. Melrose tried to buy him out before they were too bad, but Nichols refused, thinking he could save the company by taking out another loan."

"So he was angry with Edward?"

"Nope. Not at all. Edward saved him from having to file bankruptcy by taking over the company along with all the debt. Nichols felt indebted to Edward."

"Oh." One more suspect to cross off the list.

"You sound disappointed."

"No. Not at all." But I was. I wanted them to find

whoever murdered Edward and I wanted them to stop thinking Bobbi Jo had any motive at all.

"Yeah," he said. "Anyway, just wanted to let you know about it. I'll talk to you later."

"Thanks. I appreciate that." I said good-bye and hung up.

As soon as I heard Sheridan get out of her shower, I started mine. I wanted to go over to Bobbi Jo's and see how she and Lily were doing. I'd only been gone for a few days, but I missed them. I rinsed the conditioner from my hair, pulled on a robe, and wrapped a towel around my head. The sight of my bed with the rumpled sheets made me grin. Usually when I get up, I only have to smooth the sheets on my side and pull the comforter up. The entire bed was a tangle of sheets, pillows, and comforter. And with good reason. After Max got the condom packet open, I'd surprised myself, and probably him, by becoming a bit aggressive and demanding. I'd never done that before and now I couldn't imagine why not.

I pulled on shorts, a T-shirt, and sandals, and grabbed my purse. Sheridan had already left to go shopping, so I left her a quick note that I'd be at Bobbi Jo's.

Sean was just leaving when I arrived at Bobbi Jo's. His brows were drawn together in a frown, and he glanced back at the door as it closed behind him. When he saw me, he rearranged his features into a phony smile.

"Skye. Nice to see you again."

"Hi, Sean. How have you been?" Like I really cared how the little weasel was.

"Good."

"Thanks again for all the help with the wedding."

"Sure. No problem. Glad to be of help." Sean beeped the remote to his car, got in, and drove away. What the hell was he doing at Bobbi Jo's on a Sunday morning?

"Hey. Where are you guys?" I called out as I opened the door.

"Out here, darlin'."

I followed Bobbi Jo's voice to the patio where she and Lily were sipping orange juice and nibbling on bagels. I hadn't had breakfast, so I helped myself to a cup of tea in the kitchen, then grabbed a bagel as I sat down.

"Well, someone has an appetite this morning." Bobbi Jo grinned. "How was dinner with Max?"

"Fine. It was fine."

Bobbi Jo laughed and Lily smirked at me.

"What?"

"Darlin', it's written all over your face that you got laid."

"Excuse me?" What, did I have a tattoo on my forehead or something? I didn't know what to say so I frowned.

"So, how was he?" Bobbi Jo asked.

"Bobbi Jo!"

"Oh, never mind her, Skye." Lily wasn't quite able to stop smirking at me, though. "So, how is Max?"

"Yeah, how was he?"

"Bobbi Jo, that's not what I meant," Lily objected.

"Well, it's what I meant," she retorted.

"What is it? I mean, Sheridan seemed to know as soon as she saw me and now you two. How do you know when someone's had sex?"

"It's a look, darlin'. And you have it."

"If it's of any interest to you, I also have other news."

"Tell," Bobbi Jo demanded.

"I have an interview with a photographer."

"Doing what?" Lily asked.

"Photographer's assistant. Which probably means a lot of grunt work. Oh, that reminds me." I pulled the envelope out of my bag. "These are some photos I took at Jasmine's wedding."

Lily opened the envelope and I turned to Bobbi Jo. "So, what was Sean doing here on a Sunday?"

"He brought over some papers from Edward's office that he thought I might need."

"Bobbi Jo, you know he has a crush on you, don't you?"

"Sean? Don't be ridiculous. He's just feeling at loose ends. Trying to make himself feel needed until

Jimmy finds a position for him."

"I don't think that's it. And I think you need to be careful."

"Careful about what?"

"It reminds me of when that guy was stalking you."

Lily passed some of the photos to Bobbi Jo and nodded. "He does seem a bit obsessive."

"Really? You think so? I just thought he was being nice."

"That's not it. He looks at you all the time. His eyes follow you around the room, even if he's talking to someone else. And when he heard that you're pregnant—well, it wasn't a normal reaction." I smeared cream cheese on my bagel and took a bite.

"Not normal how?"

"He looked kind of pissed. Almost angry."

"That's ridiculous."

"Not really," Lily said. "I don't think his attention toward you is entirely innocent, either."

"Okay. I'll be careful. I'll keep my distance from him. But only because I don't want to hurt him. He's just got a crush. It's not like it was with the stalker. John Templeton wishes he'd ever gotten that close to me."

"Maybe you should push Jimmy to find a position for Sean as soon as he can. Give Sean something else to do." Maybe Jimmy could transfer him to Bulgaria.

Not that MMC had an office in Bulgaria.

"I can't imagine being stalked. It must have been horrible." Lily flipped through the rest of the photos and handed them to Bobbi Jo. "Skye, these photos are just incredible. Can I get some prints?"

"Of course. Just let me know which ones you want."

"I want them all. They're gorgeous."

"Well, it certainly wasn't fun. Being stalked, I mean. The worst part of it was that the cops couldn't do a damn thing about it." She looked at another photo and smiled. "I love this one, where Grant is getting ready to walk Jasmine down the aisle. And this one, where Kyle has his hand on David's shoulder."

"Why couldn't they do anything?" Lily asked.

"They said it was because he hadn't actually committed a crime. Like calling me all the time wasn't anything. You know, he must have joined the gym I belonged to because he'd call and tell me what I'd been wearing that day." Bobbi Jo shuddered. "It was awful."

"But you knew his name. Couldn't they just go arrest him for that?"

"Oh, I didn't know his name until the very end. He sent me some flowers and the cops were able to get his name from the florist because he used a credit card to pay for them."

"What made him stop?" Lily asked.

"I think that was it, actually. Somehow he found out that the cops knew who he was and he just disappeared. That was the biggest relief until I saw the headlines about him raping that girl in Louisiana."

"There's nothing you could have done to prevent that, Bobbi Jo. And they caught him," Lily said.

"Thank gawd for that." Bobbi Jo patted her belly. "I promise I'll be careful. I have more than just myself to think of now."

"How did the ultrasound go?" I asked. "I'm so sorry I missed it."

"That's okay. You can come to the next one. Everything's exactly the way it should be. And they're pretty sure it's a girl but they can't really be certain this early."

"A girl!" I hugged Bobbi Jo. "That's great! But I won't buy anything pink until we're sure."

"You should be wishing for a boy. Boys are a *lot* easier to raise."

"Oh, come on, Lily, are you saying Jasmine was a problem?" I asked.

"The six months before her first period, and the two years she wore braces were a living hell."

"Well, I don't care if it's a boy or a girl. I don't care how much trouble she, or he, is. I'm going to love every minute of it." Bobbi Jo patted her tummy and grinned. "So, really, Skye, how was Max in bed?"

The interview wasn't going well. I'd been at Benjamin Steinhart's studio for an hour and he'd been working the entire time. Barking orders at the models. Screaming because the lighting wasn't just right. He'd managed to ask me three questions, but I didn't think he'd really listened to any of my answers.

"Here." He shoved a camera at me. "Go change the film. The darkroom's over there."

I walked in the general direction he'd indicated and found a door leading to a small closet. I flipped the switch and the room glowed red. I made sure the door was closed, wound the film, removed it, and put in a new roll. This man was a maniac. Did I even *want* to work for him?

Yes. More than anything.

I walked back to the set and handed the camera back to him. He checked it and grinned. "Okay, we're done here."

The models scampered off the seamless. No doubt they were relieved to get away. Benjamin walked across the huge studio without sparing me a glance. "Roll up the seamless and come into my office."

It took me a minute to figure out how the roll of

seamless worked, but I finally got it rolled up, only to find three other layers of seamless beneath it. I put them all away, straightened my jacket, and followed him to the office.

"You want a drink?" He poured bourbon in a glass and replaced the bottle in his drawer.

"No, thank you."

"Did you get the seamless rolled up?"

"Yes. All four layers of it."

"You did okay with loading the film, too. And you can take orders. That's an important part of being an assistant."

"What if I'd put the film in wrong? Or exposed the roll that was in the camera?" His photos would have been useless.

"Oh, I was already through shooting. It was just a test."

Great. At least I'd passed.

"So, you take any photos yourself?"

"Photography has been a hobby for me for years."

"You got anything to show me?" He lit a cigarette and waited while I pulled out a large manila envelope. He took the envelope, pulled out the photos, and grimaced. "Amateur stuff." He shrugged and handed the envelope back to me.

"I didn't know you wanted a photographer. I thought you were looking for an assistant."

He laughed and took a drag on his cigarette. "I am. You're older than most of my assistants."

"Is that a problem for you?"

"Hell, I don't know. Maybe you won't go all goo-gly-eyed at the models. Be here Wednesday morning at seven. I have a big shoot so don't be late. If you're late, you're fired."

"I'll be here." I was surprised I could even speak. Benjamin Steinhart was offering me a job. A grunt job. But still.

"Hope you're stronger than you look. This isn't an easy job."

"I'm not an easy woman. See you on Wednesday."

"Wait a minute."

Damn. I should have kept my mouth shut. But he was such a jerk.

"Here." He opened a drawer and pulled out some CDs. "If you like photography, you might like these. Bring them back when you come to work."

I looked at the discs. Photo software. Great. Now I needed a computer. No problem. I could han-dle this. I tucked the discs in my briefcase and waved at Steinhart, who had picked up his phone, which I took as a dismissal. I drove across town thinking that I'd better be familiar with the software he'd given me by Wednesday. Just in case this was another test.

I walked into the Best Buy store and wound my

way through the software displays and the games to the area with the computers. I was totally out of my element. I probably should have just loaded the software onto Sheridan's computer. But I wanted my own, and I was going to buy one. I just had no idea which computer to buy. My cell phone chirped and I pulled it out of my bag.

"Hello?"

"Skye. How did the interview go?"

I melted a little at the sound of Max's voice. "It was horrible, but I got the job."

"Great. Don't let Ben intimidate you."

"Too late."

Max laughed. "Where are you?"

"At Best Buy. I need a computer but I have no idea what to buy. Should I get a laptop or one that sits on a desk? Damn, I need a desk, too."

"Skye. Don't move. And don't buy anything. I'll be there in fifteen minutes."

"Okay. .I'll just look around."

"Just don't buy anything."

I walked around the store while I waited for Max. It was amazing what was available. I looked at the software displays for a while, then meandered over to the computers again. There was a really darling little laptop I liked. I was playing with the display model when Max found me.

"You don't want that one."

"Why not? It's pretty."

"Doesn't have enough power."

"So, what do I want?"

Max took my hand and pulled me over to another laptop. This one was bigger. The screen was larger, and I figured that would be good. Especially for photographs.

"This one is better. Better processor, better software, better operating system. And it's got a wireless network card. That's nice."

Whatever. It was a shiny gunmetal blue, which I liked, and came with a nice carrying case. I paid for the computer and Max followed me home. I still didn't have a desk so Max set the laptop on the dining table and fiddled with it while I made a pot of coffee.

"Do you want some dinner?"

"No, thanks. I have a dinner date in a couple of hours."

A dinner date? He must mean one of his writing friends or an editor or something.

"Oh, who with?"

"Sandra." He finished loading the software Ben had given me. "There, you're all set."

"Sandra? Did I meet her at your party?" I was trying to not sound like a jealous girlfriend. From the look on Max's face, I was failing.

"No. She's just a girl I go out with occasionally."

"Oh, I see."

"Skye, I never said we were exclusive."

"You and me or you and Sandra?"

"Either. I'm seeing several women right now, and I'm up front with all of them. Is that a problem for you?"

Was it? If it was, I didn't want to tell him that. "I just like to know where I stand."

Max walked over and put his arms around me, kissing my temple. "Well, you stand just fine. But I'm not in the market for an exclusive relationship. Not right now, anyway. That could always change."

"Good. I'm not, either."

Max glanced at his watch. "I need to run. Call me if you have any problems with the computer."

"Sure. Thanks for the help."

He kissed me, on the lips this time, and left. I dumped my coffee, splashed some wine into a glass, and called Bobbi Jo.

"Hey, Skye, what's up? I thought you might be seeing Max again tonight."

"Max has a date tonight."

"The bastard!"

"No, not really. He was very up front about it. He sees several women, I guess. Said he isn't looking for an exclusive relationship right now."

"Bastard."

"I don't know. I mean, am I ready for an exclusive relationship?"

"What do you mean?" Bobbi Jo asked.

"I'm just out of a long marriage. I haven't dated since high school. Maybe I don't need to get into an exclusive relationship right away."

"That's a thought. So you're going to take over my Man-a-Week plan?"

"I don't think I'm ready for that, either."

"You should ask Detective Madison out. He's really cute. And I think he has the hots for you."

"Bobbi Jo! He doesn't have the hots for me. Oh, I forgot to tell you. I got the job with Benjamin Steinhart."

"That's great. When do you start?"

"Wednesday. I don't know how long I'll last. I think he goes through assistants like tissues."

"You'll do fine. Before long you'll be taking pictures yourself. It'll be a great career. You'll end up famous."

I laughed. Bobbi Jo was nothing if not supportive of her friends.

"You know, you could do me a favor. Call Detective Madison and ask him how the investigation is going. I'd do it myself, but I'm just feeling a little delicate what with being pregnant and all."

"Bobbi Jo, you have never felt delicate a day in

your life. This is just a ploy to get me to ask him out. Which I won't do." Would I? He *was* really good looking. And nice. Of course, he considered Bobbi Jo a suspect in Edward's death, but he didn't really think she did it. Or did he? It seemed to keep changing.

"You don't have to ask him out. But at least if you call, he'll have an opportunity to ask you out."

Well, if he asked, that would be different. And I wanted to know about the investigation as much as Bobbi Jo did. Really.

"I'll call him tomorrow. He's probably gone home by now."

"You want to come over for dinner?" Bobbi Jo asked. "Lily's making a roast."

"Thanks, but I'm exhausted from the interview. I think I'll just watch a movie and get to bed early. I thought I'd go shopping for some work clothes tomorrow; you want to come?"

"Of course. Pick me up around eleven."

I hung up and looked at the clock. Seven fifteen. Maybe I could call Scott and just leave a voice mail. I punched in his number and mentally went over the message I'd leave.

"Detective Madison."

"Oh. Hi. I didn't expect you to be there."

"Then why did you call?"

"This is Skye. I was going to leave you a message."

"I recognized your voice. What message were you going to leave?"

"I just wanted to know what was happening with the investigation. Bobbi Jo asked me to call you." That sounded stupid. And planned.

"Have a drink with me and I can fill you in?"

"Are you allowed to do that?"

"What? Have drinks with you?"

"I thought that because I'm a friend of Bobbi Jo's maybe it wasn't allowed."

"It would probably be unethical for me to go out with Mrs. Melrose, but I think I'm safe with you."

"Oh." I wasn't sure just how safe he was with me.

"How about tomorrow night? Say seven? I'll take you to my favorite burger joint."

"Okay. That sounds good."

"Great. I'll see you then."

"Do you want me to meet you there?"

"If you want. But I can come by and pick you up."

"That will be fine. My address is—"

He rattled off my address. "DMV records. One of the perks of the job."

CHAPTER SIXTEEN

"Y ou've got to help me decorate the nursery," Bobbi Jo said as we walked through the department store.

"Doesn't the doula do that for you?"

"Lily is a great doula but she has no decorating sense. She suggested I just put the baby in one of the drawers of my dresser."

That's Lily. Down-to-earth practicality.

"I want to do the nursery in bright colors. I heard it stimulates the baby."

"You'll probably regret that. Believe me, babies are stimulated enough all on their own."

"You'd look great in this." Bobbi Jo held up a slinky black outfit.

"I need work clothes, something with lots of pockets." I led her to the sportswear department and picked out a pair of cargo pants. "This will work."

Bobbi Jo made a face at the pants. "You should be shopping at L.L. Bean. Maybe Lands' End."

"Great idea. I'll have to get their catalogs. Or I could order from their Web sites."

"That doesn't help you now, though."

"This will do for a while. I can order something more when I get home."

"Let's look at the baby department before we go."

I couldn't refuse her. I remembered how I'd wandered through the baby department when I'd been pregnant. I paid for the pants and we walked to the other end of the store and went into Babyland. It almost smelled like babies. Maybe they scented the air with baby powder.

"Lily, what are you doing here?" Bobbi Jo asked.

"I just wanted to look at some things. I love shopping for my friends' babies, and since this is your first, you're going to need a lot."

"I want one of everything," Bobbi Jo said. "I just don't know what it all is."

"You'll definitely want one of these. It's a Diaper Genie."

"What's it do?" she asked.

"You put the dirty diaper in it and it twists a plastic bag around it so you don't have any baby poop odor," Lily explained.

"My baby's poop isn't going to stink."

"Not until you stop breast-feeding. Then, the odor is incredible."

"How long do you breast-feed anyway?" she asked.

"I nursed Jasmine and Beau until they were almost two."

Bobbi Jo looked horrified. "I'm going to have the little sucker on my tit for two years?"

"Most women nurse for less than a year," I assured her. "I think I nursed Sheridan for about six months. After that she wanted food, not breast milk. I think she was eating pizza as soon as she could crawl to it."

"Oh, look at this crib. Isn't it darling?" Bobbi Jo ran over to a brass, antique reproduction crib complete with a lacy, Victorian-style canopy.

"You really don't need something like this." Lily shook her head.

"Well, it depends on how you define *need*. If I want it, then I need it."

"There's no arguing with her, Lily. This is going to be the most overindulged child in the world."

"I'm not going to spoil the baby. I'm going to spoil myself."

I glanced at my watch. "I really need to run. It's almost four."

"What's your hurry?" Lily asked.

"I have dinner plans."

"Dinner?" Bobbi Jo asked with a big grin. "And just who are you having dinner with?"

"Max?" Lily asked.

"No. Actually, I called Scott last night to ask about the investigation and he asked me to dinner. But it's just to tell me about the investigation."

"Sure it is," Bobbi Jo said. "Although I'll be happy when the whole thing is over. Brian is driving me nuts. He's all nervous and twitchy about getting back to New York."

"Has he asked Scott about that? I mean, surely they'll let him go back as long as they know how to get in touch with him." Wouldn't they? It seemed reasonable to me.

"I like Brian and all, but he gets on my nerves after a while. And it's been a while. He's still talking to some lawyer about contesting the will, but my lawyer says he doesn't have a chance of making that happen."

"I can ask Scott about Brian leaving tonight." That would make me feel like it was less of a date. Which might make the knot in my stomach go away.

I left Lily and Bobbi Jo still browsing through Babyland and drove home thinking about what to wear to dinner.

I spent a ridiculous amount of time trying on outfits. This was beginning to feel like high school again and I didn't like it a bit. Finally, I settled on a pair of tailored khakis and a red silk blouse. I'd just slipped my feet into a pair of black flats when I heard the buzzer.

"Hey, that must be your date, Mom. I'll buzz him in."

"How do I look?" I asked Sheridan as I walked into the main room.

"You look fine. He's on his way up." Sheridan was settled on the sofa with a bowl of ice cream and the television remote. "How late are you going to be out?"

"Why?"

"Just curious. It's not like you have a curfew or anything." She grinned and spooned ice cream into her mouth. "Don't worry. I'm not going to wait up for you. I have an early class tomorrow."

"Damn. Classes."

"What?"

"I have to cancel mine. Because of the job with Benjamin Steinhart."

"Bummer."

I opened the door just as Scott got out of the elevator. "Hi, you found me. Come in."

He was wearing jeans and a light blue cotton sweater. The jeans were kind of tight and worn in all the right places, and the sweater showed off his chest and shoulders. Funny, I hadn't noticed how broad his shoulders were before. I did notice the manila envelope he was carrying, but I didn't mention it.

"This is my daughter, Sheridan. Sheridan, this is Scott Madison."

"Hi, Sheridan."

"Hey, Scott."

I walked over to give Sheridan a good-night kiss, something I'd done every night since she was born. When I leaned over her, she whispered, "Mom, I'll totally understand if you don't come home tonight. He's really hot." I glared at her, but she just grinned at me.

Scott drove a big truck and I was happy I'd worn pants when I had to almost crawl into the seat. He parked downtown and we walked a block to Fatz Burgers. The restaurant was small with a long bar and small tables crowded together. Several people greeted Scott when we walked in. He waved at them but kept his attention focused on me, which was flattering and unnerving at the same time.

"Hi, Scott." A perky girl who didn't look old enough to work in an establishment that served liquor greeted us. Actually, she greeted *him*. She ignored me.

"Could we get a table in the back?" he asked. She nodded and led us into a second room. Still small, but without the noise from the bar and with larger tables. We were seated in the corner after Scott shook his head at the first two tables the girl stopped at.

"I'll have an Arrogant Bastard," Scott said.

"I'd like a glass of Merlot." The girl bounced away, hopefully to notify someone old enough to serve the drinks. "Arrogant Bastard?"

"It's a really good beer. Comes from Stone Brewing in Southern California. Fatz is the only place that carries it up here."

"I'm not much of a beer person. I like it occasion-ally, but I don't know all the brands and which one is better or anything."

"That's good. When I have you over, you'll drink wine and leave my beer alone."

When he has me over? Oh, my. I grinned and pointed to the envelope. "So, what's that?"

Scott put the envelope on the table and opened it. He pulled out a photograph and handed it to me. The man in the photo was young, maybe midtwenties. He had long, scraggly hair and a full beard. I could tell he was short because there was a kind of measuring stick next to him indicating he was five feet, eight inches tall. Obviously a picture from an arrest or something of that nature. From what I could see of his cheeks aside from the beard, he appeared chubby. "Who is this?"

"Have you ever seen him?"

"I don't think so." Something about the man's eyes bothered me, but I couldn't put a finger on it. I rubbed at a spot on the photo and Scott leaned over to look. A waiter placed a glass of Merlot and a bottle of beer on the table. Scott nodded at him.

"I don't think that comes off," he said.

"Oh, sorry. I thought it was something on the photo." I peered closer and saw that it was a mole on the man's cheek. "So, who is this? And why did you ask me if I'd seen him?"

"No, I asked if you've *ever* seen him."

"A test of my long-term memory?" I shook my head. "No, I don't think I've ever seen him." I peered at the photo again to make sure. "I don't like his eyes, though."

"That doesn't surprise me."

"So, who is he? And why are you showing me his picture?"

Scott put the photo back in the envelope. "His name is John Templeton."

I gasped and almost choked on my wine. "The stalker? Bobbi Jo's stalker?"

"It took me a while to dig it up. I was researching all the sus—" Scott cleared his throat. "—everyone involved and I found a restraining order Bobbi Jo had filed against him."

"That was before I met her, right after she and Edward were married."

"There was nothing the police could do. He was very careful. We couldn't trace his phone calls. He never did anything threatening to Bobbi Jo."

"I thought he was in prison for raping someone in Louisiana."

"Right. We finally got a lead on him when he sent her some flowers and we were able to get his name. But, before we could locate him, he returned to Louisiana, evidently to visit his mother, now deceased. During that visit, he decided to enjoy the charms of a certain young woman. Against her wishes. Fortunately, they were able to bring the bastard to trial and found him guilty. He got twenty years."

"So, he's still in prison."

"I'm afraid not. Prisons are overcrowded. Hardly anyone serves a full term. If he keeps his nose clean and plays nice with the other boys, he's out in less than half the time of the sentence."

"When did he get out?"

"Over a year ago. We've lost track of him. He checked in with his parole officer for a while, but then he just disappeared."

"Have you told Bobbi Jo?

"No. I didn't want to upset her. There's no sign that he tried to contact her while he was in prison, or since he got out, so he could be focused on someone else now."

"Focused on someone else?"

"It happens sometimes. If they're removed from the person long enough, they often focus on someone else. Someone more obtainable."

I shuddered. The waiter approached again and I realized I hadn't looked at the menu. I picked it up, but Scott put his hand over mine.

"Let me order. There's only one thing worth eating here anyway."

"Sure."

"Two Fatz burgers and a side of veggies." The waiter nodded and left. "In addition to Bobbi Jo's reports of his harassment, there was one other report. Evidently Templeton threatened Edward Melrose at one point."

"Bobbi Jo never told me that."

"I don't think she knows. The report was made separately. I believe Edward Melrose didn't want his wife to know about it. Then when Templeton went to prison, the problem was solved."

"So, you think he might have murdered Edward?"

"It was a shot in the dark. As I said, we don't know where he is. But if he was stalking her again, it's possible he'd want to get rid of Edward so he could have her for himself."

"That's sick."

"Very. You've been spending a lot of time with her. If he was around, I was thinking you might have seen him."

"Thanks."

"For what?"

"For asking me instead of talking to Bobbi Jo."

"No reason to upset her if it was a false lead, which it appears to be." He grinned as the food was set before us. "Besides, it was a great excuse to see you."

I hoped my blush didn't show.

"This is the best burger in Portland." Scott shook the ketchup bottle, squirted some on his burger, and passed it to me. I did the same and noticed that the veggies he'd ordered were battered and fried. Mushrooms, zucchini, and onions. Well, you only live once. Besides I'd had a salad for lunch.

The burger was delicious. The veggies were heaven. Between bites I asked Scott about the investigation. He didn't tell me much, and by the end of dinner I realized that he actually hadn't told me anything I didn't already know or could easily surmise.

"You haven't told me anything about the investigation that I didn't already know."

"You caught that, did you?" He grinned and his eyes sparkled.

"You said we'd have dinner and you'd fill me in."

"I lied."

"Oh."

Scott paid the bill and we walked back to his truck. "You want to get an after dinner drink?"

"I can't. I have a new job and it starts early tomorrow morning."

"In that case, I'll take you home."

He drove me straight home and against my insistence that I could get to my apartment on my own, walked me all the way to my door.

"I'd ask you in for coffee, but I really need to be up early." It was already past ten and I had to be up at five thirty. I had my back against the door to the loft, my hand on the doorknob, but I was reluctant to end the evening, in spite of my need for sleep.

"No problem. I have an early day, too. But thanks for having dinner with me."

He leaned in and suddenly I realized that he was going to kiss me. I also realized that I had absolutely no desire to stop him. His lips grazed mine and without warning, my lips parted and his tongue was in my mouth. How the hell had that happened? But then, I was a little too distracted to think about it. His hand caressed my shoulder and trailed down across my breast to rest at my waist. One of my hands had found its way to his neck and the other one clutched his sweater, holding him close. Damn, he was a good kisser.

"I guess I should be going." Scott pressed a chaste kiss to my lips that made me want to devour him. I forced my fingers to release his sweater.

"I'll call you if there's any sign of John Templeton," I whispered. He kissed me again and I almost melted.

"Call me anyway."

"Are those muscles in your arms?" Bobbi Jo asked. She settled into the chair next to mine at the table and carefully placed her fruit juice on a coaster.

"Benjamin Steinhart is trying to work me to death," I said, taking the tall glass of iced tea she handed me. "The muscles are from hauling props and dealing with those huge rolls of seamless paper."

"Then why are you smiling?"

"Because I love it. I've learned so much from him. Just in three days." I reached into my bag and pulled out my digital camera. "That reminds me. I want to take some pictures so I can play with the new software he gave me."

"I was kind of surprised that you invited Max today." Bobbi Jo looked over to the pool where Max and Sheridan were splashing each other.

"Why?" I adjusted the lens and snapped a few shots.

"I thought you really liked Scott."

"I do. But I like Max, too." I put the camera down and sipped my tea. "I don't know that I can handle having a relationship with more than one man, though."

"Is that where you're headed with Scott? And by relationship do you mean having sex with him?" Bobbi Jo leaned her elbows on the table. "I have to live vicariously now that I'm pregnant."

"He's a really good kisser. Kind of makes me want

to know more." I waggled my eyebrows at her and she laughed.

"I'll want details."

"So, what's Sean doing here?" I glanced at the grill where Sean was turning chicken and slathering on barbeque sauce.

"I just thought he'd like to come over. He's been real nice about doing stuff for me and I think he's lonely. I need to fix him up with someone."

"Couldn't hurt. Then he wouldn't be following you around like a puppy dog."

"Skye, shush. He'll hear you. He's just lonely. I'll find someone for him and then he'll forget all about me."

"Where's Brian? Oh, damn. I totally forgot to ask Scott about him leaving."

"No problem. Brian finally called him and Scott said it was okay as long as he can get in touch with him."

"How do you feel about that?"

"I'm relieved that he's leaving tomorrow. He's still griping about having his inheritance in a trust fund. Still threatening to contest the will. I finally told him he's lucky that Edward left him anything at all."

I focused my camera and snapped a couple of shots of Max and Sheridan, who were playing something that looked like pool Frisbee. "Scott still considers him a suspect because of that argument he had with

Edward and Edward threatening to cut him out of the will."

"With the way he's been acting lately, I don't doubt that he might have been mad enough to kill Edward. I just don't think the little whiner has the balls."

"I can understand that. Besides, what about his brake line being cut? That just doesn't make any sense to me."

"I have no idea," Bobbi Jo said. "I don't think he even knows anyone in Portland. Maybe someone followed him from New York to kill him."

"Bobbi Jo, that's a terrible thought. Besides, the car he's driving belongs to you. Did you ever think that maybe someone intended for you to have that accident?"

"I haven't driven that car in over two years. Edward and I just kept it in the carport next to the guesthouse in case someone wanted to use it while they were visiting."

Lily appeared from the kitchen with a bowl of potato salad. She gave Sean a sharp glance as she passed him on the way to the table.

"There's just something not right about him," she said quietly.

"That's mean, Lily. There's nothing wrong with Sean. He's just a little timid," Bobbi Jo said.

"Timid?" Lily shook her head. "Don't you think

it's a little off that he's spending so much time with his late boss's wife?"

"No, I don't. I think it's nice. He's concerned about me. When did that become a crime?"

"Can I help you bring some stuff out?" I asked Lily.

"No, I'll just get the bread and the fruit salad and we'll be ready as soon as the meat's done."

"It's ready now," Sean called from his station at the grill. Bobbi Jo waved Max and Sheridan in from the pool and we all sat down to eat.

"What's Ben shooting next week?" Max asked as he piled food on his plate.

"We're doing another catalog shoot on Monday, a magazine ad on Tuesday, prewedding photos on Friday, and a wedding on Saturday."

Max grinned. "I guess that means a date this weekend is out."

"Probably so. But it's your own fault."

"I never should have suggested the job." He shook his head and looked morose, then laughed.

"It's hard work, but I love it. I should have done something like this a long time ago. He's going to let me shoot some of the wedding. After a few years of doing his grunt work, I might become a full-time photographer for him. His photographers make a lot of money and they get the best jobs in the city."

"I didn't know Benjamin Steinhart even did

weddings," Sean said. "He's the top photographer in the Northwest."

"He has a ton of awards. Keeps them all stuffed in a closet in his office. But you're right. He doesn't do many wedding shoots. They're paying him a fortune for about three hours of work." I picked up the digital camera and snapped a few shots of everyone at the table. "This is a good photo op, as we in the business say."

"Is there any more news on the investigation?" Sean asked Bobbi Jo.

"No. They're still working on it. I wish it would be over. It feels like something is incomplete until they find the bastard who killed Edward."

Sean placed his hand over hers and squeezed it. "I'm sure they'll find the person. Try not to think about it."

Then why did he bring it up? Sometimes he appeared to have the social skills of someone raised in a closet. Lily frowned and shot me a look, then glanced at Sean's hand still covering Bobbi Jo's. Yeah, I didn't like it, either.

Lily stood up and started gathering plates. "Sean, help me carry these into the kitchen."

I almost laughed at the look he gave her. I gathered a couple of bowls and took them to the kitchen. Sean dumped the plates he'd carried onto the counter and scurried back to the patio.

"I don't like him a bit," Lily said as she rinsed plates and stacked them in the dishwasher. "He's probably thinking he can make Bobbi Jo fall in love with him, then he'll have all that money."

"I don't like him, either, but Bobbi Jo thinks he's lonely. She wants to find someone to fix him up with."

"Somehow I don't think that's going to work."

We finished loading the dishes and went back to the patio. "Sheridan, I need to get home soon."

"Oh, Mom, I'm not through swimming. Besides, this is probably my last chance to work on my tan."

"I'll take you home, Skye," Max offered.

Bobbi Jo grinned at me and winked. "Thanks for coming over." She gave me a hug and whispered, "Remember, details." Then she hugged Max. I hoped she wasn't whispering the same thing to him.

We made love when we got back to my loft and it was good. But I kept thinking about Scott. Which made me feel guilty.

"I've got to go," Max said a couple of hours later. "I have plans tonight."

Plans. I assumed that meant a date. Of course, I could be wrong, but the fact that I'd thought it bothered me. The fact that I'd been thinking about Scott bothered me, too.

I sucked at multidating.

Monday and Tuesday were twelve-hour workdays spent running and jumping through Steinhart's hoops. Flaming hoops. I changed film, set up shots, helped the stylists, swept the floor, and changed the seamless paper so many times, my shoulders ached. All to the accompaniment of his bellowing.

I had Wednesday and Thursday off to recover, and Scott made it even better by asking me to a movie Thursday night.

"I thought you'd like this one," Scott said as we took our seats and arranged the soft drinks and popcorn bucket.

"Because it's a chick flick?" I pulled my cell phone out and turned the ringer off, setting it to vibrate, then dropped it in my pocket.

"The politically correct term is 'female-oriented comedy film.'"

"I stand corrected. You're right. I really like the actors in this one." I handed the popcorn over to him. "So, what would you have chosen for yourself?"

"Oh, definitely the Bruce Willis film. And not just because it has more depth. It also has an important social message."

"And what would that be?" I was trying to keep a straight face but failing.

"If you kill somebody, Bruce will hunt you down and kill you back."

The movie started and we stopped talking. We finished the popcorn halfway through the movie, and Scott set it aside and took my hand in his. It felt ridiculously good. Occasionally during the movie, he'd lean over and whisper something in my ear. That made me shiver, but in a good way. We stayed through the credits to let the crowd disperse, then walked out to Scott's truck.

"It's nine and I haven't eaten yet. You want to come back to my place and I'll make us an omelet?"

"That sounds great." I hadn't really meant to say that. I'd meant to say that I needed to get up early. Which would have been a lie. I didn't have to be at the studio until ten tomorrow. But I suspected that having an omelet might lead to having something else. Like sex. Not that I wasn't interested. I was. But I'd just been in bed with Max a few days earlier. I really did suck at this.

Scott lived in a small apartment in downtown Portland. I perched on a stool at the counter while he broke eggs into a bowl.

"How long have you been separated?"

"Just a few months. Seems like longer, though.

The divorce will be final in another month."

"How long were you married?" He cut bacon into small pieces and tossed them in a frying pan, then started slicing mushrooms.

"Twenty-two years."

"That's a long time. What happened?"

"Are you interrogating me?"

"Sorry, it's a bad habit."

"No, I was teasing. I don't mind. Actually I walked in on him and his lover."

"Ouch. That must have hurt." Scott shook his head. "He's probably really sorry about that now. Didn't realize what a prize he had."

"I'm not sure he feels that way."

"I'd bet he is. You're beautiful, smart, fun to be with."

"Thanks for the compliment. But his lover was a man."

"Whoa! And you had no idea?" Scott turned to me, his eyebrows lifted in surprise.

"Not really. I guess he'd been hiding it for years. Trying to convince himself that he was heterosexual."

Scott removed the bacon and mushrooms, whipped the eggs to a froth, then poured them into the pan. I was enjoying watching him. And I liked the idea that he was cooking for me.

"I can see why you were stunned."

355

"I got over it pretty easily. I guess because I could see the pain he's been going through. It might have been different if I'd walked in on him with another woman."

Scott divided the omelet, dished it onto two plates, and set one in front of me. The toast popped up and he plucked it from the toaster, juggling it from hand to hand.

"Hot," he said.

"You could use a pair of tongs, or an oven mitt."

"Wouldn't be manly. Better to burn my fingers. You want some juice or milk?"

"Juice would be good."

While we ate Scott told me stories about his work as a detective. I had a feeling he was skipping the gruesome ones and just giving me amusing incidents. When he piled the dishes in the sink and suggested we move to the living room, I got nervous. But in a giddy anticipation kind of way. Which was a lot better than a sweaty palms, stuttering kind of way.

Before long we were kissing. Scott pulled me close and started nibbling down my neck. Everything he did felt really, really good, then my phone vibrated in my pocket.

"I'm vibrating."

"Yeah, me, too." Scott grinned and waggled his eyebrows.

I laughed and pulled my phone out of my pocket. The display showed Craig's cell number. I turned the phone off and tossed it behind me.

CHAPTER SEVENTEEN

I'm a tramp," I said when Bobbi Jo answered the phone.

"Was it good?" she asked.

"Bobbi Jo, I slept with Scott last night. I can't believe I did that."

"Nothing wrong with that, if you enjoyed it."

"But I just slept with Max on Saturday."

"I think the rules state that you have to sleep with two men in a twenty-four-hour period to be a tramp. More than two and you're a slut. More than four and we're talking professional."

"You aren't helping." But she was. I was laughing.

"Listen, darlin'. It's only wrong if you feel like it's wrong."

"I know. I'm just no good at this, Bobbi Jo. I can't sleep with two different men. It's making me crazy."

"Oh, then you just need to choose one. Was Max good?"

"Of course, he was. He's funny and nice and playful."

"So, what about Scott?"

"He made me feel so wanted, you know? Like I was the only woman in the world. Like he wanted to be with me more than anything."

"Did you tell him you're seeing Max, too?"

"It didn't come up." And I felt guilty about that. "I have to run. Steinhart will have me drawn and quartered if I'm late for the shoot. Worse, he'll change his mind about letting me take some of the pictures at the wedding tomorrow."

"Come over when you're done and we'll talk. Go have fun."

I made it to the studio with ten minutes to spare. Just enough time to get Steinhart a cup of coffee when he barked the order at me. The pace of shooting prewedding pictures was a lot slower than shooting for the catalogs. We worked steadily for several hours, then a catered lunch was served and we wrapped up before five.

"That's it." Steinhart handed me the camera. "Send this out, then take off. And don't forget to be at the hotel at noon tomorrow."

Like I would forget. I mumbled a few curses under my breath while I removed the film and dropped it into the bag for processing. Steinhart was a brilliant photographer, but he was a pain-in-the-ass jerk. No wonder he couldn't keep an assistant.

I dropped the bag on his desk. "All done."

"Is the studio clean? One of the other photographers has a shoot here tomorrow."

"It's clean."

"You played with that software I gave you yet?"

"It's really something. I took some shots last weekend and played around with it. I was amazed at what it can do. Retouching, cloning backgrounds. Pretty incredible."

"Yeah, I like to draw mustaches on the models I don't like."

Somehow that didn't surprise me. "I'll see you at noon tomorrow."

"Wear something nice. You don't want to stand out too much," he called after me.

Bobbi Jo was looking at a photo album and crying when I got there. I sat down beside her and put an arm around her shoulder. I held her for a few minutes and let her get it out.

"I don't know if it's missing Edward or being pregnant." She took the tissue I offered her and blew her nose.

"Probably both. I remember crying for no reason at all when I was pregnant."

"I just wish they'd find out who did it. Then maybe it would be easier, you know?"

"I know. And Scott will find out. It's just taking some time."

I wasn't sure I believed what I told her. It had been almost ten weeks and the investigation seemed stalled. Scott told me he was doing background checks on everyone in the hospital who might have had access to Edward's room. I knew that was a last-ditch measure. Jimmy McLaughlin didn't appear to have a reason to kill Edward since his financial difficulties had been short-lived and easily solved. Sean Castleton had no reason to want Edward dead. In fact, having Edward die had put the skids on his career. That left Brian. But there was no proof that he'd done it, and he hadn't cracked during the interrogations with Scott. I hated to think someone would get away with murdering Edward. I hated to think that Bobbi Jo would have to always wonder about it.

"I'm over it. At least for now." Bobbi Jo dabbed at her eyes. "Let's talk about you and your love life."

"Do we have to?"

"What are you going to do?"

"I don't know. I mean, I don't even know if Scott is seeing anyone else."

"Dating used to be easier when we were younger, wasn't it?" She got up and walked into the kitchen. "You want some tea?"

"I'd love some." I followed her and sat on a stool at the counter. "I don't know if dating was easier. I never did much of it. Maybe that's my problem now. No experience. Maybe it was easier when we were young because we didn't have sex when we dated. At least not in high school. Well, not until the end of high school."

We took our tea out to the patio. It was still warm, but the temperature would start dropping soon. And then the rain would come. I was kind of looking forward to it this year. I'd noticed a fireplace in Scott's apartment and I could see myself curled up with him watching the flames. Building some flames of our own.

"But not Max," I murmured to myself.

"What? You lost me." Bobbi Jo leaned back in a chaise and put her feet up.

"I was just thinking about winter and that I could see myself sitting in front of Scott's fireplace in his apartment."

"And?"

"Well, why didn't I see myself sitting in front of Max's fireplace?"

"Aha! Because you'd rather be with Scott."

"Exactly. Problem solved. Now I just have to tell Max."

"Just give him the, I-still-want-to-be-friends line. It'll make up for some of the men who did that to me."

The wedding shoot had gone fine until the very end. Steinhart had let me take as many pictures as I wanted. He kept an eye on me to make sure I wasn't being intrusive to the guests, and he kept interrupting me to change film and cameras for him, but I thought I'd gotten some good shots.

Fortunately he didn't fall off the table and break his leg until the very end of the reception. The bride had changed clothes and come downstairs to throw the bouquet. Steinhart had thought his best shot would be from standing on a table in the corner. It probably was a pretty good shot until the table leg gave out and he crashed to the floor and broke his leg. I had to hand it to him, though. He didn't scream until after the bouquet had been tossed and caught. At least I was taking pictures of it so the bride would have something for her photo album.

The ambulance had arrived and carted Steinhart off to Mercy Hospital, and I'd gathered up all the equipment and gone home.

Now I was in his office trying to sort through all the bookings he had for the next week. Fortunately there weren't many and I was able to cancel them all, giving everyone the names and phone numbers of other photographers or rescheduling the shoots for another time. Steinhart had assured me that he'd be back at work in a week. Which was good, because we had an important location shoot that week for the Carson Agency.

I'd spoken to Emily Carson often enough to know she wouldn't take kindly to having the shoot cancelled. Her agency produced an enormous number of catalogs and ads. Of course, Steinhart would be in a cast and I'd have to do everything for him but go to the bathroom. The phone rang. I cursed and picked it up.

"Steinhart Studio."

"Emily Carson. I'm calling about our shoot that's scheduled for next week."

Speak of the devil.

"Yes, Ms. Carson?"

"We've had a change in our print date. I need the shoot to take place tomorrow. I've already notified the modeling agencies and cleared the location permits."

"Mr. Steinhart isn't in the studio right now. Could I have him call you back?"

"Tell Steinhart that if a photographer from his studio isn't there, he can forget about any more work from the Carson Agency."

That didn't sound good. I punched in the phone number for the hospital and asked for Steinhart's room.

"Emily Carson's a bitch," Steinhart said when I relayed the message about moving the photo shoot. "All the photographers are busy, so she's just going to have to wait."

"But she said—"

"I don't care what she said. Call her back and tell her we'll shoot as scheduled."

"Maybe you should call her. She said she had to move the shoot because of a change in the print schedule."

"She's lying. I can't call her back because these quacks have decided they need to do surgery on my leg and they have to do it right now. I'll talk to her when I get out of the hospital and smooth everything over with her."

Steinhart hung up the phone, and I was left sitting there listening to a dial tone. Great, now I'd get to give Emily Carson the bad news myself. I punched in her phone number.

"Emily Carson, please. This is the Steinhart Studio."

"Ms. Carson isn't available at the moment."

"Could I speak to her assistant?" That would be better. Let the assistant get her head chopped off.

"She isn't available, either."

"I really need to speak to someone. Ms. Carson wants a photo shoot moved and—"

"Ms. Carson is out of the office and unavailable until Friday, as is her assistant. She left me a note that the photo shoot has been rescheduled and that everything is arranged."

"I see. Thank you." I hung up the phone. What the hell was I going to do? Steinhart was in surgery.

Carson was unavailable. The models would show up at the location tomorrow, and there would be no photographer. Steinhart would lose the account and I'd lose my job.

Unless I did the shoot.

What was I thinking? I wasn't a photographer. At least not in Steinhart's eyes. But how hard could it be? I'd gone over the layouts, and the art director would be there to tell me what kind of shots she wanted. The stylists would take care of the models and the clothes. All I'd have to do is point the camera. Okay, it was a little more than that, but surely I could do well enough to save the account. Couldn't I?

The shoot took two days. I worked my ass off, but the art director was a doll. She helped set up the shots, she talked to me about lighting; she guided me to exactly what she wanted. I thought the photos were going to at least be usable. But I wouldn't know until I got the proof sheets and transparencies back tomorrow morning.

I didn't dare call Steinhart and tell him what I'd done. At least not until I knew if the photos were any good. If they were, I might be able to save my job. If they weren't, then I could just leave my resignation on his desk and go take the basic computer skills class at

Portland Community College.

Sheridan had gone out with friends so I was alone with my thoughts. Finally I opened the laptop and pulled up the photography software Steinhart had given me. Maybe playing with it would eat up the hours until I could go to bed and hopefully not have nightmares about what I'd done.

I brought up a few photos I'd taken of Steinhart. I clicked on an icon and started drawing a moustache and goatee on him. Then I drew horns. If it had been a full body shot, I'd have put a tail on him. I chuckled at the image, then decided I'd better use my powers for good rather than evil. I opened the shots I'd taken at Bobbi Jo's barbeque and started to fiddle with them. I had a really good shot of Sheridan diving into the pool and one of Max talking to Lily. I played around with them for a while, softening some edges, eliminating some shadows. Sean seemed to be in almost all the shots I'd taken of Bobbi Jo. If he wasn't right next to her, he was in the background watching her. It was downright creepy. I erased him from a couple and cloned in the background. I brought up another one of Sean and drew a moustache on him. Then I added a goatee and the horns.

As creepy as he was, he didn't make a good devil, so I gave him long, scraggly hair. I filled in the goatee so it was a full beard. The picture looked so familiar, I

stopped and considered it. Then I remembered where
I'd seen it before. There was only one thing missing. I
carefully placed a mole over the little white scar he was
always touching. I was looking at John Templeton. I
started shaking all over, and realized I needed to do
something immediately.

I called Scott, but he didn't answer his cell phone.
When I got his voice mail, I left a message.

"Scott. Sean Castleton is really John Templeton.
I'll tell you about it later. I'm going over to Bobbi Jo's to
tell her. I don't want her to be alone." I pressed the key
to mark the message as urgent and headed for the car.

I started to call Bobbi Jo on the way over to her
house, but decided not to. This was going to upset her,
and I didn't want to tell her over the phone. It was
almost dark when I rang her doorbell.

"Skye, what are you doing here?" Bobbi Jo turned
and walked down the hall. "Not that I'm not happy to
see you. It's just a surprise. Lily is working late at the
shop and I was just going to—"

"Bobbi Jo, sit down. I need to talk to you."

"Okay. What's wrong?" She sat on the sofa and I
sat next to her.

"I was playing on the computer with the photos I
took. No, wait, let me start at the beginning. Scott
showed me some photos of John Templeton. He
wanted to know if I'd seen anyone like him around

recently."

"You couldn't because he's serving a twenty-year sentence in Louisiana."

"No, he isn't, sweetie." I took her hands in mine and they were ice-cold. "He got out of prison a couple of years ago. Scott thought he might have been the one who killed Edward because when he was stalking you he also made threats against Edward."

"Edward never said anything about that."

"I know. Scott thought that he probably didn't want to worry you. Anyway, I was playing with the pictures I took at your barbeque. I put a beard and long hair on Sean's picture. Bobbi Jo, Sean Castleton is really John Templeton."

"No! He can't be."

"He's lost weight and shaved, but it's definitely him. Did you ever see John Templeton up close?"

"No. But I saw his picture in the paper when he was on trial." She paused and I could see her remembering the pictures she'd seen. "Oh, gawd! Skye, you could be right."

"I know I'm right. The pictures Scott showed me were very clear. It's him, Bobbi Jo. I think he murdered Edward. And I think he cut the brake lines on Brian's car."

"He's here," Bobbi Jo whispered.

"What? Where?"

"Right over here, actually," Sean said from the dining room.

Bobbi Jo and I both rose and turned to him.

"Skye, I really, really wish you hadn't done that. Now I'm going to have to do something about you."

"What do you mean?" I thought I knew what he meant, but the longer I could delay it the better.

"I can't have you ruining all my plans, can I? Everything was going so well. So very, very well." He looked at Bobbi Jo. "You were falling in love with me, weren't you?" He smiled when she didn't answer. "I knew you would, if you just had enough time with me, and once I got Edward out of the way. You never really loved Edward, you know. You only enjoyed his wealth. Now we can enjoy it together. Just like I planned. That's why I tried to kill Brian. He wanted to take your money away from you. That would have been wrong."

Templeton had undergone a complete change from Sean Castleton. His voice and movements were different. He even looked different. I felt my phone vibrate in my pocket. I turned a little so Templeton couldn't see my hand and slipped it into my pocket. I snapped the phone open and put my thumb over where I hoped the little receiving holes were. I prayed that Templeton wouldn't hear whoever was calling and that they would figure out what was happening. I also prayed that the caller was Scott.

Bobbi Jo's face was pale and pinched; her breathing short and shallow. "You killed Edward?" Her voice was thin and squeaky. "You killed my husband?"

"I did it for us, love. So we can be together." Sean shrugged. "He was dying anyway."

"He had at least a couple of months left." Bobbi Jo's voice was stronger and I could hear her anger, although Sean seemed oblivious to it.

"I couldn't wait any longer. What if he'd recovered or gone into remission or something? I couldn't take that chance. Not when I could have you sooner."

"You took him away from me. I hate you!" A tear trickled down her cheek and her hands were clenched into fists.

"No, don't say that. You don't hate me. Not really. You'll see. It'll be all right soon. I just have to take care of Skye first. Then we can be alone together. All the time."

Damn. He was back to taking care of me. I didn't like the sound of that. Especially when I noticed the knife in his hand. "You'll never get away with it."

Sean turned back to me. "I don't see why not. I got away with killing Edward. Of course, your death will have to be sudden and I'm afraid violent. Like that Natalie chick." He shook his head. "That was a shame. I really thought it was the personal trainer. How was I supposed to know they wore the same hooded sweatshirt?"

"You killed Natalie because you thought she was David?" I asked.

"Of course. I couldn't have that man coming to see Bobbi Jo all the time. Now for you. I won't let you suffer. Because you're Bobbi Jo's friend."

"No!" Bobbi Jo screamed.

"Now, love, it won't be bad." He smiled and it was pure evil. "How about a little accident in the pool? I've heard that drowning is a very pleasant way to go." He grasped Bobbi Jo's arm and motioned me toward the kitchen with the knife. I walked as slowly as I thought I could without pissing him off.

"Go on." He motioned to the patio door. "Let's all go out to the pool."

"You don't want to do this," I said, trying to stall for time.

"You're right. I really would prefer not to, but, I can't afford to have you around."

"They'll know you did it. Even if you take Bobbi Jo away with you. They'll find you."

We were at the stone patio that surrounded the pool now. Templeton reached down and picked up one of the decorative rocks at the edge of the concrete. I was afraid that Bobbi Jo would try to stop him. And I was sure that Templeton would hurt her if she did.

Templeton nudged me to the edge of the pool. I

looked down at the pattern of light playing across the water and went into that strange state where time slows down. I turned back to see Templeton's arm rise slowly in the air, his knuckles white from gripping the rock. Just as his hand started to lower, Bobbi Jo moaned and collapsed. I watched her body crumple slowly to the concrete. Her head rolled to the side and back, and there was a bloody scrape on her cheek. Templeton turned toward Bobbi Jo.

A loud crack split the air and I plunged into the pool.

When I surfaced, gasping and sputtering, Templeton was lying next to Bobbi Jo, a dark stain slowly spreading across his shoulder. I climbed out of the pool and knelt down next to Bobbi Jo. Her eyelids fluttered open.

"Is she all right?"

I looked up at Scott standing over Templeton. He bent over and placed two fingers against his neck, then pulled his hands behind him and slapped handcuffs over his wrists.

"I have to call this in." He flipped open his cell phone and punched a speed dial button. While he spoke to the dispatcher, I got Bobbi Jo up and away from Templeton.

More cops arrived within minutes, along with an ambulance. The EMT cleaned the scrape on Bobbi Jo's cheek and recommended that she go to the hospital, but she refused. A couple of the cops took preliminary statements from us, but Scott said we didn't need to go to the precinct.

Lily came home in the middle of all the confusion and called the doctor to come over and take a look at Bobbi Jo, then hustled her off to bed. By the time the cops had left, I was emotionally exhausted.

Lily came out of the bedroom, closing the door softly behind her. "She's fine, just exhausted."

"God, I've never been so scared in my life." And I never wanted to be that scared again.

"How did you know that Sean Castleton was really John Templeton?" she asked.

I explained about Scott showing me Templeton's picture and then playing with the software Steinhart had given me.

"I'm just glad it's all over and everyone's safe." Scott squeezed my shoulder and I patted his hand. I had a special thank-you in mind for him later.

"I should have figured it out just from his name. Sean Castleton. John Templeton." He shook his head. "It was right in front of me."

"Don't beat yourself up about it," I said.

"You're right. The captain will take care of that for me. But right now, I want to get you home."

"That sounds wonderful." Scott took me to his apartment, and I was okay with that. It felt good to sleep with some strong arms around me.

CHAPTER EIGHTEEN

The next morning, Scott dropped me off at home on his way to work. I drove over to the studio and picked up the transparencies and proof sheets that had been delivered.

It took me a good half hour to get up the courage to put the transparencies on the light table and look at them. But they were pretty good. At least I thought so. There were some duds, but that happens with every shoot. I'd been looking at them for an hour when the art director came by.

"Hey, Skye. How do they look?"

"You be the judge." I stood and gestured for Connie to sit on the stool at the light table. She glanced at the ones I had laid out, then pulled out her loupe and checked the transparencies closer. She removed them and spread out more, checking each one. Finally she looked at the black and white proof sheet.

"I love these. You're really good. Want to do another shoot with me?"

I couldn't speak so I just nodded my head like an idiot.

Connie gathered the transparencies and proof sheets and slid them into an envelope. "I'm going to call Steinhart and tell him how good you are."

Steinhart. I still had to talk to Steinhart. I swallowed the lump in my throat and followed Connie outside. When I got home, I put on some water for a cup of chamomile tea and sat down by the phone.

It rang forty-five minutes later.

"Skye, you are one ballsy bitch. I told you to cancel that job."

"I tried to cancel the job, but Ms. Carson—"

"I don't want to hear your damn excuses. This is not what I expect from an assistant."

"But the photos are good. Connie loved them and she wants to work with me again."

"I don't give a rat's ass what Connie wants. I can't work with an assistant who disobeys a direct order. I don't want an assistant who takes matters into her own hands."

I was guessing I wouldn't need the formality of a resignation letter.

"Effective immediately you are no longer my assistant, is that clear?"

"Yes. Absolutely clear."

"Good. I expect you to be in the studio at seven tomorrow. We have a shoot and Paul is sick."

"What?"

"You're shooting the *Northwest People* layout tomorrow."

"I am?"

"Well, if you don't, you're fired. Try to look like a professional photographer when you show up."

The phone clicked and I sat there staring at it. Then I started laughing a little hysterically.

Steinhart had promoted me to photographer.

When I left Craig, I had been looking for a new life. And I'd found it. I had my friends, I had my daughter, I had Scott, who was becoming more than a friend, I had a great place to live, and I had an actual career now. But I'd also found what I'd really been looking for all along and just didn't know it.

I found the woman I'd left at the altar twenty-two years ago.

A special presentation of *Breeding Evil*
by L I Z W O L F E

CHAPTER ONE

"Since when is the FSA hiring private investigators for black ops?" Shelby Parker closed the file and placed it back on Ethan Calder's desk.

"It isn't really a black op, Shelby."

"And I'm not really an FSA operative." She'd tendered her resignation to the Federal Security Agency six months earlier, after ten years of living on the edge. One op after another. Having no job skills that really applied in corporate America, other than being sneaky and nosy, she'd opened her own security and investigative firm. And here she was, back at FSA headquarters in Denver letting her former handler talk her into one more op.

Ethan hadn't changed a bit since she'd been gone, other than a little more gray at the temples of his dark hair, and a few more lines at the corners of his dark eyes. He leaned his elbows on the desk and tapped his long, slender fingers together. No, he hadn't changed. He would wait for her to come around to his way of thinking,

1

to agree to his proposal.

She had no doubt that he knew she needed this job. The check for her advance lay on his desk, and even though Shelby couldn't see the exact amount, the number of zeros she counted made her a little giddy.

For six months she'd been struggling to survive by keeping tabs on wayward spouses, investigating fraudulent insurance claims, and providing bouncer services to a local bar on wet tee shirt night. If she didn't get some decent cases soon, she'd be living on the edge of poverty. Still, it was an edge that *she* had chosen. She hadn't left the FSA because of Ethan, or even because she didn't like the work. At thirty-three years old, she'd decided that she wanted to run her own show. She wanted something that was hers, something that she controlled.

Shelby leaned back in her chair and looked at the majestic Rocky Mountains through the ceiling-to-floor windows behind Ethan's desk. If she decided to take the job, it would have to be on her own terms.

"I can give you whatever support you'll need," Ethan said.

"You just said that no one in the FSA knows about this. That you can't even use an FSA operative."

Ethan sighed and folded his hands on the desk. "I need you on this one, Shelby."

Shelby stood and moved to stare out the glass wall of his office, turning her back to him. Ethan Calder was the best handler in the Federal Security Agency. He had been hers the entire time she'd worked for the FSA. No one was more aware than Shelby that, while she was out saving the world, he was back at headquarters saving her butt with the latest intelligence and best support he could cajole, bribe, or beat out of anyone who might be helpful. But he was distant and cold, and he leaned a little too heavily on the need-to-know theory of information disbursement for her comfort.

Still, there was no doubt he would come up with some creative way to provide whatever she might require.

On the other side of the glass wall, people were hunched over computers, speaking urgently on phones or to co-workers. No one just strolled down the hallways created by the cubicles. Footsteps on the utilitarian beige carpet were hurried and purposeful. The FSA offices were always intense. Because there was always something important on the line—like lives and national security.

Shelby reluctantly admitted that she missed being a part of it—but not enough to give up on her fledgling agency. And her fledgling agency could certainly use the chunk of money Ethan was offering for this job.

It wasn't like she was going back to the FSA. It would just be a case—a lucrative case—and wasn't that exactly what she needed and wanted?

"So, will you do it?" Ethan walked back to his desk and sank into the chair. It took her a second to bring her mind back to the conversation.

"Why me?"

"The op calls for a chameleon. And, you're the best."

"Is that your idea of a compliment?"

Ethan had often noted that her appearance was one of her greatest assets. Exceptionally plain was the only way she could describe it. Neither attractive nor unattractive. Five feet six inches tall, neither slender nor plump. Although she tended to have more muscle than most women, that wasn't noticeable in street clothes. Hair that was a combination of dark blond and light brown, eyes that were neither green nor brown, but somewhere in between. Her face might as well be a blank canvas. Eyes, nose, and lips in proportion to each other, and none of them outstanding in any way.

Shelby looked at her reflection in the glass wall. Totally unremarkable and utterly forgettable. Someone who was easily lost in a crowd. But given a few products readily available at the drugstore, she could transform herself into just about any kind of person she chose.

"Fifteen people missing so far?" Shelby turned away from her reflection and walked back to Ethan's desk. She slid a finger under the folder and flipped it open, scanning the first page.

"At last count. Including Shannon Masterson and her son, Sam. No death certificates. All of them had some connection to The Center."

"Dr. Jonah Thomas is the head of The Center?" She

turned over another page in the file. "I've heard his name before. A scientist, right?"

"Years ago he headed up a government-funded research facility. He was supposed to verify the existence of psychic phenomena, which he did."

"Really?" That woo-woo stuff was a bit much for her to believe in. "I remember him losing the funding for some reason."

"Right. It turned out that not only was he verifying the existence of psychic phenomena, he was performing experiments on some of the research subjects. The government dismantled the research facility and sealed all the records."

"So, he's an evil scientist."

"And an egocentric megalomaniac." Ethan leaned forward. "We know that he's been doing research on psychics for years, along with Dr. Ruth Carlson. He has contacts outside the country that are less than reputable. The Center seems to have unlimited funds that we can't trace. What we don't know is what the hell they're up to."

"You're really hopped up about this." Shelby couldn't help grinning at him.

Ethan sighed and leaned back in his chair. "Shannon is a friend. She was my wife's roommate in college."

"Charlotte wants you to find her?"

"No, she doesn't know that Shannon is missing. Shannon's aunt is married to the Ambassador from the United Kingdom. The aunt called me about it because of Shannon's friendship with Charlotte."

"Has she ever disappeared before?"

Ethan swiveled his chair to look out the window. "Shannon's what you'd call a free spirit. She's taken off before, but never without telling her aunt."

"So there was no indication she was taking off on some trip or whatever?"

"No. In fact when Shannon took trips in the past, she usually asked Charlotte to watch Sam for her."

"So, the niece of an Ambassador. Why, exactly, is this a black op again?"

"It isn't a black op."

"OK, not a black op. Just a secret between you and me." She lifted her eyebrows in blatant disbelief.

Ethan turned his chair back, sighed, and shook his head. "All right. The deal is that Ambassador Watkins has already called in the FBI to investigate.

"So, it's a black op because the FBI is already investigating? Why not just let them handle it?" The boundaries between the FSA and the FBI were blurred at times, but if one agency already had control, the other agency usually didn't interfere unless they were asked. Professional and political courtesy.

"It's not a black op."

"Ethan, if the FBI is already investigating The Center, then sending me in could be the end of your career."

Ethan stared at her for a moment, frowned and pressed a hand to the back of his neck, kneading the tense muscles. Shelby bit back a smile. That was a sure sign that he was about to resign himself to actually giving her the information he'd been trying to withhold. She sat down in the chair across from his desk and leaned back, waiting for the story.

"FBI Director Fields and Ambassador Watkins have a history that is less than congenial. The Ambassador's wife is concerned that the FBI won't do everything they can to find Shannon and Sam."

"Must have been something pretty heavy in their history to make her feel that way."

Ethan nodded. "Ambassador Watkins. Evidently he's a hard dog to keep on the porch. He had an affair with Director Fields' niece."

"Oh. Isn't Ambassador Watkins around sixty or so?" Shelby bit back a smile, knowing that Ethan was sensitive about the fact that he was twelve years older than his wife, Charlotte.

"Fifty-eight. He's also tall, handsome, and debonair. Not to mention that he is an excellent gift giver."

"I see. And Mrs. Watkins is okay with all this?"

"I wouldn't presume to ask, but evidently she's learned to live with it. I believe she's willing to overlook certain behaviors that aren't entirely acceptable to her."

"So, she called you because of Shannon's friendship with Charlotte?"

"Precisely."

"Did you mention this to Chambers?"

"As director of the FSA, he can't do anything that would step on the FBI's toes." Ethan shrugged. "However, he made it clear that he doesn't want Ambassador Watkins accusing the U.S. of not doing everything in its power to find Shannon."

"I see. Chambers doesn't want to step on Fields' toes so he's letting you bring in someone from the outside. If Fields finds out, he can't accuse the FSA of anything."

"I'm just investigating the disappearance of my wife's friend." Ethan spread his upturned palms and smiled.

Shelby shifted in the chair across from Ethan, picked up the file, and looked at the picture stapled to the inside. Shannon sat on a porch swing in a sundress, her strawberry blond hair curling softly around her face, and one arm around her towheaded son who stood next to her, blowing bubbles. It was obvious from the look on her face that her son was the most important thing in the world to her. What would it have been like to grow up with a parent like that?

Crap. She knew she was about to agree to the job.

"You know someone could recognize me in Tucson. I lived there for a while."

Ethan nodded. "It's about time you agreed."

"I would have agreed two hours ago if you'd just told me everything," she shot back. "You know, I totally trust you when I go on an op. Don't you think it's about time you returned that trust? Don't you think that maybe our collaboration would work even better—"

Ethan cut her off with a wave of his hand.

"We need to get you inside."

Shelby leaned back and sighed. "I can't believe I just agreed to a black op."

"It's not a black op." Ethan gave her a rare, one-sided grin. "Maybe a little gray, but it's not black."

ISBN# 9781932815054
Mass Market Paperback / Suspense
US $6.99 / CDN $9.99
Available Now

BREEDING
EVIL
LIZ WOLFE

Someone is breeding superhumans …

…beings who possess extreme psychic abilities. Now they have implanted the ultimate seed in the perfect womb. They are a heartbeat away from successfully breeding a species of meta-humans, who will be raised in laboratories and conditioned to obey the orders of their owners, governments and large multi-national corporations.

Then Shelby Parker, a former black ops agent for the government, is asked to locate a missing woman. Her quest takes her to The Center for Bio-Psychological Research. Masquerading as a computer programmer, she gets inside the Center's inner workings. What she discovers is almost too horrible to comprehend.

Dr. Mac McRae, working for The Center, administers a lie-detector test to the perspective employee for his very cautious employers. Although she passes, the handsome Australian suspects Shelby is not what she appears. But then, neither is he. Caught up in a nightmare of unspeakable malevolence, the unlikely duo is forced to team up to save a young woman and her very special child. And destroy a program that could change the face of nations.

But first they must unmask the mole that has infiltrated Shelby's agency and stalks their every move. They must stay alive and keep one step ahead of the pernicious forces who are intent on …

ISBN# 9781932815054

Mass Market Paperback / Suspense

US $6.99 / CDN $9.99

Available Now